THE ONLY CHILD

MIRANDA RIJKS

INKUBATOR
BOOKS

PROLOGUE

She comes to slowly and knows immediately something isn't right. She's not waking up in bed but sitting up, hard wooden slats digging into her aching back. She forces her eyes open and blinks several times to make sure she's really awake.

She glances around, adrenaline pumping through her veins, and then she screams, but the only thing that comes out of her mouth is a pathetic, muffled moan. She can move her head from side to side, but it hurts, a bit like waking up with a horrendous migraine, a searing headache splitting her skull in two.

'Help!' She hears the word in her head, but her voice just sounds muffled. Her fingers are numb with pins and needles, and her wrists are tied to the chair behind her, the muscles in her forearms contracting painfully. As she glances down at her feet, she sees that her ankles are bound to the chair legs, with what looks like plastic ties. Who is it that is holding her here? Who has knocked her out and bound her to this chair?

She tries to wriggle around, to shift the chair, make it fall to the ground perhaps, and then maybe she will be able to free herself, but it doesn't move; all she does is cut and chafe her wrists. She tries to gulp in a lungful of air through her mouth, but it feels like she's going to suffocate.

She tells herself to calm down. Her nose isn't covered, so she should be able to breathe. She closes her eyes again, because perhaps this is a dream, and when she wakes up, she'll be at home in bed. She counts to ten in her head: *One elephant, two elephant, three elephant ...* And then she opens her eyes.

She's not asleep.

She has no idea where she is. This looks like a shed or a small warehouse, but the windows have been covered up with newspaper taped haphazardly to the window frames.

It smells musty in here, unloved and unused, big bulky things covered in dust sheets, weak daylight permeating through the newspaper covering the windows. She strains to read the headlines, but the words blur. She can't tell if she's been unconscious for days or even weeks, or maybe she has memory loss.

Is she going to die here? She doesn't want to die. She has too much of her life left to live, too much to do. She feels tears dripping down her cheeks, the wetness being absorbed by the cloth in her mouth. *Why? Why am I here?* The words are on repeat in her head. None of this makes any sense.

And then she hears footsteps and the turning of a key in a door, and it makes a creaking noise as it opens. She tries to twist her head around to see who it is that is keeping her here, tied up like a hostage.

What? Her eyes pop wide open. Of all the people in the world to keep her captive, this person would be the very last on the list ...

1

CHANTAL – NOW

I know you're not meant to have favourite clients, but I do. Carla is an impressive woman. She broke through the proverbial glass ceiling to become a main board director of a publicly listed company. Statuesque, with platinum hair and azure eyes, she is frequently photographed and cited as a role model, and her opinions on anything, from business to lifestyle, are widely taken as gospel. It's even been suggested that she would make a good prime minister. But this morning, that Carla was unrecognisable. She sat in my office, makeup-free, livid bruises around her wrists.

'Thank you. Thank you so much, Chantal,' she said, her voice tremulous.

I had just succeeded in getting a non-molestation and occupation injunction to stop her ten-years-younger, coercive, violent live-in lover from going anywhere near her. For the past eighteen months, Carla has been living in hell. Yet no one, absolutely no one, would think it credible that a woman as successful and overtly confident as her would be subject to coercive control. It just goes to show, you can never ever know what goes on behind closed doors. And that's why

I love my job. As a matrimonial lawyer, I am my client's saviour. I've got their backs, and I'm good at my job.

It's exhausting, though, and today the fatigue has caught up with me. After Carla left, I worked through a mountain of paperwork. Now I tidy up my desk, slip my laptop into my red leather bag and put on my raincoat. I take a quick glance around my office. It looks more like a comfortable living room with leather armchairs, a floor-to-ceiling bookcase and fresh flowers in vases, placed next to boxes of tissues on the two side tables – necessary because a lot of tears are shed in here. I close the door and walk out into the open-plan area.

'I'll be out of the office for the rest of the day,' I say to Alicia, my secretary. 'If there's any fallout from Carla's case, call me immediately.'

'Of course, will do.' She smiles at me before carrying on typing.

Client confidentiality is everything, particularly for my high-profile clients. The only people who know about Carla's nightmare are me, Alicia and the judge. For now, at least. Of course, I can't be responsible for what her aggrieved ex-partner is going to do or say.

WE LIVE IN SUSSEX, which is not ideal for Stuart. My husband is a television presenter, and he has to get to the studios in London most days. But it's home and the perfect environment for bringing up our son, Alex. Neither Stuart nor I have moved far from our roots, but our house couldn't be more different. Both of us were raised in council accommodation; we now live in splendour in a five-bedroom, modern home. The architect won awards for our house, because from the outside, it looks like a large, converted stable block. Its true beauty is what lies within. The back of the house is built into the hillside, with glass ceilings linking the front to the rear, and there are magnificent views to the South Downs through the large sliding patio doors. Oak floors throughout the downstairs lend warmth to the house – something that, in my opinion, is often lacking in modern design.

At the same time, we have all the mod con features: built-in coffee machine, air conditioning, a beautiful kitchen with a curved island unit, and outside, a manicured garden with concealed water system and three individual garages, one for each of our cars. We've even got a summerhouse at the bottom of the garden, with a hot tub, which none of us have used in years.

Stuart and I have both worked incredibly hard, and our home is the visible fruits of that labour, hopefully not in a show-off kind of way, but in quiet good taste that demonstrates how far we have come. What both Stuart and I like about our home is that it's just on the edge of the village and looks fairly modest from the outside. But when visitors walk in for the first time, their jaws drop.

It's 3 pm by the time I get home, and when I put my key in the lock, I'm surprised to find the door unlocked. Perhaps Gail, our cleaning lady, has come this afternoon rather than this morning.

I take off my raincoat and hang it up in the cupboard under the stairs and walk through the long, light-infused hallway with reclaimed flag stone tiles towards the kitchen. It's then that I hear noises coming from the living room. I stop and tiptoe to the door, which is slightly ajar. I push it open. Alex is on the sofa with a girl, both of them half-dressed, kissing.

'What the hell!' I say.

They spring apart. I've never seen the girl before. She is mixed race with numerous piercings, in her nose, her lip, her tongue and all the way up her ears. Her black hair is braided in tight cornrows, and she has several tattoos on her back and down her arms.

'What are you doing here?' Alex asks, hastily pulling on his discarded T-shirt. He's filled out a bit more during the past year and no longer looks like a gawky bean-pole adolescent.

'You are asking me what I'm doing in my own home?' I exclaim. 'You should be at school.'

'School?' The girl sniggers as she brazenly fastens her bra.

'College,' Alex says gruffly.

'I thought I could trust you,' I say quietly.

Alex rolls his eyes at me and turns towards the girl. 'Sorry, babe.'

The girl throws daggers at me. She slowly puts on a black shirt, all the time holding my gaze. Despite being petite, she's got a hardness to her. One thing is for sure, she doesn't attend the private sixth-form college where Alex is meant to be finishing off his school years. Tattoos and piercings are strictly prohibited.

'Do you need a lift home?' Alex asks as she stands up.

'You're going nowhere,' I say, crossing my arms. 'Your girl-friend can make her own way home.'

'It's okay, bae, I'll walk. Let's nifock later, okay?' she says. Alex grins. He accompanies her to the front door, and I stand back in the hallway with my arms crossed, watching them to make sure she really leaves. Alex gives her a quick peck on the cheek and then turns around to face me, his jaw set forwards.

'You could at least be nice,' he says.

'What does nifock mean?'

'None of your fucking business.'

'You don't talk to me like that! And you don't bring back random girls into our home when you're meant to be at school. Do you understand? You've got your A Levels soon, and your whole future depends on your grades. Surely I don't have to spell that out to you?' I swallow hard to rein in the disappointment. I'm not being unreasonable, am I? I know Alex's timetable, and he should be in classes this afternoon.

'I'm nearly eighteen, Mum. You've got no right to talk to me like this. I can do what the hell I like. It's my life. You don't even know Luna, but you've decided you don't like her because you've got a thing against piercings. You're so predictable!'

'I haven't said a word about how she looks,' I say, thinking that he has a point. She isn't the sort of girl I hoped he'd bring home, but I'm certainly not going to express my thoughts; otherwise I risk pushing him away.

'I object to you skiving off school. And I don't want Luna here, certainly not when you're alone in the house. You're grounded.'

He rolls his eyes at me. 'Fuck you!' he mutters under his breath, grabbing his car keys from the bowl in the hall. And before I can say another word, he's out of the door, slamming it behind him and racing away. For a moment, I consider running after him, but what would that achieve? Even if I wanted to, I'm not strong enough to restrain my son. I hear the garage door opening, and then I walk to the window, where I see his little red car reversing out of the garage. Gravel flies up from underneath his tires as he skids out of our driveway.

'Oh, Alex,' I murmur to myself. 'Drive carefully.'

I walk into the kitchen and pour myself a large glass of white wine; then I take out my phone and search for nifock. After a while I work out that it's NIFOC. My shoulders sag when I learn it's an acronym for *Naked In Front Of the Computer*.

· · ·

WE ARGUE A LOT THESE DAYS, Alex and me. The boy infuriates me, but I love him with all my heart. I get that he's trying to push the boundaries, but this is too much. He's got loads of girls from school to choose from, so why can't he go out with someone from there? And where did he meet her? I suppose he's doing it to shock Stuart and me, and if so, he's succeeded.

I leave my half-drunk glass of wine on the kitchen table and glance around the room. It's a big kitchen with a bank of dark green cabinets on one wall, inset with the ovens, the coffee machine and extra-wide fridge. A large island unit with a white marble counter houses the double sink. It's looking tidy in here, thanks to Gail, who clears up after us three mornings a week.

I walk upstairs, passing the wall of etchings, and turn left along the corridor to our bedroom, which is a bright yet calming room with a taupe plush carpet and silk curtains in a slightly darker shade. We have a large en suite bathroom with a rain shower, double sinks and separate bath, and I have my own dressing room with built-in wardrobes. I change into my gym wear, then pad back downstairs to our home gym. All the equipment is lined up so that I can look out of the wide window with views across our garden and onto the hills in the distance. The exercise helps me clear my mind and will stop me from worrying about Alex, and, of course, there's the added bonus that it keeps me trim. Does it make me vain to care about my appearance? I frequently get told I look a decade younger than my forty-two years. It takes work to maintain this body, but it's worth it.

After a gruelling hour's workout, I try calling Alex, but his phone is switched off. So I text him:

Please come home, darling. We need to talk.

I start making supper; just a simple tray bake with

chicken and sweet potato. I'm not very interested in cooking, and these days, Alex frequently chooses not to eat with us. He turned vegan about six months ago. I tried to accommodate him, but I was forever getting it wrong, so in the end he said he'd make his own meals. He eats lots of rice and mung beans and vegetables that I don't know the names of.

An hour later, I hear the crunch of wheels in the driveway, but it's Stuart in his Porsche, not Alex in his Fiat. My husband strides into the kitchen, a big grin on his face. Stuart is conventionally good-looking, with a square jaw and straight white teeth that he regularly whitens. His dark hair is peppered with grey now and, much to his dismay, is thinning on the top. It's his eyes that are the most compelling feature of his face. They remind me of tortoiseshell, changing in colour from burned umber to mahogany, depending upon his mood, lined by dark lashes that some have suggested must be enhanced with mascara. We laugh about that. Stuart hates makeup, particularly the stuff he has plastered onto his face before facing the television cameras. But the one thing that is particularly special about Stuart is he has that unique ability of looking at you as if he's really seeing you, as if you're the most important person in the world. I suppose that's what makes him such a good interviewer, and why the camera loves him. What the cameras rarely show is that Stuart is only five feet eight inches, barely taller than me. These days, Alex towers above him. Stuart's height has never bothered me, but I know it bothers him.

'Good day?' I ask.

'An excellent day.' Stuart grabs a tumbler from the over-head cupboard, walks to the sink and pours himself a glass of water from the purified water tap. He takes a long swig of water. 'What about yours?'

'All fine until this afternoon, when I walked in on our son making out with some girl on the sofa in the living room. She was covered with piercings. I sent her packing, and he's stormed off too.'

'Oh, Chantal. Did you shout at him?'

'Of course I did. He should have been at school.'

'So long as he's predicted to get reasonable grades, I think you're overreacting.'

'Excuse me!' I say, scowling at my husband. 'He'll only get reasonable grades if he actually puts the work in. It's not going to happen by osmosis.'

'At least he brought the girl home. They could be out doing drugs or goodness knows what.'

'I can't believe you think it's okay. He swore at me and stormed away. And now his phone is off, and I've no idea where he is.'

'I'm sure he's absolutely fine. It's what us boys do at that age, push the boundaries, wind our parents up. He's just a normal, hot-blooded lad, no doubt thinking about sex every minute of the day. When he comes back, apologise to each other and let it go. Anyway, do you want to hear my news?'

To be frank, I don't. I'm upset that Stuart isn't supportive of my reaction towards Alex. It's as if he's condoning the bad behaviour. Our son needs to learn discipline and respect, and I certainly don't think it should be me who should be apologising.

'I'm on the shortlist to be the new anchor on the breakfast show.'

'You're what?' I swivel around to face Stuart, my annoyance from a moment ago dissipating.

His face lights up as he reaches for me and pulls me into an embrace. 'If I get it, I'll be interviewing politicians and celebrities. And it's a massive salary hike.' He murmurs into my hair, 'It's everything I ever dreamed of.'

'That's amazing,' I say, extracting myself from his arms. 'Fingers crossed.' I don't mention all the negatives that will undoubtedly come with the position. The horrendous early starts, the fact he'll be even more recognised, the worry that he'll think that his job is more important than mine. We've never been in competition with each other work-wise, and have shared the load in all things child-raising and domestic, so I don't have any reason to complain, but of course, that might change now.

'What's the next step?' I ask.

'One further interview, and the decision will be made next week.'

'That's fantastic.' In many ways it is, but I'm not sure that I want the additional scrutiny of the public gaze or the worry that Stuart might want us to relocate to London to be nearer the television studios. Nevertheless, I'm not going to worry about it now. He may not get the job.

AFTER OUR MEDIOCRE SUPPER, we sit together in the living room, watching a Scandi crime series, but Stuart is distracted. He's forever on his mobile phone, sending messages.

'Can't you leave that thing alone?' I ask, the tapping of the keys frustrating me.

'I need to stay on top of all the news, and I need to know everything that's going on. Be happy for me, Chantal. This could be the best thing ever.'

'I am happy for you,' I say, 'but have you actually watched any of this programme?'

'You're right. I'm too buzzed. Let's go to bed.' He shoves the phone in his pocket and grins at me. I know exactly what that look means. I haven't seen it in ages.

As I switch off the television, I hear the crunch of tyres, followed by the slamming of the front door and heavy footsteps as Alex runs upstairs. I breathe a sigh of relief. Our son may be angry, but at least he's safely home.

Stuart stands up and stretches, then walks towards me, brushing his lips against my forehead. We have an unspoken ritual, a bit like the dance that birds do when getting ready to mate. Stuart throws me particular looks, touches me in a certain way, and even though it's the last thing I feel like, I know I'll enjoy it when we do make love. In fact I can't remember the last time it happened.

'I'll have a shower,' he says. 'Can you lock up?'

As I walk around the house, switching off the lights, I can hear the thumping of music coming from Alex's room. The difficult conversation with him can wait until tomorrow. I know I'm lucky. I have a handsome, successful husband, a son whom I love, even if he pretends not to love me back, a fulfilling job and a beautiful home. As I climb into bed a few minutes later and Stuart pulls me towards him, I let him make love to me. If I'm honest, I haven't really enjoyed it for years, but I'm doing this for him, for our family. What I can't do is dwell on the compromises I've made over the years, because something always has to give in order to achieve perfection.

And what I certainly can't do is think about the fly in the ointment. What happened eighteen years ago.

2

CHANTAL – THEN

It rains too much in Manchester. When I first arrived here, I thought it would be the perfect balm, so very different to the little market town where I grew up in Sussex. Not that I lived a middle-class existence. Mum and Dad brought Debbie and me up in a council flat with one bedroom and a box room just large enough for our bunk bed and nothing else. Dad died from cirrhosis of the liver when I was fifteen. It was a relief. My childhood had been filled with loud, drunken rows, and while I don't think he ever hit Mum, it certainly wasn't a happy marriage.

Even so, after he died, she fell apart. When she passed away, just three years later, Debbie said she'd died of a broken heart. I think Dad had destroyed Mum years previously, that her shocking pulmonary embolism was the result of an unhealthy lifestyle combined with co-dependency. I reckon Mum had simply come to rely on their emotionally harmful relationship and didn't know how to live without it. It's what prompted me to want to become a family lawyer. My view is, get out of the relationship before it really destroys you. Anyway, Debbie and I have agreed to differ about Mum's death. I suspect my sister suffered more, being two years older than me. Ever since we became orphans, she's taken on the responsible older sister role, insisting that we stick together come what may. We were close in those early years; not so now. I feel a sense of freedom being away from her, here in Manchester. She's still in West Sussex doing her thing as a primary school teacher. I'm sure all the kids love big, bubbly Debbie.

I'm officially a family lawyer, although still just a junior associate, but I'm sure I'll work my way up the ladder soon enough. The firm I work for was happy to facilitate the move to their Manchester office. Today, I've had to come home from work early because I thought I was going to throw up due to the pain. It's a cliché that we've all come to expect – it's *de rigueur* to have a horrid boss, particularly in your first job. But Lorna Stephenson is no stereotype; in fact, she's lovely and empathetic. When I knocked on her door, she knew straight away something was wrong.

'Goodness, you're as white as a sheet. Are you alright, Chantal?'

'I'm sorry, but I don't feel very well.' I leaned against the door frame, unable to stay upright.

'You must go home straight away. Order a taxi and put it on the firm's account. And get better soon,' Lorna said. I had to blink away the tears that welled up in my eyes. I'm not used to people being kind like that.

Now I'm back in my one-bedroom flat, lying on the bed, having taken painkillers, and hugging a hot water bottle. I miss Stuart so much. I thought it would be better moving to the opposite end of the country, where there were no places or people to remind me of our years together. But running away doesn't make any difference. I want to call him and tell him how nice my boss is, and how the grey weather is getting me down but the people are warm and welcoming, and that this flat is lovely with shining leather and chrome furniture and in a great location in the centre of the city. But I don't. We've agreed that a break means a break. No contact at all for twelve months.

Stuart and I fell in love in our last year at school. He was a new boy, and the second I saw him, I knew we were meant to be together. It was difficult for him joining the school in the final year of A Levels, but what made us unusual in our friendship group was we each had a clear vision of what we wanted to do and the paths we had to take to achieve that. I went to university to study law, whereas Stuart went to another university to do a degree in journalism. Somehow our relationship stayed strong despite living in different parts of the country. I never doubted him. And then, when we both started our first jobs, we rented a bedsit in south London and moved in together. He carried me over the threshold, and it was the best night of my life, the first time I felt truly secure and grown up.

But there have been pressures on us during the past couple of years, and we have argued. A lot. Stuart said he wanted out of the relationship. I was devastated, and when he saw how broken I was, he suggested we take a year's break. After all, we were so young when we got together. I tried to be philosophical about it. I'd rather he sows his wild oats now and then come back to me, and I am confident that he will. The night before he left for Dubai to work as a junior reporter for an English-speaking newspaper, we both cried as we made love, clinging to each other as our bodies juddered and released.

'I need to do this, for myself,' Stuart said. 'You do understand, don't you?'

I nodded tearfully. As the old saying goes, *If you love someone, set them free.* I am still praying that he will eventually come back to me, that it will be of his own choosing, and I won't have to beg or cajole.

So for now, here I am, alone and miserable. I'm just drifting off to sleep, the pain easing somewhat, when I hear keys in the front door. I sit up, my heart racing.

'Who's there?' I shout as I climb out of bed.

'Oh, sorry. You've never been home before,' the young woman says as she walks into the flat. She looks younger than me, probably aged nineteen or twenty to my twenty-five. She's got black spiky hair and thick kohl around her eyes that makes them look almost panda-like against her pale skin. 'I'm the cleaner,' she says, tugging the waistband of her black leggings, which are slipping downwards. My eyes are drawn to her distended stomach. She's very pregnant.

'Yes, sorry,' I say. 'I forgot that you come on a Wednesday afternoon. I'm not feeling well, which is why I'm home.'

'Do you want me to go away? It's just I really need the money with the babe on the way.' She places her hands protectively around her belly. 'I'll work around you and be as quiet as I can.'

'Yes, of course, that's fine,' I say. 'I'm Chantal, by the way.' I feel silly as soon as I say that. Obviously she knows my name. No doubt she's snooped around and seen my things, and the landlord, who hired her, will have passed on my details.

'I'm Jade, and I'd better get on. You don't pay me to stand around having a chat.' She walks out of the hall and disappears into the living room. There's a basic kitchen built into the back wall, and I can hear her turn on the taps. I return to bed.

An hour later, she knocks on my door and pokes her head around. 'You okay if I clean in here?'

'Yes, sure,' I say, wrapping a long cardigan around me and walking with bare feet out of the room.

'What do you do, then, when you're out at work?'

'I'm a solicitor. I'm in Manchester on a year's secondment.'

'Yeah, I can tell you're not from around here. The way you speak and all.'

I smile. 'Would you like a coffee or a tea?' I ask. 'I'm going to boil the kettle.'

'Thanks, a brew would be good. Milk and two sugars.'

An hour later, Jade has finished cleaning. The flat smells lemon fresh, and it's spotless.

'That's me all done,' she says, wiping her damp hands on her grubby T-shirt. 'I've got some mates who could do with your help.'

'I'm a divorce lawyer.'

'Oh, so you don't do theft and drugs and the like?'

I try to stop myself from smiling. 'No, I help couples separate.'

'That's sad. So you can't help our Kev? He's up before the magistrates for a petty theft charge. It's a load of bullshit, because he's not a thief.'

'I mean, I could. But I wouldn't be the best person.'

Jade shrugs. 'Anyway, how are you liking Manchester? Been to any good clubs?'

'I don't have much of a social life,' I say. That's the understatement of the year; I have no friends here, and when I'm not working, I wander around the shops or stay in the flat, declining any invitations to work socials.

'You'll have to come out with me and my mates. We'll show you a good time.'

'Thanks,' I say, but I don't imagine I will.

IT'S NOW ten days later, and I'm driving along a street somewhere off Cheetham Hill, all because of a note that Jade left me on my kitchen counter. It was written in lower case with letters that didn't join up.

dear chantal, my mate realy needs ur help. I know u said u just do divorcies but can u call me. Tnx 0749746320 jade x

I didn't want to snub Jade, who seems like a nice girl, and of course she has the keys to my flat, but I really didn't want to get involved in her friend's problems. I wondered how I could say no politely. That evening, I made myself an omelette, all the while staring at her note. When I finished, I rang her number.

'It's well kind of you to call,' Jade gushed. 'What are you doing Friday night?'

'Um, nothing,' I said before realising I should have made up some excuse.

'Come over to mine, and we'll have a few bevvies. Is this your phone you're calling on?'

'Yes,' I said, wondering who else's it might be.

'I'll message you my address. Come around seven. Byee.'

And so it is that I've found myself here, grateful for any friendship that I'm offered, even if it's in return for my legal services. I'll out price myself so as to avoid any awkward situation.

I find a parking space on the run-down street and lock up the car. I'm being eyed by a gang of youths, and despite dressing in old jeans and a sweatshirt, I suppose I look out of place. I just hope that my car is in one piece when I return. Keeping my head down, I hurry along the pavement until I locate Jade's house. It's a scruffy, flat-fronted red-brick semi-detached house with white-framed windows and doors that look like they haven't been painted in several decades. Not that it worries me. Where I was brought up wasn't much better.

I ring the doorbell to flat 2A, but it doesn't seem to work, so I ring Jade's mobile. A moment later, the front door swings open, and she's standing in front of me with a wide grin on her face. She's wearing a cropped top, which exposes her protruding belly. I try not to look at it and just keep my eyes on her face. She has a gold stud in her cheek just to the left of her lips. I wonder how painful it was when she had it done.

'Come in. It's not a fancy place like yours, but we make do.'

I follow her up the stairs. The paint is peeling off the walls in little curls, and the brown carpet is totally worn through and fraying. She opens a door on the landing, and I follow her through. I was wrong: this place makes our old family home look like a palace. It's little more than a squat with exposed floorboards, patches of mould on the walls and ragged furniture that looks like it was salvaged from a tip. There are pieces of black fabric stapled to the wall, improvising as curtains. But it's surprisingly clean. There are no old pizza boxes or discarded cans of beer, just a hookah on the floor next to the sofa and some rolling paper on top of a plastic box.

'I've got wine or beer. What do you want?'

'I'll have a beer, please.'

Another girl appears in the doorway. She has clear, ebony skin and a perfect heart-shaped face with wide, sparkling almond eyes. Her hair has been shaved on the left-hand side, leaving long coiled braids that hang down over her right shoulder. She's wearing a white miniskirt and a black leather jacket paired with vertiginously high-heeled black patent leather boots that extend up and over her knees. But even if she had been wearing torn leggings and a ragged T-shirt, she would look stunning.

'I'm off now, Jade,' she says, ignoring me.

'Have fun, babe,' Jade says as she appears holding a can of

Fosters in each hand. 'Don't do anything I wouldn't.' She roars with laughter and turns to me. 'Melody's the good girl. I'm the baddie, which is how I got banged up, and our other flatmate, Tammy, should be back in an hour or so.' She rubs her stomach, then hands me a can, grabs a cushion from the sofa, and slips down onto the floor.

I sit on the sofa and wriggle around to try to avoid my backside being pierced by a piece of coil.

Jade laughs again. 'That's why I sit on the floor. So why did you want to move to Manchester, a posh girl like you with a hoity-toity voice?'

I try not to cringe. The irony is I don't have a posh accent; if anything, I've had to work on pronouncing my *t*'s and making sure I don't speak like the working-class southerner that I really am, so my clients feel at home around me.

'Don't tell me. It's man trouble, isn't it?' she says before I can formulate an answer.

I wonder if she's been looking through my things, seeing the photographs of Stuart and me.

'Go on then,' she prompts.

'Yup. I'm on a break from my boyfriend, and I wanted to move away for a year.'

'You're lucky. The furthest I've ever been from Manchester is Liverpool. Never even been to Blackpool. Oh yeah, went up into the hills a couple of times, but that's it.'

'You haven't been to London?' I ask.

'Can't afford the train fare, and anyway, what would someone like me do in a place like London? One day I'm going to get on an airplane and go far away. Australia perhaps. But for now, Manchester's my home, and as shitty as this flat is, at least me, Tammy and Melody have a roof over our heads. Tam's my bestie, and I'm lucky she wants to hang around me. She's got a proper job working in Selfridges. Mel is trying to be a model, but that's a tough nut to crack. I tried to get off benefits, but with a baby on the way, no one wants to employ me. I'm just grateful for the couple of cleaning jobs I've got.'

'How long have you cleaned my flat?'

'About a year and a half. The man who owns your place is some rich guy and is a mate of a mate. I clean his house and your flat that he rents out.'

As hard as I try not to look at her pregnant belly, my eyes are drawn towards it. 'Are you still with the father of your child?' I ask.

Jade laughs again. She has one of those infectious laughs, and I can't stop myself from grinning.

'No. Don't think I'm a slut, but I don't even know who the father is. I thought about getting rid of it, but I want something to love. Me and the baby against the world. Neither Mel nor Tam want to live with a baby, which is fair enough, so I'm going to have to find somewhere else to stay. I might get a council flat if I'm lucky, or else I'll get some money from somewhere and fly off to Australia to start a new life. What about you? What are your dreams?'

'Nothing fancy. I just want to settle down with Stuart, have a family and get a partnership in a law firm. Boring, traditional, I suppose.'

'You don't look like the boring type,' Jade says.

I'm glad about that, and she's right. I can be a social chameleon when I need to be. Around someone like Jade, I can relax into the real me, the old Chantal I was before Mum died. But to get on in the law, I had to adopt the etiquette of the middle classes, wear the right clothes and develop the patter. And now I fit right in with the privately schooled folk I work with. I'm a good actress and have often thought I'd be at home on the stage except, that is, that I don't like the limelight. I prefer to be watching from the side.

'Do you fancy a joint?' Jade asks.

'No, thanks,' I say. 'I'm driving home.'

'They wouldn't stop someone like you.'

I smile. She's missing the point.

'You don't mind if I do?' It's obviously a rhetorical question, as she stands up, walks to the chipped mantlepiece, and reaches inside a biscuit tin to remove a bag of weed. I wouldn't blink an eyelid about her smoking weed generally, but she's pregnant. Surely she must know how it'll affect her baby?

'Should you be doing that whilst you're pregnant?' I try to keep my tone of voice jovial and non-judgemental, but I can't help myself from asking the question.

'It'll be fine. Mum did all sorts of drugs when she was pregnant with me, and I came out okay.'

There's nothing I can say to that, and what's the point of showing my disapproval when Jade is being so welcoming to me?

It isn't until a couple of hours later, after Jade has drunk three more beers and smoked two joints, that I realise I've had the most relaxing evening since before Stuart and I split. I can just be me around Jade. She's funny and street-smart, and I can imagine myself being like her if I hadn't had teachers who recognised I had the potential to do well in exams. I got lucky and used education to help me make my way in life. Jade has had a tougher time.

'You know you shouldn't be drinking or doing drugs when you're pregnant,' I can't help myself from saying once again.

'Yeah, I know, and I'll stop soon.'

'How about tonight? Perhaps you've just had your last smoke for the next few months.'

'Come on, Chantal. We're having a laugh. Don't get all lawyer-ish and preachy with me.'

'Sorry, I don't mean to. It's just that life is precious.'

'Hello, babe!' A loud, female voice startles me, and I can see that Jade is relieved that our conversation has been interrupted.

'Hiya! Who are you, sweetheart?' Tammy walks into the room and dumps several shopping bags onto the floor. She is also a black girl, with her hair cropped closely to her head; bright blue eye shadow and huge fake eyelashes make her eyes pop. Her long fingernails are painted in the same bright blue. She's wearing a very short white dress that barely covers her buttocks and high-heeled, white peep-toe sandals. Her well-toned legs are covered in goose bumps, unsurprising since it's cold outside.

'Chantal meet Tammy; Tammy meet Chantal,' Jade says.

'Nice to meet you,' Tammy says, kicking off her shoes and leaning in to give me an air kiss. She smells like she's sprayed herself with every scent in the perfume department of Selfridges.

'Chantal's been giving me stick for smoking when I'm preggers.'

'Too right. She's an idiot, is our Jade,' Tammy says. 'And she doesn't listen to me.'

'Okay, you two, stop giving me a hard time,' Jade groans.

'Has Kev turned up yet?' Tammy asks.

'No.' Jade turns towards me. 'He's our mate who got busted, and I told him you'd help him.'

I had totally forgotten that was the pretext Jade had for asking me over, and I'm relieved that he hasn't shown up. At least I don't have to disappoint Jade and Tammy by turning Kev down.

'I'm hungry. Anyone want a kebab?' Jade says, rubbing her stomach.

'You're always hungry,' Tammy says. 'I suppose you're going to want me to nip out to get it?' She rolls her eyes. 'Do you want one, Chantal?'

Jade yawns, which I take as my cue.

'No, it's kind of you, but I should be getting home.' I glance at my watch. 'It's been great getting to know you, Jade, and fun to meet you too, Tammy.'

'And you,' Jade says, hauling herself to her feet. 'You're not what I expected.'

'What did you expect?' I ask as I pick up my bag.

'We often don't get what we expect, do we?' she says rather enigmatically. But I think I know what she's trying to say. 'Your shout next time.' Jade winks at me, and Tammy waves.

I smile. I don't think there'll be a next time.

3

CHANTAL – NOW

I'm at my desk, finishing off some paperwork, when the phone rings.

'Hi, Chantal, it's Debs.'

I sigh. I've asked my sister numerous times to call on my mobile, not my office phone, but she's worked out that I'll always answer my direct line and I'll ignore my mobile when her name flashes up. It's not that I want to be mean, it's just that when I'm working, I don't need my personal life getting in the way.

'Can I come over this evening?'

I'm not in the mood to have her come to our house, especially as the tension between Alex and me hasn't dissipated, and Debbie always sides with Alex.

'Is everything alright?' I ask.

'Yes, but I've got some things I want to discuss with you.'

'How about I stop by yours on my way home?' My rationale is that if I go to her house, I can leave after a short time.

Debbie moved into the same village as us four years ago. Her philosophy is still the same: blood is thicker than water, and family should stick together. Sometimes it feels as if she thinks our blood is coagulating. She may be fine with that, but I find it oppressive, ironic, even. If Mum and Dad hadn't stuck together, they both might have been happy and alive today, but Debbie doesn't see it that way, and no doubt never will. I love Debbie because she's family, but we're so different. If I'm being brutally honest, I wouldn't choose her to be my friend.

Nevertheless, I look out for her, as she looks out for me. She comes over for Sunday lunch once a month, and, to be fair to her, she's always had a good relationship with Alex. As she was free during the school holidays, she used to look after him for me, and even today, Alex has a soft spot for his aunt. I know Debbie wishes she and I were closer, best friends as well as sisters, but we have little in common. She's never understood my ambition and my desire to have a harmonious family.

Debbie did get married. She was twenty-three; Jim was her first boyfriend. It was a small wedding in a registry office, followed by drinks in the local pub. Jim was a carpenter and – as Debbie proudly said to me – good with his hands. I thought it odd that he had a woman as his best man. During the marriage ceremony, she held out the ring and a look passed between her and Jim that made me uneasy, but this was Debbie's happy day, and I wanted the best for my sister. At the pub, the best woman – I can't even remember her name – hung on Jim's every word; I could tell that Debbie was also uncomfortable. But Jim took Debbie by the hand, and they left together in a taxi to go to a hotel in Brighton.

Three months later, Jim left Debbie. Six months after that, he was shacked up with the best woman with a baby on the way. It broke my sister. She blamed herself, said that she was too fat, too ugly, too serious and a long list of other negative traits. I tried to tell her that Jim was a bastard and that he was to blame, but to this day, I think she feels that she was the reason their marriage failed.

By the time I finish my work, only Kathleen and I are left in the office. I'm an equity partner, whereas my friend Kathleen is a salaried partner. In practice, that means that so long as the law firm stays profitable, I earn more money than Kathleen and have a say in the running of the business. Although our clients aren't aware of the difference, within the firm I am Kathleen's senior. It's been the cause of some awkwardness in the past, but that seems to be all behind us now. Kathleen and I are close, professionally and personally. I pop my head around the open door to her office.

'I'm off now. See you tomorrow.'

'I was hoping you'd have time for a quick drink,' she says, swiping her blonde hair away from her forehead.

'I've got to pop in and see Debbie on my way home. She's been hassling me.'

Kathleen rolls her eyes at me. She knows all about my relationship with Debbie and is perfectly aware that I would prefer to spend an hour with her than my sister. 'Good luck with the familial duties,' she says. 'I need to get back home to the girls. If Trisha knew I'd gone for a drink rather than going straight home, I'd be in serious trouble. You've probably saved me.'

We say our goodbyes, and I run down the two flights of stairs and walk outside into the cool early evening air, walking around the block to the car park. I let out a sigh as I relax into the driver's seat of my silver Mercedes Cabriolet. I bought it as a present to myself when the firm made record profits two years ago. I wondered if it was a bit ostentatious, but I actually think it gives my clients confidence that I'm good at my job. The car and I certainly turn heads when I pull up into the court car parks with the roof down and designer shades over my eyes. This evening, it's not warm enough to put the roof down.

Egerton Brook Steading is a medium-sized law firm with offices in London and various affluent towns in the southeast. I head up the Family Law department, and I'm lucky that I can work mostly out of our Horsham office, just ten minutes' drive away from where we live. I take the train up to London on average once a week, to meet clients or for board meetings, or on occasion to attend court hearings. I don't like to think about the past, but from time to time, I indulge myself. If I'm feeling particularly upbeat, I'll give myself a silent pat on the back for achieving all of my dreams. Unfortunately, Debbie hasn't been quite so lucky, or perhaps she simply didn't dream big enough. She is still single and still a primary school teacher for a mediocre local school.

I pull up in front of her small house. She lives on a new housing estate where the houses were built so quickly, it seems impossible that they will be robust enough to stand the test of time. Debbie has a two-bedroom house with a postage-stamp-sized garden and neighbours on both sides who have become close friends. Everyone loves Debbie. She's obviously been keeping an eye out for me, because the front door swings open the second I get out of the car.

'You look lovely,' she says. 'Is that a new suit?'

I glance down at my pale grey trouser suit. It always surprises me that Debbie notices when I'm wearing new clothes or if I've had my hair done, because she cares so little about her own appearance. I feel bad judging her, but if she ditched her wardrobe staples of M&S elasticated trousers, which she matches with floral-patterned blouses, and chose clothes that actually fitted her, it would make such a big difference. I'd love to pay for her to have a proper haircut and colour, but I know she'd take it the wrong way if I offered.

Instead she chops her own hair, and on the very rare occasion she asks what I think of her latest hairstyle (which is normally just a choppy fringe and hair down to her shoulders because she can't cut it when it's any shorter), I tell her she's done a good job.

I follow her into the house and through to her small kitchen at the back, where she has a table wedged up against the wall and two chairs.

'What would you like to drink?' she asks.

'A coffee, please.'

'It's a bit late to be drinking coffee, isn't it? You won't sleep well.'

'It's fine,' I say, sinking into her plastic kitchen chair. At least I know I'll get a proper coffee. I gave her a Nespresso machine last Christmas along with a coffee subscription that I'll keep renewing. 'What have you been up to?'

'Nothing much. It's busy at school, and I've taken on a new pastoral role. We're auditioning for the year six musical, and I've offered to support the kids who don't win the roles they hoped for.'

'That's kind of you,' I say. Debbie is always on the lookout for the underdogs.

'What about you?' she asks. 'How are Stuart and Alex?'

'Stuart might be getting promoted to be an anchor on the breakfast show.'

'Oh my goodness!' Debbie exclaims, dropping the coffee pod she was about to insert into the machine. 'That's so exciting. You really will be a celebrity couple. I hope you'll have time for your boring old sister.'

'He might not get it, so please don't say anything to anyone.'

'Come on, Chantal. You know I can keep a secret.' We're silent for a moment whilst the machine spurts out my coffee. 'What cases are you working on?'

I know I shouldn't tell Debbie, but she's right, she can keep a secret; she's never betrayed my confidence before. 'I've just been appointed to represent the husband in what will be a very high-profile divorce. They're the multimillionaire couple who own LALO Clothing.'

'You're joking!' she exclaims. 'Lauren and André Lowaski?'

I nod.

'But they were only featured in last month's *OK! Magazine*. They seemed like such a lovely, solid couple.'

'Don't believe everything you read in the press,' I say. 'Anyway, how are things with you? Been on any more internet dates?'

Debbie slumps into the chair opposite me. Despite my suggestion to use a photo-enhancing app, Debbie's profile on the various internet dating sites is a very accurate representation of herself. I know it sounds mean to even think it, but it's probably why she gets so few likes.

'I've given up on internet dating. It's too sordid. I've had two lousy dates in the past couple of months. The first one expected me to go around to his house after the drink for a bit of "hanky-panky", as he called it. The second one took one look at me and turned around and walked back out of the pub. He wasn't even subtle.'

'I'm sorry,' I say, and I genuinely am. I wish Debbie could find herself a kind, steady partner, because she deserves some luck, and she would be the sort of wife who would put her husband on a pedestal, catering to their every need. Over the years, I've tried to set her up on dates, but nothing has worked. I think the main reason is Debbie's lack of self-esteem.

'Look, the reason I wanted to see you is the IVF didn't work again,' she says, sighing deeply.

'Oh, Debs, I'm so sorry.'

'I want to do another round. It might be my last chance, Chantal. I'll be forty-four next month.' She sniffs, and her shoulders sink downwards. After a moment, she looks up at me with tear-filled eyes, her chin trembling ever so slightly. 'Would you pay for another round?'

I squeeze her hand. I've seen the pain that Debbie has put herself through: the selection of donor sperm, the medical appointments, the injections, the hope ... only for it to be dashed. And then there's the cost, which I've paid for twice now. My heart bleeds for her, because if there's anyone who would make a good mother, it's Debbie. She loves kids, and they love her back, but some things are not meant to be.

'Oh, Debbie. I'm sorry,' I say again quietly. 'Are you sure that's really a good idea? I'd hate anything to happen to you or the baby because the risks of pregnancy are so great at your age.'

'It's not my fault I didn't find a partner or have the opportunity earlier.'

'Of course it's not. If I could wave a magic wand and give you a family, that's the first thing I'd wish for.'

She throws me a watery smile.

'You need a holiday,' I say. 'Let me treat you to a break, a lovely luxury holiday to a health spa. You could go somewhere gorgeous during the October half-term. I can speak to a travel agent and find somewhere perfect for you.'

A tear drips onto the table. 'A holiday isn't going to fix this, Chantal. I want a baby, not a trip to a health spa. You don't understand,' she says under her breath.

But Debbie's wrong. I do understand.

4

CHANTAL – THEN

Stuart has been gone for two hundred and seventeen days. My friends lied when they said it would get easier with time. It doesn't. I miss him as much today as I did on the first day he left. We promised each other that we wouldn't stay in touch, that we would make a clean break of it, but I haven't been able to do that. We've still got mutual friends, a couple of whom have visited him in Dubai. Our mutual friend, Amira met up with him when she went on holiday to Dubai. I quizzed her on her return and she says Stuart hasn't found a replacement for me – or if he has, he didn't tell her. I don't think I could bear it if I saw photos of his smiling face with his arms around another woman. But according to Amira, rather gallingly, he's having a great time. Bronzed from the sun, she showed me photos of him on a groomed beach and one weekend, she and Stuart went with a bunch of expats on a Bedouin safari, sleeping in tents in the desert, racing 4x4s across the dunes. It should have been me doing that with him, having a wonderful time around a romantic campfire. I am still waiting for him to send me a postcard telling me he can't live without me and asking me to buy a plane ticket to fly out to join him. I think it's a forlorn hope.

Amira said that he eats out at super fancy restaurants, and she showed me a photograph of Stuart with a neon-lit wall of fish tanks behind him and a table laid with white linen and silver cutlery. His plate was piled high with lobsters and seafood I don't recognise, and he was holding a glass of champagne. My typical meal is a ready-made lasagne from Sainsbury's.

It's Saturday today, and like normal, the weekend stretches out empty and miserable. I decide to explore the Northern Quarter and have a wander around the hip, alternative shops in Affleck's Palace. I've just entered the building when my phone rings. I fumble around in my crossbody handbag and see that it's Jade calling. Although she's been to clean over the past couple of weeks, I haven't spoken to her since my visit to her flat. It's my fault, really. I like her, but it's not easy for me to be around her at the moment, and I don't want to have to explain why.

'Hi, Jade.'

'Chantal,' she gasps. 'I ...'

'What's happened?' I ask, stopping still underneath a board plastered with notices and flyers just inside the entrance of the imposing red-brick building.

She moans. 'My waters have broken. I ... Can you come over?'

'What? Why me?' I step to one side to let people walk past me.

She sounds breathless. 'There's no one else.'

'I don't think–'

'Please, Chantal.'

'Shouldn't you call 999?'

'Please. I beg you.' And then she starts sobbing.

Oh, god. This is the last thing I want to do. Be with

someone I barely know who is going into labour. But how can I say no? She sounds desperate, terrified and inconsolable.

'Alright,' I say, against my better judgement. 'I'll be with you as soon as I can. Leave your door on the latch, but if the contractions get worse, call for an ambulance.'

I want to scream as I walk quickly back to my place. It seems crazy that Jade, who has lived in Manchester the whole of her life and claims to have a great social life, hasn't got someone else she can call upon. I suppose I'm the most respectable person she knows. What a joke. I'm tempted to call an ambulance for her, but I don't. I go back to my place, run up the stairs to my flat and find my car keys, which I leave in a little ceramic bowl on the kitchen counter.

Fifteen minutes later, I'm in the car and driving towards Cheetham Hill, where, fortunately, I find a parking space very near Jade's house. The front door looks closed, but when I push on it, it opens. I hurry upstairs and can hear Jade moaning inside.

I open the door to her flat. She's doubled over, her knuckles white as she grasps the edge of the plastic table. It judders precariously as she sways backwards and forwards. She takes one look at me and bursts into tears.

'I don't know anything about labour,' I say. She throws me a look of horror mixed with terror. But it's true, I don't. And I'm the world's most squeamish person. Seeing someone else's blood makes my legs go weak. 'Have you rung your midwife?'

'What?' she mumbles.

'Your midwife. The nurse who's been doing your check-ups.'

'I haven't seen nobody. Don't like doctors,' she gasps.

Great. I suppose she isn't even registered to a doctor's practice. I just hope that this baby is going to be alright, bearing in mind she hasn't had any check-ups and has carried on drinking and doing drugs. It would be too awful if her irresponsible behaviour has affected the baby's health.

'How long between contractions?'

'Not long,' she pants.

'We'd better get you to the hospital.'

If she was pale before, she's even whiter now. What did she think? That she could give birth all alone here on her grubby, carpet-less floor?

'Have you got a bag packed, clothes for you and the baby?'

She shakes her head. This is getting better and better. I sigh. 'Right, lean on me, and I'll get you to the car.'

Somehow, we make it down the stairs and out to my car. I'm surprised how large she's got since I last saw her, but she manages to sit down on the front passenger seat. I help swing her legs around and, with difficulty, stretch the seatbelt across her vast belly.

'You need to direct me to the nearest hospital. I don't know my way around here,' I say.

I drive quickly, terrified that she might give birth right here in the footwell of my car. Not only am I squeamish in the extreme, anything to do with babies drives a spear through my heart.

When we arrive at North Manchester General Hospital, I park haphazardly at the front and rush inside to get someone to help us. A man comes out with a wheelchair, and I stand back as he gently lowers Jade into it.

'Good luck,' I say as he starts to push her away.

'No,' she yelps. 'You can't go. You have to stay with me.'

'Don't you have a friend or some family who can help you? There must be someone, Jade.'

'No. Tammy's away, Melody has moved out, and there's no one.' And then she cries big heaving sobs. I'm embarrassed that it's the orderly who takes charge of the situation.

He stops and points his finger at me. 'You, go and park

your car and then make your way to the maternity unit. I need to check your friend in. She needs you.' He gives me a look as if to say, *Don't you dare shirk your duty.*

Five minutes later, I'm walking in through the entrance and following the signs to the maternity ward. I hate hospitals. I know it's irrational, but all they've done is fail me. They weren't able to save Mum's or Dad's lives, and the only thing I get when I go to hospital is bad news. The last time was the very worst.

I've had period pains all my life. Not ordinary cramps that can be alleviated by popping a few over-the-counter pills, but agonising, scream-inducing pain that cripples me for up to a week every month. It was shortly after Stuart and I moved in together that he became aware of how much I suffered.

'This isn't normal,' he said as I rocked from side to side on the bed, hugging a hot water bottle to my stomach.

'It's normal for me,' I said.

But Stuart insisted that I should see a doctor, and before I knew it, I was swept up in the system, with my GP referring me to a gynaecologist. She took it very seriously; it was the first time anyone had mentioned endometriosis. 'I want you to have a laparoscopy,' she said. When I went home and told Stuart, he looked terrified.

'It's only because she thinks I might have endometriosis,' I said. 'It's not like it's cancer.'

But Stuart had already Googled it, and he knew the implications. Stuart being Stuart, he didn't tell me what it might mean. He just hugged me, and we rocked from side to side. But I knew Stuart; it was obvious he was worried. So I Googled it too, but I convinced myself that I didn't have a really bad version, and what was the point in worrying until we knew for sure? If Stuart thought it odd that I insisted we make love every night, sometimes twice a night, he didn't say anything.

Three weeks later, after I'd had the procedure, I sat in the gynaecologist's consulting room, Stuart by my side.

'I'm afraid it's not good news,' she said. Stuart grabbed my hand. 'You have a severe form of endometriosis, and really the only way to cure it is to have a hysterectomy.'

'A hysterectomy? But I'm twenty-three years old! I want to have children,' I said as the blood whooshed loudly inside my ears.

'I need to manage your expectations, Chantal. I think it's extremely unlikely that you will be able to conceive. If you don't want to have a hysterectomy, I can give you hormone therapy to reduce the symptoms.'

'And will that help me get pregnant?' I asked. Stuart squeezed my hand; we had talked about children, and I knew he wanted a family as much as I did. Perhaps not quite then, but certainly by the time I was thirty.

She threw me a sympathetic smile that looked more like a grimace. 'I'm afraid not. It will do the opposite, in fact. I know it's an awful lot to take in, but, Chantal, the chances of you bearing a child are almost zero.'

'But they're not zero,' Stuart said.

The consultant shrugged. I burst into tears.

Over the next eighteen months, I had just one goal: to prove the consultant wrong and get pregnant. But my obsession with my fertility cycle became too much for Stuart. He didn't want to have sex at the dates and times dictated by my ovulation calendar, and the more determined I became, the greater the disappointment was when, month after month, I failed. I knew that I was pushing Stuart away, but what could I do? All my research suggested that the younger you try to become pregnant, the easier it should be. I still had time on my side.

I may have had time, but I didn't have Stuart. Oh, the sweet irony. The man whom I desperately wanted to be the father to my children, my one true love, needed time out, and I had no choice other than to grant him his wish.

So that is why being in a maternity ward, acting as the birthing partner to a woman I barely know, is so utterly cruel. Because it should be me having a baby.

'I'm here with Jade,' I say through the intercom at the door to the maternity department. I don't even know her surname. Obviously, she's told them that I'm on my way, as I'm buzzed in and a nurse accompanies me along the corridor to Jade's birthing room. This is torture. I can hear babies wailing and women screaming. It isn't until we get to Jade's room that I realise it's not other women, it's in fact just her making all the noise.

'You got Jade here just in time,' the nurse says, standing outside the closed door. 'She's fully dilated, and the baby will arrive any moment. Two of my colleagues are in there with her now.'

'I think I'd rather stay out here in the corridor.'

She frowns at me. 'Jade said you're her birthing partner.'

And so it is that she opens the door, and I see Jade lying on a bed, her legs wide apart, a midwife bending over her. And I want to gag, to run away from here. To unsee the horror of what I just saw.

I know that sounds selfish when it's Jade who is having all the pain, but hers will ease when the baby is born, whereas mine is permanent heartbreak and monthly agony. Her pain will end in happiness. Mine just serves to remind me what I've lost.

Somehow I get through it. I try to imagine that I'm in a forest, surrounded by beautiful trees, Stuart at my side as we build a bonfire, the scent of pine and freshly burning wood taking away the overwhelming scent of antiseptic and metallic blood. And then just when I think I can't bear it any longer, I hear the high-pitched yelp of a newly born infant. I'm tugged back into this room of horror.

'Congratulations, Jade, you've got a beautiful baby boy!'

When they place the baby on Jade's chest, she looks at him with an expression of pure adulation. Then she turns her head towards me.

'Thanks, Chantal,' she says. 'I don't know what I would have done without you. You're a real friend.'

I smile awkwardly because I can't say that the feeling is mutual. She just backed me into a corner. Frankly, I'm feeling a wave of resentment.

'Chantal, meet Noah.' She puts a finger into the baby's curled fingers and smiles at me. 'Noah, meet your new aunty. Aunty Chantal.'

5

CHANTAL – NOW

Stuart gets the job. He rings me just as I am about to go into a client meeting. I've never heard him sound so happy.

'We need to celebrate,' he says. 'They're putting out a press release this afternoon.'

'Would you like me to organise a party?' I know the answer will be yes, because Stuart is the extrovert in our family. He loves nothing more than hosting lavish jamborees.

'Great idea. See you later.'

I don't even get the chance to say congratulations. As I put the phone down, I am a maelstrom of mixed emotions. Of course I'm happy that Stuart has achieved what he has always wished for, but I'm concerned about the implications such notoriety will have on our family. Stuart is currently a B-list celebrity, getting recognised from time to time, but this will thrust him onto the A list. He'll be the focus of gossip; he won't be able to do the supermarket shop anymore, and when we go out together, we'll be photographed and gossiped about. I know I have to take it on the chin; it's part of the package that I signed up for all those years ago when I first fell in love with Stuart. I'm incredibly proud of him, and his ambition and success just add to his attractiveness, but I'm nervous of the spotlight falling on Alex and me. How will we cope?

I drive home via Waitrose and pick up some sirloin steaks, a vegan burger and chocolate pots for supper. I pop a bottle of champagne into the basket as well, although we've got plenty stashed in the wine cellar fridge in the basement. That's Stuart's domain, and I wouldn't want to choose a bottle that he's saving. Back at home, I put the food in the fridge and walk upstairs. I knock on Alex's bedroom door. Getting no answer, I open it. He's hunched over his laptop.

'Darling, can I have a word?'

I get no response, so I walk over to him and tap him on the shoulder. He jumps. For a moment, I wonder if he's watching something online that he shouldn't, but fortunately, he doesn't slam the lid down.

'Bloody hell, Mum, you gave me a fright. Can't you knock before walking in?'

'I did.'

He removes his earbuds. I wonder how loudly he's playing music and hope he doesn't damage his hearing.

'Dad got the promotion. He's going to be a lead presenter on the breakfast programme.'

Alex shrugs. He clearly doesn't understand what a big deal this is.

'I'm making steak for supper. I know you're not eating meat at the moment, but as it's a celebration, I was wondering if you'll join us.'

He throws his hands up in the air in a gesture of exasperation. 'You just don't get it, Mum. I'm a vegan now. It doesn't mean I eat meat one day and none the next. It means I don't eat meat ever again, and the thought of watching you eat the flesh of a cow makes me sick.'

It was worth a try, I suppose. 'I thought you'd say that,' I admit. 'I bought you a black bean burger.'

'Stop trying to make me eat meat. I'm not going to.' He turns back to his computer, pops his earbuds in, and I'm dismissed.

Stuart is normally home by 7 pm, but this evening, it's nearly 8 pm and he hasn't appeared. I'm starving, and by the looks of things, so is Alex, because he lopes into the kitchen, asking, 'When's supper?'

'Whenever Dad gets home. I want us to eat together, as we're celebrating.'

'I'm starving.'

'I'm sure he'll be here any moment. He's probably gone out for drinks with his colleagues.'

'Nope. He'll be shagging his mistress. A quick celebratory fuck before coming home to his family and pretending that he's a good dad and husband.'

'How dare you!' I say, swivelling around and narrowing my eyes at Alex. 'Never speak about your father like that.'

'Sorry, Mum, but it's true, and I don't know why you put up with it.'

'I don't accept it because it's not true.' I turn away from my son and rummage in a kitchen drawer because I don't want him to see my face. I don't know why Alex thinks his father has a mistress, but I've suspected that Stuart might be having an affair for a few weeks now. He's been coming home late, smelling of soap, defensive when I ask him where he's been, keeping his mobile phone out of reach. And the biggest signal of all is the flowers that he's picking up at the station. Stuart never brings me flowers.

I've confronted him; of course I have. It was last week when he returned home late with a big bouquet of white lilies.

'Why the flowers?' I asked.

'Just because.'

'Are you feeling guilty about something?'

'No. What do you mean?'

'Are you having an affair, Stuart?'

He held my shoulders and looked me straight in the eyes. 'Of course I'm not. I never want to do anything that would hurt you, Chantal. There's just a lot that's been going on at work. You have nothing to worry about.'

And then he'd hugged me so tightly, my face was squashed into his neck, and I told myself that I was being stupid. Just because I spent so much of my life surrounded by divorcing couples and cheating partners didn't mean that my own husband had fallen into that camp. The thing with Stuart is that he may be a presenter, but he's also an actor. When he's interviewing someone, he can't afford for his own feelings or thoughts to show on his face. Instead, he has the unique ability of hiding his expressions and just locking eyes with the person he's interviewing, tilting his head to one side, mirroring their body movements and smiling at them, encouraging them to open up while he offers them the safety of his gaze. And it works. I fear that it even works on me.

I've tried to take Stuart at his word. The last couple of weeks I've assumed that he's just been stressed about getting the new job, and that my suspicions aren't warranted. If he really is having an affair, then I need to think things through logically, plot out all my options, present him with real evidence and have a solution lined up. But it seems unlikely. Would he really risk an affair, and possibly a messy divorce, now he's got his dream promotion? Surely that's the very last thing he would want now he's in the public eye. I can just see the headlines: 'Love rat! Newly appointed breakfast TV presenter, Stuart Heaton, caught in a love tryst with Apple' (or Onyx or Dream or some other name suitable for a flighty young female influencer twenty years his junior). No, Stuart isn't going to do that; there is no way he will want to risk sullying his public persona, especially not now.

From my part, our marriage is the most precious thing in my life. I will do everything I can to preserve it. There is no way that I will end up in a rancorous marriage like my parents did, or go through an acrimonious divorce like most of my clients. I need to be the role model for marriage, so my only option is to chart a way forward to make Stuart realise that we are bound to each other for ever. Despite my reservations, I decide that his promotion will be a good thing for our marriage, and that's why I want to bolster his ego, throw a lavish party and shout to the world what an amazing husband I have. Because he is amazing, and I love him.

Fortunately, I hear the crunch of Stuart's tyres on our gravel drive, and I don't have to continue a dialogue about the state of our marriage with Alex. Stuart comes bounding into the kitchen, a champagne bottle in hand. He sweeps me up into an embrace, and I hope that Alex can see that he's wrong. Stuart and I still love each other very much.

The rest of the week is intense. I juggle working on the divorce for André Lowaski with tidying up the paperwork for Carla and planning the party for Stuart, although I've handed much of the of the organisation to a party planner. There is a flurry of increasingly hostile letters between myself and Lauren Lowaski's solicitor, although there's one thing we can all agree on: The division of their assets is going to be a nightmare. The Lowaskis have a complicated network of offshore trusts, plus houses in every continent, as well as joint ownership of their clothing empire. On top of that, they are contesting custody for their three young children and the two family dogs. André is determined to prove that Lauren is a bad mother, an alcoholic who is more obsessed with her wardrobe than her children. So far I haven't found any concrete evidence of that, but however unsavoury it is, it's my job to make sure I unearth the facts my client is seeking. This week, I have appointed both a private investigator and a forensic accountant.

By Saturday morning, I'm exhausted, yet I have to be up early to oversee all the deliveries for this evening's party. I had rather hoped that many of our friends would decline the short-notice invitation, but it seems our parties are legendary, and the majority of our sixty invitees have accepted. The marquee, complete with a starry ceiling made from twinkling LED lights, has been erected over our back terrace, and the interior has been fitted out with round tables covered in white tablecloths and chairs bedecked with large gold ribbons. This afternoon, the caterers will arrive along with the florist, followed by the live band and DJ with lighting equipment. It's impressive that Nathalie, my party planner, has been able to organise all of this within the space of a week. Money and the whiff of fame helps, I suppose.

It's now 7 pm, and I'm dressed in a shimmering silver maxi-dress that shows off my toned body. My chestnut brown hair is swept up in an artfully tousled style, thanks to a quick visit to the hairdresser earlier this afternoon, and I'm wearing the diamond necklace that Stuart gave me for my fortieth birthday. He is looking dapper in a starched floral shirt and dark jeans. We're standing together at the entrance to the marquee.

'Chantal, this is Jake Goodway,' Stuart says. 'He's a freelance photographer. I invited him to take snaps of us and our guests tonight. Annie suggested it would be a good idea.'

Annie is Stuart's agent, and she creams off a nice percentage of all the work that Stuart gets, particularly for any gigs beyond his main contract of TV anchor. I had thought this was a private party, a celebration with our friends, so I'm a bit disconcerted that Annie has sent us a press photographer.

'Can you stand together? Stuart, put your arm around your wife's shoulders,' Jake orders. 'Move to the left. Smile at each other. Stuart, can you get your wife to sit down, and you stand behind her?'

'Hello!' I say. 'My name is Chantal, and I'm right here. No need to talk to me through my husband.'

'Sorry, love, just trying to get as many shots in as possible before your guests arrive.'

I wonder in which gossip magazines our photo will appear over the next couple of weeks. I hate having to smile for the camera. In fact, the only photo I like of myself is the black-and-white profile picture on the firm's website, where I'm looking straight at the camera, my head slightly tilted to one side, my lips together, looking professional yet also approachable. And nothing like my twenty-four-year-old self. I've never done the celebrity thing before, and just hope that I'm not simply described as Stuart Heaton's wife, but as a leading family lawyer. I must remember to give Jake the photographer my business card before he leaves.

Debbie is the first to arrive, accompanied by a school-teacher friend of hers, both of them in floral day dresses. I feel bad that I didn't tell Debbie that the dress code was formal. And then all the guests start arriving, and I plaster on a smile and make small talk with our friends and well-wish-ers, a glass of champagne in my hand, which I barely touch. Mostly these are Stuart's friends. I enjoy their company, but unlike my husband, I'm a happy introvert and could easily go for days without any social interaction. It's probably why our marriage works; we complement each other.

It isn't until nearly 8 pm that I realise Alex is nowhere to be seen. In fact, I can't recall seeing him since lunchtime. I accost Stuart, who is being patted on the back by a journalist friend from the days when they used to work together at the *Times*.

'Have you seen Alex?' I whisper.

'No.'

'I'm not sure where he is. He knows the party was starting at 7 pm.'

'He's probably out with some mates. He'll be here. Stop worrying, love, and enjoy all of this.' He waves his hands around. I wonder how much he's already drunk.

And so, for the next hour, I meander amongst our guests, chit-chatting, accepting everyone's congratulations for Stuart's success. There is a grand buffet with a sumptuous array of foods, and people start tucking in, sitting in little clusters around the tables, chatting with acquaintances. Kathleen is the only person here who is my friend. She's sitting at a table with her wife, Trisha, and I pull up a chair to sit with them. It's the first time I've had the chance to have more than a passing conversation with Kathleen for well over a week, and I haven't seen Trisha in months.

'You're looking gorgeous,' Trisha says. 'How are you feeling about Stuart's new role?'

I look at her with surprise. No one has asked me that; there's an assumption that I'm delighted about it.

'Honestly, I'm not sure that the publicity will be great in my job. I've always felt that I should keep a low profile so that my clients shine. If I'm outed as the wife of Stuart, I'm nervous as to how that will pan out.'

'I disagree,' Kathleen says, laying her cutlery neatly on her plate. 'I think you're worrying about nothing. You'll be a celebrity divorce lawyer because people love to be associated with fame. I've told Trisha about the Lowaskis – hush-hush, don't worry.' She winks at me and motions as if to zip up her lips. 'If all goes well with his divorce, that's going to really put you on the map. He'll talk to his multimillionaire friends, and before you know it, you'll be the go-to solicitor with the famous husband.'

I laugh uncomfortably. Yes, it would be great to get more high-profile family clients, because the reality is, the wealthier they are, the more complicated the division of assets is and the larger their legal fees are, which all feeds into both my take-home pay and my profile. Although I can only admit it to myself, it's exactly where I envisaged my career going.

'You must come over for supper one evening. It's been ages since I've seen you properly, and you need to see the twins. They're changing every day,' Trisha says. 'I know you see Kathleen at work, but that's not the same, is it?'

Before I can answer, there's a commotion at the entrance to the marquee. I stand up to see what's happening. Alex is weaving his way towards me, his eyes sparking, his right index finger pointed at me and his upper lip snarling. Luna is behind him, clutching his left hand, trying to pull him backwards to no avail.

'You're a disgrace,' he slurs.

'Look, everyone!' He waves his arms around as he stumbles into a chair, knocking it over. 'My mother.' Our guests fall silent, and gazes are drawn to Alex and me.

And then Debbie is there, throwing her arms around Alex, leading him away, standing on tiptoes so she can whisper something into his ear as Luna follows them. She looks totally out of place in a torn black T-shirt and black leggings with rips in them, but at least her expression is one of embarrassment. Alex, on the other hand, is so outrageously drunk he can barely stand up. His trousers are slipping down, exposing the top of his boxer shorts. Our guests start talking amongst themselves again, but I can sense the judgement, and I want to sink into the floor. How could Alex do this to us, this evening of all evenings?

I wend my way through our guests, passing Stuart.

'I can't believe it,' I mutter.

'He's just a hot-blooded teenager. Everyone will understand. It's quite funny, really.'

'I don't think it's the slightest bit funny.'

'Chill, Chantal. Have another glass of wine.'

Infuriated, I leave Stuart and stride inside the house, where Alex is slumped on a kitchen chair, and Debbie is making him drink a large glass of water.

'You choose your moments, don't you?' I say, crossing my arms.

'You've sold out,' he slurs.

'What?'

'You've sold out. I thought you had a bit of moral backbone, but you don't, do you?'

For someone so drunk, he is talking surprisingly coherently. I hope this isn't about the possibility of Stuart having an affair, because that's the last thing I want to discuss in front of Debbie and Luna.

'LALO Clothing.' And then he starts to retch, and Debbie pulls him towards the sink just in time for him to be violently sick.

'How much has he drunk?' I ask Luna. 'And is it only drink, or drugs too?'

She looks affronted. 'He's been drinking beer all afternoon, ever since he found out that you're representing André Lowaski in his divorce. He thinks you've sold out.'

'I don't understand.'

Having purged himself, Alex drinks water from the cold tap, wipes his mouth with a tea towel and turns to me. 'That's exactly the problem. You don't even know what you've done. LALO Clothing is one of the biggest polluters on the planet. Fast clothing, workers living in squalid conditions earning a pittance, plastic consumption, encouraging people to buy cheap clothes and chuck them away, whilst the Lowaskis swan around the world in their private jet, not giving a fuck about their carbon footprint. They're scum, and you're working for them, so what does that make you?'

'Don't talk to your mother like that,' Debbie says. I'm glad of her support, but it's futile.

'Go to your room, Alex,' I say. 'Luna, it might be best if you leave now.'

'You think you can treat me like a little boy or one of your minion employees, don't you? But I'm an adult now, and I know what's right or wrong more than you do. We're the next generation, the one who are going to inherit the shit that you're leaving behind. You're a spineless fraud, Mother.'

'Alex!' Debbie exclaims.

'I'm only representing André Lowaski in his divorce,' I say. 'It's not like he's a friend.'

'You're endorsing what he does, and it stinks. You could have refused to represent him, but no, money and prestige are all that matters to you. I've lost all respect for you.'

'That's enough, Alex,' Debbie says.

'I'm going to bed.' Alex crosses his arms in front of his chest and stomps out of the kitchen. Luna has already scarpered.

'Tonight of all nights,' I murmur, pouring myself a glass of wine from an open bottle in the fridge. 'He seems to hate me at the moment. I can't do anything right.'

'I'm sure that's not true,' Debbie says. 'He's drunk and self-righteous. Forget about it and enjoy the party.'

But I can't forget about it, and I don't enjoy the party, because Alex might be right. Maybe I am a fraud.

6

ALEX – NOW

I wake up with a thumping headache and reach for my phone. I've slept through the whole morning; it's already 2.30 pm. And then I remember last night and the look of horror on Mum's face when I walked towards her in the marquee, with all of their fancy friends staring at us. I groan and find a couple of paracetamols, which I knock back with a gulp of water from a glass that I don't remember putting on my bedside table. I wish I'd had the chance to tell them the truth about her, and I should have called Dad out, too. There he was, all pumped up and pleased with himself for becoming a superhero, but doesn't he realise what the implications of fame are going to be? I don't want to be the son of a celebrity when people are going to want to befriend me for who my father is. How the hell am I ever going to know whom I can trust or not? At least Luna couldn't give a toss about all the trappings. She's the real deal; she hates all the display of wealth and lack of values of people like my parents. We get each other.

I get out of bed and fling on some clothes. It's quiet in the house, and hopefully Mum and Dad are both out. I walk downstairs to the kitchen, and it's all tidy in here, any remnants of last night's party long gone. I look outside and see that Dad is directing the marquee people who are taking it down.

Dad hasn't given a second thought as to how his new job is going to affect me. It's all been about him, as it always is. He should have asked me how I felt about it before accepting the position, because life is never going to be the same for me. I don't want to be in the spotlight; I just want to fight for what I believe in, quietly and under the radar. Both my parents are so very bourgeois, worried what other people think about them, wanting to impress the great and the good. It's bullshit. They've both sold out, but Mum especially. At least Dad has always been open about what he wants, but Mum claimed she wanted to do good, help people play happy families. I thought she cared about the environment, too, but it's all show. She probably only recycles the rubbish because it's trendy to have a compost bin.

I eat a few slices of bread and then head out, relieved that I get to the car without seeing anyone.

I'm pissed that I haven't got a message from Luna, although I can't really blame her. She'll be angry that she was shoved out of the house again last night like a second-class citizen. If my parents actually bothered to get to know Luna, they'd realise what a special person she is. Or perhaps they're so superficial that they will never see beyond her tatts and piercings.

Before starting the car, I see I've got some messages on Snapchat. A few of my mates are meeting up in the woods, so I send a message to my best friend, Josh, and tell him that I'll join them.

My parents think that everyone who goes to the private sixth-form college I'm attending are well-behaved teenagers. Neither of them went to fee-paying schools, so they don't know what it's really like. The kids are definitely worse behaved than at the local comprehensive, because they've got access to money and to the well-stocked wine cellars of their parents, who don't notice when a bottle or two of tequila goes missing. They use their obscenely large sums of pocket money to buy dope and ecstasy from the local dealers who hang around the school gates at the end of each day. Honestly, our parents must be blind, not realising what really goes on. Because I got chucked out of my old school, I'm part of the in-crowd, not that I particularly want to be. I think I fit in better with Luna's friends, who are seriously cool activists and are determined to make a real difference. But this afternoon, all I want to do is chill. Smoke a couple of spliffs and lark around with Josh and the crew.

I drive a few miles out into the countryside, along narrow and winding country roads with overhanging oak trees and hedgerows that back onto farmland. I leave the car in a remote car park mainly used by local dog walkers, although I've never actually seen any walkers when I've been here. It's the sort of place that you wouldn't know existed unless you were a local and someone had shown it to you. I recognise a few of the cars already parked up, including Josh's Polo. Most of us have our own cars, courtesy of our rich parents, and I'm not turning my nose up about that. It gives me freedom, although as soon as I can afford it, I'll buy myself an electric car. I don't know who found the spot where we congregate, but apparently it's been used by a few generations of sixth-formers from our school. There was a hiccup a couple of years ago when one of the school leavers became a police officer, but fortunately he was posted to Hampshire, so our not-so-secret spot remains covert.

I lock the car and walk through the dense wood of beech and silver birch trees, following the small crosses that have been slashed deeply into tree trunks, marking the way to the clearing in the woods. I love these woods and the singing birds and the network of tree roots that protrude from the earth. It reminds me that trees have an innate wisdom that I think humans are missing. Luna would agree with me, but it's not a sentiment I can share with my college friends. Four of my mates are already there. They've lit a small bonfire and are lounging on old blankets, smoking weed and drinking beer. I slump down next to Josh.

'Can your dad help me meet Holly H?' Zak asks.

'What?'

'Josh told us that your dad's the new presenter on breakfast TV, and he's going to be interviewing loads of famous people.'

'For fuck's sake, Josh. Can't you keep your mouth zipped?'

'It's hardly a secret, is it, when your dad's sitting on the sofa gazing out of the TV screen as we're eating our breakfast?'

I shrug my shoulders. He's right, and I'm pissed about it, but I'm certainly not going to ask Dad if he can introduce my mates to some idiot influencer. I open a can of beer and take a swig. I'm not stupid enough to drink and drive, so I'll go easy on the beer.

We while away the rest of the afternoon with banter and smoking, and as the light fades, a couple of girls join us. But I'm not interested in them; I've got a girlfriend. I check my phone often, but Luna hasn't messaged me.

As it gets dark, I feel cold and hungry and decide it's time to go home. I use the torch on my phone to follow the path back to the car park, and I walk quickly, stumbling on tree roots a couple of times. It's one thing enjoying the woods during the day, but being alone out here in the dark creeps me out a bit, as the trees creak and the wind whispers through the leaves. It's a relief to reach the car.

I manoeuvre out of the car park and turn up the music to

full volume before heading towards home. It was good to get away from the crap with my parents and have a few relaxed hours with my mates. I'm singing along when there's a massive thud.

Shit. Oh my god. I've hit something.

I'm thrown forwards, and the glass on my driver's side window shatters. I scream. I slam the brakes on, and the car skids to a halt. My heart is hammering in my chest. What was it? It happened so quickly. I sit for a few moments, trembling from head to foot, shaking off bits of glass from my lap. The side window is cracked but not completely broken. I peer outside, but I can't see a thing in the pitch black. Was it an animal, a deer, perhaps? And then I have a horrific thought.

What if it was a person?

Have I just killed someone? My life will be over, and so will Mum's and Dad's. It's so dark out here in the woods, and I know I've just got to get away. Quickly. Before anyone else drives past. I've been smoking weed all afternoon. I probably stink of it.

And so I put my foot on the accelerator. With my head trembling on my neck, and my hands slick with sweat as they grip the steering wheel, I drive. I don't give a second's thought as to where I'm driving to. All I can think about is what the news will say tomorrow. *Person found dead on side of road in a hit-and-run; the police are asking anyone who drove on Trowbridge Lane to come forwards.*

And then I realise that I can't go home. If my parents see the car, they'll want to know what happened, because there's bound to be a massive dent in the car. And what if there's blood on the front bumper? What the hell am I going to do? I can't stop. If I stop to look, then someone might see me and ask questions. I've just got to carry on, driving carefully, and get out of the dark so I can take a proper look without drawing attention to myself.

I make my way to Aunt Debbie's house. It's not even a very conscious decision, but it's somewhere I feel safe. It's not late, just gone 9 pm on a Saturday evening. She'll be home, and she'll know what to do. I'm still shaking as I park my car as closely to her bright blue Toyota Yaris as I can. As I get out and put weight on my leg, it hurts like hell, but it's only when I look down at myself that I realise blood is pouring down my shin and puddling in my trainer. I walk around the car. There's a lot of damage to the bodywork on the side door and side bumper, and the light is smashed. Shit. I'm going to have to get this sorted without Mum and Dad knowing. But there's no blood on the outside of the car. Thank god for that, at least. I groan. It feels like I'm going to puke.

I take in a couple of deep breaths and knock on Aunt Debbie's door. Fortunately for me, she doesn't have a life; she's inside watching telly. I can see her shadow getting up from the sofa in the living room and walking through to the hall.

'Alex!' she exclaims as she opens the front door. 'What are you doing here?' And then she glances down at my leg, and I follow her gaze. My shin is covered in blood. 'What happened? Come in. Quick, come in.'

I burst into tears the moment she shuts the door behind us, like some pathetic, snivelling kid.

'Hey, it's all going to be okay,' she says as she hugs me. But I'm too tall for her now, and she pulls away, takes my hand and leads me into the kitchen. 'Take a pew and let me have a look at that leg.'

It's really hurting now, and I can't look at it. I freak at the sight of blood; it's making me feel dizzy. I look away as Debbie tries to roll up my jeans.

'This isn't looking too good,' she says. 'What happened?'

'I had a car accident. I think I hit a deer.' At least, I *hope* I hit a deer. Surely a person wouldn't have been walking along the side of that narrow country road in the middle of nowhere.

'Oh, you poor darling. This cut is deep, and it looks like it's going to need some stitches. There might even be some glass in it. We'd better get you to the hospital.'

'No!' I groan.

'Sorry, darling, but it needs looking at. Why did you come here and not go home, sweetie?'

I roll my eyes at her. 'You know what Mum's like. She'll go off the deep end. I can't tell her what's happened, not with everything that's going on at the moment. She'll probably confiscate my car.'

'Alright. Let's get you to the hospital, and I'll send her a message to say you're staying over with me tonight.'

'Thanks, Aunt Debbie.'

My leg is really throbbing now. Debbie gives me some paracetamol and wraps a clean towel around my leg. I lean on her as we limp towards her car.

Forty-five minutes later, we're at the hospital, hobbling into the Accident and Emergency department. Aunt Debbie registers me, and we sit down on plastic chairs and wait to be seen.

'Are you going to tell me what really happened?'

'I've already told you.' But I can't look her in the eyes when I say that. All I can do is hear that horrible thud. Was it a deer or a fox, or could it have been a person? Have I just left someone out there on the side of the road to die a slow and painful death from horrific internal injuries? I'm feeling increasingly petrified, and am just plucking up the courage to tell Aunt Debbie, when my name is called.

We follow the nurse into a cubicle, where she gets me to sit on the side of a trolley bed. She's hot, with wavy blonde hair tied back and a cute gap in her front teeth. Her name badge says she's called Mia.

'That's a nasty cut you got there. Let's get you up on the bed and clean it up, and then we'll get the doctor in to see if you need stitches.'

I grit my teeth and squeeze my eyes shut and try not to cry out as she cleans up my leg. When eventually I open my eyes, Aunt Debbie has that worried look on her face. Shit. I hope she keeps her promise and doesn't ring Mum or Dad.

'I'm going to get the doctor in to have a look at your leg, Alex,' Nurse Mia says. 'You stay lying here, and we'll be as quick as we can.'

'What's the problem?' I ask Aunt Debbie as the nurse leaves, pulling the blue curtain across the cubicle.

'It's bleeding a lot, so I'm sure you'll need stitches, and that has to be done by a doctor. Not the end of the world, but you'll probably have a scar. Battle wounds.'

Aunt Debbie gets me a glass of water, but we still have to wait another fifteen minutes or so. Then a young doctor who looks barely older than me comes into the cubicle with Nurse Mia. He takes one look at my leg and confirms that he's going to stitch up the wound. He wheels in a trolley with all sorts of medical paraphernalia on it. Once again, I have to swallow bile and try to think of something else. I keep my eyes squeezed close as the doctor injects me and does whatever he needs to do.

'How did this happen?' he asks, chatting away, probably to take my mind off what's happening, but it doesn't work.

'Hit a deer in the car. It wasn't a bad accident, and the deer got away, but the glass in my window broke.'

'Ouch. Did you call the police?'

'Should I have done?' I exclaim.

'Keep still, Alex,' he says. And now I'm panicking all over again. I've just told this doctor that I hit a deer. What if a person is found dead on the side of the road? This doctor will remember what I've said and will put two and two together.

I've watched enough crap TV programmes to know that I'll be done for murder and fleeing a crime scene. My life will be over.

'Hey, sweetie,' Aunt Debbie says, squeezing my hand. 'Don't you worry.'

'Right,' the doctor says. 'All done here, but I want you to stay lying down for a while, Alex. Nurse Mia will be back in to check up on you.'

When they've both left, Aunt Debbie asks, 'What's going on with you and your parents?'

'Can't say,' I mutter. 'Not here.'

'Later, then?'

I nod.

The nurse comes back a few minutes later and frowns. The wound is still bleeding, and I can tell she's a bit worried about that. She doesn't pull the curtain completely closed, and I see her talking to the doctor and glancing back at me. Shit. What's going on?

Nurse Mia comes back in. 'We're going to take a little bit of blood, Alex. Nothing to worry about.' But I'm not a little kid; of course there's something to worry about. She puts a needle into my arm. I can't look as she fills up a phial of blood, and then she's gone again. Eventually, I doze off, and when I wake up, the bright lights hurt my eyes. Aunt Debbie isn't in the cubicle with me, but there's a new gauze over the wound on my leg, and there's no blood seeping through it, so I must be okay now.

I sit up, but feel a bit dizzy. And then Aunt Debbie is back with Mia.

'How are you feeling now?' the nurse asks.

'Okay. Can I go home?'

'Yes. Your aunt has signed some papers on your behalf, as you're not eighteen yet.'

'I'll be eighteen in two months' time.'

'And I hope you have a wonderful celebration!'

I smile at her awkwardly.

'Now get down off the bed carefully, and let's see if you can walk on your leg.'

I stand still, then walk cautiously towards the curtain.

'Seems alright.'

'Good. Now, if it starts bleeding again, I want you to come back to the hospital or go and see your GP. Try to keep your weight off it for a day or two. Plenty of rest and relaxation, please.'

'Can I skive off college?'

She laughs. 'Maybe for a day or two max.'

It's almost three in the morning now, but I don't feel tired. All I can think about is what I might have done. The hospital is really quiet, and the air is cold outside. When Aunt Debbie has started her car and we're back on the main road, she glances at me. 'Are you going to tell me what really happened?'

'What do you mean?'

'How you smashed up your car?'

I can't control a little sob. 'I don't really know if it was a deer I hit. I didn't dare look or get out of the car, because it was pitch black. I might have hit someone. What if I killed someone?'

'Oh, Alex,' she says, her voice laden with disappointment.

'Where did this happen?' she asks.

'On the road coming out of Barkinghurst Woods. Trowbridge Lane.'

'Do you think you'll recognise where exactly?'

I nod.

'In which case, I think we'd better go and take a look.'

For the next half an hour, I bite my nails, drum my fingers on the door handle, and try to stop that horrible churning feeling in my stomach. And then we're driving along the road where I hit something. It's pitch dark, but Aunt Debbie is driving really slowly, and the car headlights are illuminating the hanging branches and black hedges.

'Somewhere around here,' I say, but now I'm not absolutely sure. Aunt Debbie drives even slower at a snail's pace. 'There. You can see the tyre marks in the verge.' My heart is thudding, and I think I'm going to throw up. She pulls the car up onto the side of the road and puts on her hazard lights, leaving the main beams on, lighting up the verge and the hedgerow behind it. She reaches into the passenger pocket and pulls out a torch. Typical Aunt Debbie, prepared for every occasion. I can't imagine Mum being so practical. Instead, she'd be having a hissy fit and would have carted me off to the police station.

I tear the skin off the side of a nail until it bleeds. Aunt Debbie gets out of the car and I watch as her torchlight bobs up and down. Three minutes or so later, she's back in the car.

'There's nothing there. No traces of blood. Absolutely nothing.'

'What if the person got rescued?'

'If there had been a hit-and-run on this stretch of road, the police would be here. It probably was a deer or a fox, Alex. I don't think you've got anything to worry about.'

'It's still a living being,' I mutter. I'm just so relieved that Aunt Debbie thinks I'm wrong.

7

CHANTAL – THEN

Several weeks on and I'm still haunted by baby Noah's birth. The blood, the gore, the screams, the nauseating hospital smells. And Jade's euphoric smile as she lay there with baby Noah in her arms. Obviously she hasn't been to clean my flat, and I haven't bothered to find someone else. I'm quite capable of cleaning myself, and it's not like I make much mess. But now I've got a message from Jade.

> *Hiya chantal I'll clean ur flat as normal on wednesday. C u then. Jade x*

> *Thanks, Jade. I hope you and Noah are doing well.*

She's sent me a couple of texts over the past few weeks, along with photos of little Noah and asking when his aunty – i.e., me – is going to come over for a visit. I sent her a pack of baby grows and a teddy bear, and she seemed almost pathetically grateful. But I've got no desire to actually see her. I don't want to be mean. It's just it hurts too much being around little babies.

So when I get home at 6 pm, my heart sinks to find the door unlocked. I hope that she's just forgotten to lock up properly after herself, but no, the vacuum cleaner is going in the living room. I brace myself and walk in.

'Chantal!' she exclaims, switching the machine off and striding towards me, her arms open wide. 'Hey, Noah, it's your aunty.'

I glance down and see that the baby is strapped into a car seat, sucking hard on a dummy. He looks at me with big dark eyes, and then his little face crumples, and he bursts into tears. That's the effect I have on babies, I suppose.

'Hey, sweetie,' Jade says, bending down and lifting him up out of the chair. He looks small to me, pallid and kind of scrawny, not a chubby little baby with rosy cheeks. Then again, what do I know? 'You don't mind me bringing him to work, do you? It's just I've got no one to look after the little man.'

'Don't you have anyone who can help you out, babysitting and stuff?'

Jade laughs. 'It's me and Noah against the world, isn't it?' She puts him back in his car seat, but Noah is still grizzly. Jade restarts the vacuum, ignoring the baby, whose wails seem to increase in volume and pitch to match the vacuum.

'Is he hungry?' I ask, shouting over the racket.

'He'll have to wait. We've run out of milk.'

'Aren't you breastfeeding him?' I'm trying not to be judgemental, but it's hard to ignore the message that breast is best.

'I need a drink in an evening, and I don't want to get him pissed. Besides, it's bloody painful breastfeeding, and I don't want droopy tits. After all, these two babies are my best assets.' She wriggles her chest, then stops the vacuum and winds up the cord, seemingly unbothered by Noah's cries.

'Where are you living now?' I ask.

'Tammy chucked us out, which is fair dos, so we're in a squat, but it's okay. You don't need to worry about us. I'm hoping to get a council flat, or else we might just run away somewhere far from here. My mate said it's easier to get council places over Chesterfield or Derby way.'

'Do you know people there?'

'No.' She shrugs, apparently not fazed by a totally new start. I wonder what it must feel like having no one in the world to help you. Whatever our differences, I know that Debbie and I will always have each other's backs, and I'm sure that Stuart would come to my rescue if I was really in trouble. 'Anyway,' she says, changing the subject, 'how long have you got before you're out of here?'

I bite the side of my mouth to stop myself from grinning. It's fifty-nine days until the year is up, until Stuart and I will decide if our future will be together. It fills me with a mix of excitement and terror.

'Just under two months,' I say.

'We should go and do something together. Have fun.'

I'm not sure that Jade's idea of fun and mine are the same thing, so I take a punt and suggest something that I hope she'll turn her nose up at. 'How about a drive out to the hills and a picnic if the weather is good?'

She claps her hands and does a little jig. 'That's an awesome idea! I've only been out of the city twice. The first time when I was in the children's home, and we went to the Peak District, but it pissed with rain the whole time. The second time was to a rave in a disused quarry. Best night of my life, that was.' She bends down and tickles Noah under his chin, whose crying becomes a gurgle. 'We're going to the countryside, and you're going to breathe in fresh air. Shall we go this weekend?'

'I'm busy this weekend,' I say, which isn't true, 'but let's stay in touch, and we'll do it before I leave.'

'Sure thing.'

She disappears for a moment to put away the vacuum in the hall cupboard and the cleaning materials into the cupboard under the sink. Noah is wailing now, so I disappear into the bathroom to stop my head exploding from his cries.

'See you soon, Chantal!' Jade shouts.

I feel bad when I emerge into my now silent flat. Jade has got no one, and it's not her fault that I can't bear to be around other people's children.

She rings me ten days later. 'The forecast is great for the weekend. Shall we go for our picnic on Saturday?'

I hesitate. 'I'm not sure–'

'Please!' she cries. 'Me and Noah have been so looking forward to it.'

I suppose I have nothing to lose, and besides, I could do with getting out of Manchester. It's unlikely that I'll ever see Jade again, so I decide to be kind and remind myself that I'll be able to cope for a few hours with her and the baby.

'Where do you suggest?' I ask, assuming she won't know anywhere.

'A mate was telling me about this cool reservoir near Buxton. It's bright blue and really pretty.'

'Sounds good. Where would you like me to collect you from?'

'You don't need to. I've got myself a car.'

'You have?' I'm taken aback. She hasn't even got anywhere to live, so how come she's got a car? And then I wonder whether perhaps she's living in it.

'I'll message you the address and meet you there. Noon on Saturday.'

'Wouldn't it make more sense for us to go in the same car?' I ask, but she's already hung up on me.

It is one of those rare bright-blue-sky days, and frankly, if Jade doesn't show up, I won't mind. I've bought a selection of picnic foods from M&S, little sausage rolls and sandwiches and pots of coleslaw and salads, and I'll be quite content sitting on the side of Jongleur Hill reservoir by myself, soaking in the rays, of which I've seen very few this past year. Perhaps I can even take some selfies and post them online to show Stuart what he's missing.

The drive is quite long, but the scenery is spectacular, with dramatic hills and heather-filled moors and rocky outcrops all in shades of greys, greens and mauves. Behind me, there are views right across the Cheshire plain, with sparkling rivers weaving into the distance and tiny trains snaking along impressive viaducts. Thanks to my satnav, I arrive just gone midday. Jade is right. It really is lovely up here, and the immediate vista is quite different to the land-scape I've just passed through. It's almost as if I'm in a different country, with white cliffs descending down into a green-turquoise lake that looks like it's come out of a scene from an exotic travel programme.

I get out of the car and stretch, turning my face up towards the warm sun. The place is deserted, surprisingly so for a weekend. I leave the car and stroll around the edge of the reservoir, enjoying the views and watching a bird of prey swoop downwards into a distant field. The lake itself was obviously a quarry at some point, but as I walk around it, I'm taken aback to see a sign that says *Danger*. I wonder what's so dangerous about this place other than the steep drop down to the lake. I walk back towards my car, wondering if I should find somewhere else for us to go.

And then Jade arrives. She's driving an old silver Metro car that is covered in dents and rust and frankly looks like it's been rescued from a tip. The car comes to a shuddering halt, and I realise she's stalled it. I wonder if it's roadworthy, and if she's even got a driving license.

'How was the journey?' I ask.

'Crap. It's a horrible car.'

'How long have you been driving?'

'What's it to you? I got here, didn't I? I'm just out of practice, that's all.'

I bite my tongue because I'm not here to have an argument with Jade. She climbs out of the driver's seat and chucks a bunch of chocolate wrappers onto the floor well on the passenger's side. She's looking pretty in a summery, pink floral dress and has bare feet. Noah is asleep in his car seat in the back, but he awakens when she takes him out of the car. She puts the car seat on the gravel, ignoring his cries.

'I got us some booze and crisps,' she says, taking an Asda bag out of the boot.

'We're both driving,' I murmur.

'Yeah! I know.' She rolls her eyes at me. 'But a couple of glasses isn't going to do any harm. I need it. Had a shit week.'

I take out the bags of food that I brought, along with an old blanket. We walk together towards the edge of the quarry, about twenty metres from the car.

'It's pretty here,' she says as she sinks down onto the blanket, placing Noah in his seat next to her. He's sucking hard on a dummy and is blinking furiously in the bright sunlight.

'Have you got anything to protect him from the sun?' I ask.

'If you're going to have a go at me, Chantal, I'm out of here.'

'Sorry,' I say. 'Ignore me.' I don't want to wind Jade up, and I need to remember that this baby isn't my responsibility. I take the food out of the plastic bags and place the packages on the blanket. Jade grabs a chicken sandwich.

'Thanks for this. Haven't eaten properly in days.'

'Why?' I ask. 'What's going on?'

'All my friends have deserted me now I've got the baby, and my benefits aren't enough to get us by. I can't go out in an evening because there's no one to look after Noah. The council says it could be months or even years 'til I get a property, and they want me to go into some shitty shelter. And your landlord is selling your place, so I won't even get any more cleaning money. So yeah, things are a bit crap at the moment, to say the least.'

'I'm sorry,' I say. 'Do you need any money?'

'What, you think I'd take your money? What I need is a life. A proper roof over my head, a man in my bed, some real mates and a job would be good. Benefits don't go far when I've got to buy stuff for the baby. But you wouldn't understand none of that.'

I don't know why she wanted to meet me out here if she's going to be like this, but I hold my tongue. And actually, yes, I do know what it's like to be on benefits. Mum was on benefits after Dad died.

Jade opens a screw-top bottle of white wine and takes a long swig from the top. It makes me very uncomfortable. I don't want to argue with her, but this is wrong. She shouldn't be drinking.

Noah starts crying again, and Jade completely ignores him.

'Shouldn't you–?' I say, but she cuts me off.

'Don't be like all the others, telling me what I should or shouldn't do.' She sighs and takes another swig of wine. 'It was a massive mistake,' she says, lying back on the blanket, her eyes closed.

'What was a mistake?'

'Having a baby. Keeping him.'

'You don't mean that really, do you?' I ask, horrified. I know some people find motherhood hard, but to actually regret keeping him and saying it out loud, in his earshot, just seems all wrong.

'Yeah, I do mean it. Most days, I wish it could just go back to how it was before, me and my mates having a laugh, getting by. But you wouldn't understand. Someone like you would be fine having a baby, because you've got money. You wouldn't have to worry about having a roof over your head or begging for food or being billy no-mates.'

We're both silent for a while, listening as her baby's cries morph into screams.

'Noah seems really distressed. Does he need a nappy change, or is he hungry?' I ask.

'How the hell do I know?' She jumps up from the ground. 'I'm doing me best, alright? I'm going to the car for a smoke. Look after the baby, will you?' she says, not waiting for me to reply.

This is not what I expected. Jade seems both angry and disconsolate. It must be hard for her being all alone with a baby, but drink, drugs and cigarettes aren't going to help either of them. I wonder if I can get some help for her, but I know the last thing she'll want is to have social services involved. I watch her as she saunters to her car, her shoulders sagging, the soles of her bare feet black with grime. When she's disappeared into the car, I turn to the baby.

'Hey, you poor little thing,' I say, feeling compelled to try to calm Noah. I undo the strap of his car seat and lift him out. His nappy feels heavy; I suppose he needs a change. I jiggle him up and down on my hip. His little fingers reach out and grab my hair, and then he nuzzles his head into my neck. Even though he isn't mine, I feel a jolt of longing. Poor little Noah, with a mother like Jade.

'Come along, sweetie,' I say. 'Let's go and see if your mamma has got some spare nappies for you.' As I bounce him up and down on my hip, his grizzles turn into chuckles.

It does nothing to ease my longing for a child of my own. To my surprise, it seems that I'd be good at mothering; it comes naturally.

Jade is sitting in the driver's seat of her battered car, her eyes closed, smoking a spliff. I can't believe she's smoking dope and drinking alcohol when she's meant to be looking after her baby and when she's going to be driving. Life may be tough for Jade, but this is outrageous.

I knock on the window, and she winds it down.

'What?' she asks, with a glazed look on her face.

8

CHANTAL – NOW

They send a driver for Stuart on the mornings that he has an early start. It's not much fun, having to get up in time to be collected at 4 am; he's taken to sleeping in a spare room so as not to wake me. His chauffeur navigates the drive to the London studios in a black Mercedes, while Stuart sits in the back, reading the morning papers to make sure he's fully up to date on current affairs. After just a couple of days, I can see that this routine is going to be hard for Stuart, and for me. We can no longer have a quick chat over coffee in the mornings, and he's eager to get to bed by 9 pm every evening, so it's not like we have the chance for a proper talk then. Although his snoring used to annoy me, now the bedroom feels empty and strange. It's 9 pm on the second week of his new job, and I'm tidying up the kitchen when he comes in to get a glass of water.

'I've got a work dinner tomorrow evening, so I'll stay the night in a hotel near the TV studios. You don't mind, do you?'

Obviously I do, but I don't say anything. We're going to have to negotiate our way around Stuart's new hours, and if it means we all need to relocate to London, then I suppose I'll have to consider it. But not until Alex has finished his A Levels. Next year he'll be off travelling, and the year after he'll be at university, so it would be the perfect time for a change.

As if on cue, our son lopes into the kitchen, grabs a banana and rifles around in the fridge.

'Night, Alex,' Stuart says. 'I'm off to bed now.'

Alex grunts in return while Stuart leaves the room without saying goodnight to me. A few seconds later, Alex follows him upstairs, a banana, a bar of chocolate and a piece of bread in his hands.

It hits me then how very lonely I feel. I'm in a house with two men, yet I may as well be living alone. Something is going to have to change.

The next morning, I'm driving to work, listening to the news on Radio 4, and my heart sinks. Carla, the woman for whom I got the restraining order, the woman who many say should be prime minister one day, has been severely beaten by her ex-boyfriend and is currently being treated in hospital. It isn't clear from the news whether her boyfriend has been remanded in custody, or whether Carla is going to be okay. I ring Alicia.

'Can you get hold of the custody desk at the police station and find out if that bastard is in a police cell?' I drum my fingers on the steering wheel. This is bad for me; my job is to protect my clients, and although I couldn't have done any more than get the restraining order, I feel terrible. I park the car hurriedly and rush into the office.

'Yes, he's in custody,' Alicia says as soon as I arrive at her desk.

'Good. I hope he gets locked up for a long time. Can you order a big bouquet of flowers to be sent to Carla in the hospital?' I don't suppose she'll be allowed to have flowers, but it's the thought that counts. And I have no doubt that as her solicitor, I'll be hearing from the police.

'Have you seen the papers yet?' Alicia asks.

I shake my head. She points to an article about LALO Clothing.

'Their shares have taken a nosedive this morning. The story is in all the broadsheets, and the markets have taken fright.'

I sigh. This is bad news. I skim read the article and see that LALO Clothing has been accused of using cheap labour in shocking conditions in Bangladesh. Perhaps Alex has a point. At the end of the article, it quotes a statement from a supposed family friend. 'Rumour has it that the Lowaskis' marriage is in trouble, and Mr Lowaski has appointed Chantal Lacey of Egerton Brook Steading to represent him.' The article concludes that the couple's impending divorce may have an additional negative impact on the company's value.

In another paper, the financial journalist's tip is to sell LALO shares now before they sink any further. Damn. And double damn that they've mentioned me and our firm's name. My partners won't like that one little bit, as it implies – quite erroneously of course – that I'm something to do with the nosedive of the shares.

I stride into my office and am about to call André Lowaski, but he beats me to it. Reception rings and tells me that he's here and wants to see me now. I sigh and agree for him to be allowed in. A minute later, Alicia escorts him into my office.

'It's a fucking disaster. I thought I employed you to keep my personal affairs out of the public eye.'

'No, Mr Lowaski. I am your lawyer, not your PR agent. My job is to help you and your wife end your relationship as amicably and equitably as possible. I understand that the commentary in the press must be very distressing, but–'

There is a commotion outside in the corridor and a loud rapping on my door. It swings open.

'I'm sorry,' Alicia says, looking very flustered. A glamorous, blonde-haired woman wearing a fawn coat with oversized lapels and high-heeled boots strides into my office.

'What are you doing here?' André Lowaski asks, narrowing his eyes at her.

'I don't hate you, André,' she says, pulling up a chair and sitting down next to him. 'I just don't love you anymore. What we're doing is ridiculous. We'll lose the company, all our money and destroy our children's lives. Is that what you really want?'

'Have you been drinking already?' He makes a big show of looking at his Rolex watch. 'It's barely 9.30 am.'

'Stop the nonsense, André. I know you're trying to make out I'm an alcoholic, but we both know I'm not. Am I talking sense, Mrs whatever-your-name is?'

'Chantal Lacey,' I say, glad that I still use my maiden name for professional purposes. 'This is very unconventional, you turning up here without your solicitor,' I say. 'Are you willing to try mediation?'

They both answer at the same time. He says no; she says yes.

'In which case, Mrs Lowaski, I strongly recommend that you go and visit your own solicitor.'

'He wants to take away my children. Has he told you that? Yet I'm the one who has done everything for them, who gets up in the night when they can't sleep, who had to have an abdominoplasty after their births, who makes sure they do their homework and eat healthy food.'

He interrupts. 'Bullshit! That's what we have a live-in nanny for.'

She ignores him. 'I'm their mother. I carried them; I love them. He does nothing for the children except give them money and pose for photographs of them when they're wearing their best clothes. My children need to stay living with me, their mother. Do you have children?'

'This isn't about me,' I say.

'I'm asking you a question as one woman to another. Do you?'

I nod.

'So imagine what it would feel like if your child was wrenched away from you. How would you feel?' She turns to face her husband. 'I will fight you, André, with every ounce of my being. And if it means destroying your beloved company and showing the world what a shit you really are, then so be it.' She stands up, flicks her hair over her shoulder and storms out of the room.

We're silent for a moment.

'I don't want you to bite my head off, André,' I say. 'But is it genuinely in the children's best interest to remove them from their mother?'

'Yes. The little display you saw there will have been practised in front of the mirror all morning. She's quite the accomplished actress, is my soon-to-be ex-wife.'

'If you will accept some advice from a very experienced family lawyer, I beg of you not to use your children as pawns in your divorce. They are the innocent parties in the breakdown of your relationship. Whatever their age, whether they're young like yours, or even grown-up and in their twenties, the emotional fallout from divorce is huge. They will feel confused and extremely anxious. As they watch you both lose respect and love for each other, they may well worry that you will stop loving them. They might blame themselves for the family split. Many children suffer with mental health issues or even physical health problems as a result. It's common for school grades to decrease and for poor behaviour to increase. These aren't just stresses that will affect your children now, but ones that will have a far-reaching effect on them for the rest of their lives. I'm not saying that you should reconcile with your wife, as it's obvious that you both want to go your separate ways, but I beg of you, think about your children in all of this. What is best for them? Not you, not your wife. What is truly in their best interests?'

I hold my breath. My little speech tends to go one of two ways. My client might storm out, or he may truly listen to what I'm saying. Whether he acts on it is another matter altogether.

André Lowaski does neither. 'I hear what you're saying,' he says. He stands up, nods at me and leaves my office.

It's not even 10 am, but I feel emotionally wrung out. That is the trouble with my job. I'm not just a lawyer; I'm a psychologist and the protector of children. Perhaps that's why I was drawn to this career. But my vocation is that of a warrior. Words are my weapons. Whether I'm filing petitions or talking to judges, I have to fight all day every day. And yes, it's exhausting having to assist and protect people, because I have to suppress my own feelings, and if a child's future is at stake, everything else has to go on hold.

I know that Alex has suffered over the years, because what am I to do if I have to file an emergency protection order to ensure the safety of a vulnerable child and it needs doing straight away? Do I save that child's life or go to Alex's parent-teacher meeting? And I never switch off. I cannot afford to lose a case, because that might mean my client's life is destroyed for ever. I work very hard, and I earn lots of money in return, but sometimes I just want to stop. To stop and breathe and nurture myself and my family.

I wonder whether I need a sabbatical. I've been doing this job a very long time. It's never boring, but it's draining taking on other people's problems, and of course the irony lurks at the back of my brain twenty-four seven. The world thinks I'm a good person. The Legal 500 is the go-to list of top lawyers by practice in the UK, and I'm right up at the top of the list of family lawyers. And that's a problem, because when you climb to the top of the ladder, it's a heck of a long way to fall back down. It can take twenty years to climb to the top, but one disastrous failure in court that leads to the tragic death of a woman or, worse still, a child, and my career could be destroyed overnight. That's why, just occasionally, I resent Stuart's job. Yes, he might have to work hard, but he does what his producer tells him to do. It's not like he's saving lives or making a real difference.

By lunchtime, I have a pounding headache. I've been squinting at documents for hours; I need to get out of the office. I put on my coat, swing my handbag over my shoulder and grab my phone from the desk.

'I'm going out to get a sandwich and get some fresh air,' I say to Alicia. As I'm walking down the stairs, my phone vibrates. It's a message from a withheld number.

I WANT MONEY. I KNOW YOUR SON ISN'T YOURS.

9

ALEX – NOW

I t's weird sleeping at Debbie's house. I haven't stayed here in a while, but I used to love it at her old house. She made her second bedroom into the perfect room for a young boy, with Thomas the Tank bedlinen and a box of Legos stored under the bed. Kids' books lined the bookshelves, and when I refused to go anywhere without my teddy bear, she bought a replica, which she kept sitting on top of the pillow on the bed.

But since she moved to the same village as us, I've never had a reason to stay over. I'm a bit freaked that she's turned this room into an almost-near-replica of the one at her old house. I'm nearly eighteen now. I've got no desire to sleep under a Thomas the Tank duvet cover. I don't say anything, because she's being super chilled about helping me out, and perhaps it's the only spare linen she's got.

I'm exhausted after the accident and the hanging around in hospital and sleep like a log, only waking up when she knocks on my door and says it's lunchtime.

'How come you're here?' I ask, sitting up and rubbing my eyes.

'I popped back from school to check you're alright.'

'What have you told Mum?'

'Just that with everything that's been going on, you wanted to stay with me for a couple of nights.'

'So you didn't tell her about the car accident?'

'Nope. But she'll spot that big plaster on your leg, won't she?'

I shrug. It'll be no big deal to keep it from her, as it's hardly the weather to be wearing shorts. I'm more concerned about my battered car. If they know I've damaged it, both Mum and Dad will go apoplectic.

'Can you lend me some money to get the car fixed?'

Debbie sucks air in through her teeth. 'I don't know about that.'

'Please, Aunt Debbie. I've got to get it repaired without them knowing. I'll pay you back.'

'And how are you going to do that?'

'I'll get a newspaper round or something. I'll find a way, I promise.'

'I don't know, Alex. Money is really tight at the moment. You'd better get some quotes in for the repairs, and then we'll decide.'

'What did you tell college about me not going in today?'

'That you have a stomach bug. So if you go out, make sure no one spots you.' She winks at me. 'I need to be getting back to school. There's a spare key for you on the kitchen table, and a lasagne for you in the fridge that you can heat up in the microwave.'

I grin at her. Thank goodness for Aunt Debbie.

I go online and find a garage about ten miles away. I can't risk getting the car fixed anywhere nearby. I call them, and the man tells me to drive over, and he'll take a look at the damage before giving me a quote.

I feel sick when I look at the damage in the light of day.

What if I did hit a person? I do a quick search of the local news online, but nothing comes up, so hopefully I've got away with it. The car starts fine, and I drive carefully towards Crawley, keeping well within the speed limits.

The garage is a shabby place in the back end of nowhere. A man in overalls comes out to have a look at the damage to my car. He tuts a lot. 'Worse than it looks, I'm afraid. We'll need to replace this panel, the bumper and the front light.'

'How much will it cost?'

'A grand, or eight hundred if you pay cash.'

Shit, that is huge. I wonder if I'm doing the right thing by keeping the accident hidden from Mum and Dad, but then I remember the thump and my fear that I might have hit an actual person. I've got no choice but to get it done, and fast. 'How quickly can you do it?'

He rubs the stubble on his chin. 'A week.'

'Can you do it sooner? I can't be without the car.'

'I'll do it as a rushed job for twelve hundred. You'll have it back the day after tomorrow.'

I know I'm being ripped off, but I say yes. Hopefully, Debbie will lend me the money and I won't face any aggro from the parents.

'Okay,' I say as I hand him the car keys. 'Can you order me a taxi?'

He rolls his eyes at me and strides away. 'Order one yourself, snowflake,' he shouts over his shoulder.

By the time I'm back at Debbie's, she's returned home from school.

'All sorted?' she asks as she settles down at her small kitchen table with a cup of tea, a massive donut and a pile of kids' exercise books.

'It's more expensive than I thought. Twelve hundred.'

Her jaw drops open. 'Is the car even worth that much?'

That never crossed my mind. I feel a kernel of panic.

'Why can't you put it on insurance?'

'Because Mum and Dad will go apeshit. Please, Aunt Debbie. You will lend me the money, won't you?'

'I haven't got that sort of money lying around, Alex. I'm not rich like your parents.'

'Please,' I beg her, wringing my hands. 'I'll pay you back really quickly. You're the best, you know that, don't you?'

'Stop trying to be a charmer like your dad. I'll lend it to you, but I need to have it paid back before the middle of next month. Otherwise, I'll have to pay exorbitant charges on my credit card.'

'Thank you so much!' I say, giving her a kiss on the cheek. I then go into the living room and check the local news. There's been no report of a hit-and-run, but I still can't rest easy. That's the real reason I don't want anyone to know about the accident, in case I did something really bad. I send Luna a message. To my relief, she replies, and we agree to meet up in an hour.

I take Aunt Debbie's bike, which I doubt she's ever used. I don't want to be mean, but she's probably too big to use it anyway. My leg hurts a lot as I cycle into town, but I try to ignore the worry that I might be messing up the stitches. I don't want to be late to meet Luna in the park, so needs must.

'I'm sorry about what happened at my parents' party,' I say.

'Yeah, you were a jerk.'

I hang my head. I thought Mum was more of a jerk for chucking Luna out of the house, but I'm not going to get into an argument with her. I tell her about the car accident and how I'm staying at Aunt Debbie's, and how I need to get hold of the money to pay her back.

'Got any bright ideas?' I ask.

'You could steal it.'

'What!' I laugh, because she's joking, surely? But Luna looks deadly serious.

'I've got some mates who nick stuff, and they've got mates who can sell it on. Don't look so shocked. They never hurt anyone, and they choose people who can afford to lose it. It's the only way you'll get hold of that much cash in a short space of time.'

'Will they do it for me?' I ask.

'Eh, no!' She looks at me as if I'm an idiot. Perhaps I am.

'I can't steal things,' I say. We're both silent for a while.

'What about nicking things from your own house? Make it look like it's a burglary, and I'll get the stuff sold for you.'

'Seriously?' That isn't such a terrible idea. If I just take things, then Mum will accuse me or Luna or our lovely Gail, the cleaning lady, of stealing, but if I make it look like a break-in, then it'll be more authentic. 'That might be a goer,' I say before leaning over Luna and taking her in my arms.

It's three days later, and I've plucked up the courage to do it. Luna has come along for support and to be my lookout. I think she's also here because she's worried I might bottle at the last minute.

'It's the only way,' she reassures me, stroking my forearm. 'It's not like you're doing anything really bad. It's not as if you're breaking into a stranger's house. It isn't a crime to break into your own home, so you've got nothing to worry about.'

I don't know about that. I just don't know if I can do it. I've dreamed of being many things, but never a burglar. But is it really theft if you're taking from one sister who is loaded to give to another who isn't?

Luna picks up on my hesitation. 'If you do it, I'll give you a special treat.'

'What exactly?'

'Blow-your-mind sex stuff. You won't regret it. How else

are you going to get the money? I've told you; I've got a good contact who will buy the stuff from us. Go on. I dare you.'

And so I leave her standing there on the pavement, and I pull the hood up over my head and walk with my shoulders hunched, keeping to the shadows underneath the hedgerow that leads into our garden. The hammer she has given me weighs down my jacket and bumps against my leg, the same leg that is still hurting from the accident. Mum and Dad are both at work, so I know I'm safe, but it doesn't stop my heart from thumping out of my chest. I could just walk in using my key, take the stuff and break a window on my way out, but Luna says I've got to be an authentic thief, and that means breaking in from the outside so that the glass shatters in the right way, and I have to leave by the same route. I suppose she's right, just in case they get the police involved. I don't have to worry about my fingerprints or footprints, because they'll be there anyway, but Luna's given me a pair of black rubber gloves, nevertheless. They're tight around my fingers, and my palms feel sweaty inside them.

I open the intricate wrought-iron garden gate that leads from the front drive to the right-hand side of the house, leaving it slightly ajar so I can make a quick getaway, and then I tiptoe along the paving stones. The birds are singing, and it's a perfectly normal day ... except it isn't. I glance from left to right, even though there is no one here and our house isn't visible to any neighbours; plus we don't have any security cameras. I take the hammer out of my pocket. The downstairs toilet window shatters surprisingly easily, although the noise pierces my skull. I make a fist and push the glass through. It tinkles as it lands on the floor. I haul myself up onto the window ledge, making sure I don't cut myself. I've learned that lesson. Then I'm inside. It's a small room with a white toilet and sink and walls painted in dark blue, with lots of gold-framed photographs on the walls, mainly of Dad shaking hands with C- or B-list celebrities. I suppose these photos will be replaced with the A-list folk soon enough.

I walk along the downstairs corridor to the hallway and up the stairs, heading straight for Mum and Dad's bedroom. It's a big room with fluffy carpet and curtains in a dull colour that Mum says is sophisticated. They've got a huge bed, and the headboard is really tall and covered with velvet in the same colour as the curtains. Mum has a dressing room that leads off the bedroom, and there's a safe in there. I know the code, but obviously I can't use it, so I have to choose things that aren't safely stored away. There's no jewellery lying around in the dressing room, so I walk back into their bedroom and open Mum's bedside table drawer. There's a pair of diamond earrings inside that sparkle. I'm about to pick them up, but I can't, because Mum loves these earrings. Dad gave them to her when she was made a partner in her law firm. I can't choose something that she cares about. I open Dad's bedside table and take a watch. It looks expensive, but I don't know if it is. I walk over to the chest of drawers, and there's a necklace just lying there next to a photograph of me as a toddler in a silver frame. I'm not sure if the necklace is worth anything, but I stuff it in my pocket anyway. It feels wrong being in here, grubby almost. I'll try the living room instead.

I run back down the stairs and into the living room. There's a big antique dresser on the back wall, and it's full of stuff. I realise that even though I've looked at it a million times, I've never noticed what's really there. I pick up a silver dish and a small antique clock. I've no idea where they've come from or what they're worth. It's crazy, isn't it? That we can live somewhere all our life, but not really notice what's inside. I glance around, wondering what else I can take.

And then I hear the crunch of tyres on the drive.

Shit. There's someone here. I hope it's just a delivery or

something, but then I hear the whirring of the garage electric doors as they lift open. It must be Mum home early. I am frozen. A text message pings on my phone from Luna.

Get out NOW. Ur mum home.

I race back to the downstairs loo, my trainers crushing bits of glass on the tiled floor, fear making my breathing shallow and quick. I haul myself up onto the window ledge and somehow throw myself out, landing with a thud on the paving stones. I can hear Mum's footsteps now. She's on the phone, and although I can't see her, I can imagine exactly what she looks like, her phone wedged between her ear and shoulder, wearing her beige raincoat, holding her bags in one hand and fumbling for the house key in the other.

'Hold on a sec. I think I heard something.'

My breath catches in my throat. I stand right up against the house, under the shadow of the eaves. With trembling knees, I brace myself for her to walk around the side of the house and see me standing there like an idiot. What will I say? How can I explain the broken window? It's not like I'm a little kid playing ball and accidentally broke the glass.

But she doesn't walk around the side of the house. She opens the front door, and I hear it slam behind her, and the sound of her voice disappears as she goes into the bowels of the house. And then I sprint, running as fast as I can, the way I came in, until I'm out on the road. Luna emerges from her hiding place in the bushes, and we both collapse in a fit of hysterical laughter as I realise what I've done.

'What you get, then?' she asks.

I take the items out of my pockets.

'Oh,' she says as her face falls.

10

CHANTAL – NOW

I t was futile trying to concentrate today. All I can think about is the text message. And why now? Why is someone sending me that now, after all these years? What do they want? Is this the precursor to blackmail, or is it just to scare me? It must be something to do with my name being printed in the press today, although I'm a high-profile lawyer and it certainly isn't the first time that's happened. It simply doesn't make sense.

I return to the office, but spend the next hour or so staring at my computer screen and constantly glancing at my phone, waiting to see if I get another message. After a while, I realise trying to work is futile, so I decide to go home and have a workout in our home gym. Perhaps that will clear my mind and ease the tension in my neck and the churning in my stomach. I'm on the phone to Alicia when I park the car and walk to the front door with the phone wedged between my chin and shoulder. I hear something.

'Hold on a sec,' I say to Alicia. I strain to listen, but there's silence now. It's probably nothing, a fox perhaps. Besides, my nerves are on edge today. I finish my instructions to her and walk into the house, dumping my bags and going straight through into the utility room to collect the pile of washed and ironed clothes that Gail has left me. And then I do a double take. The door to the downstairs loo is wide open, but I was the last to leave this morning, and I have a thing about shutting doors before leaving home. Gail knows I do, and she's always diligent about shutting every door before she leaves. In the six years she's been cleaning and ironing for me, she has never left a door open. As I step inside the doorway, I immediately see the broken window, glass all over the floor, fragments scattered across the toilet seat.

I have to lean against the wall to stop the dizziness. My god. Someone has broken in. Is this related to the text message? And now I'm scared. What if the person is still here? I left my handbag with my phone in the kitchen, so I have to creep back that way, my ears hyper alert. But all I hear is my own ragged breathing. I grab my phone out of my bag and shove it in my jacket pocket. I take a carving knife out of the drawer.

'Is anyone there?' I shout, but my voice reverberates through what seems to be an empty house. I strain to listen, but hear nothing except my pounding pulse. No footsteps or creaking floorboards. I walk into every room of the house, the knife outstretched in front of me, but there is no one here. From a first glance, it doesn't look as if anything has been taken. The safe is still firmly closed in my dressing room, and my diamond earrings are in my bedside table drawer. Letting out a loud exhalation, I walk back downstairs and put the knife back.

I telephone Gail. 'Hi, Gail, it's Chantal. I assume that the window in the downstairs toilet wasn't broken when you left.'

'Goodness,' she exclaims. 'I left about 1 pm and made sure all the doors were shut as normal. Everything was fine in that bathroom. I used it and cleaned after myself. Has anything been taken?'

'No, that's what is so weird. Thanks, Gail. I'm sure there's no need to worry.'

I put the knife back in the drawer and fill up the kettle.

Is someone just trying to scare me? Is it related to the text message? I decide that a cup of tea won't pass muster and pour myself a brandy, tipping it back in one swig, burning my mouth and throat, and then I pace up and down the kitchen. Under normal circumstances, I would call the police, but I can't. Not in light of that message.

And then I wonder: Perhaps it was Alex. Maybe he has lost his key, and rather than being sensible and calling me, he's broken in. He has been behaving so strangely of late. First of all, there was his terrible behaviour at our party, and then he spent three nights at Debbie's. I wouldn't mind, except I've never got to the bottom of his supposed problem. I get that he's angry with me because I'm representing LALO Clothing and because I haven't exactly been welcoming to his girlfriend. He's probably annoyed with Stuart, too, although I'm not sure why ... but there must be more to it than that. I'm sure that Luna, Alex's girlfriend, is behind much of his latest bad behaviour. I ring his number, but he doesn't answer. Hopefully, he's at school with the ringer turned off.

I call an emergency glazier who, for an outrageous sum, says he can be with me in two hours to replace the broken window. In the meantime, I get changed and walk downstairs to our home gym. I hope that exercise might clear my mind.

In my heart of hearts, I have always known that the truth might get out. Alex may be our son, but biologically, of course he's not. As I'm running at full speed on the machine, I think back to seventeen years ago. I was bold back then, finding someone to get me fake ID so baby Noah could be turned into Alex. For years, I waited to be found out, but after a decade, other than the occasional nightmare, I stopped thinking about it. Alex is our child; we've given him a wonderful life, and he cemented my relationship with Stuart.

I sent Stuart a message a week before he was due to come home from Dubai, although I didn't know for sure if he still was coming home. I knew I had to play it cool and not come across as the needy ex-lover.

I hope you've had a wonderful year. When are you coming home?

When he replied almost instantaneously, I leaped around the room, jumping with joy, even though after reading it a dozen times, I realised his reply was very muted.

Wednesday 14th. Hope you're well. Let's meet up when I'm back.

I rang his mother and found out the flight time and told her that I'd be meeting Stuart at the airport. As she worked full-time, she seemed relieved. Next, I had to persuade Debbie to look after Alex for the day. As it was the school holidays, and she seemed as obsessed with him as me, that didn't require too much persuasion. I got my hair done and purchased a new red dress that hugged my curves. I knew I looked good and confident as I strode through Heathrow's arrivals hall, but inside, I was a quivering wreck.

I saw Stuart long before he saw me, and I had to breathe hard to keep my legs from buckling. A year in the sunshine suited him. He was tanned, and his hair was longer, and he had an air of confidence about him that made other women take note.

'Hey,' I said as he passed just a foot away.

'Chantal!' I couldn't decipher if his immediate reaction

was shock or delight, but within a couple of seconds, he threw his arms around me and hugged me tightly. The passionate kiss I longed for wasn't forthcoming, but I knew there would be a time and a place for that. 'I wasn't expecting you,' he said.

'No,' I replied coyly. 'I've got something really important to tell you, and I had to do it in person.'

'Okay.' A flicker of worry creased his face. 'And it couldn't wait?'

'Not really. Did you have a good flight?'

We made small talk as he pushed the trolley with his two large suitcases towards the car park. I don't remember what he told me. All I can recall are the nerves that were sloshing around my stomach. We got in the car, and he turned to face me.

'You're looking lovely,' he said, but he still didn't touch me.

'I'm just going to say it, as it will come as a shock. We've had a baby.'

There was a long pause as he tried to process the information.

'What? What do you mean?'

'The last night we were together before you left for Dubai, do you remember it?'

'Of course.'

'I got pregnant. We have a baby boy called Alex.'

I wondered if Stuart was going to faint. His tanned face faded instantly to white, and his jaw hung open.

'He's mine?'

'Of course he's yours, Stuart. You are the only man I've ever loved, and I've missed you every single day you were away.'

'I don't understand. That doctor said you'd never be able to conceive.'

'She was wrong.'

'Wow. But why didn't you tell me you were pregnant? I would have come home.'

'I thought about it long and hard and decided that you needed your year away. I didn't want to deprive you of that, because I was worried you might feel resentful later in life, and we needed to know whether we were destined to be together or not. I suppose that's what really scares me. Don't answer me now, but do you want us to be a family? You, me and Alex?' I took a deep breath, because I knew what I was about to say was a lie. 'I won't ask anything of you if you don't want to be my partner or Alex's dad.'

Stuart turned towards me and put his hands on either side of my face, drawing me towards him.

'But this changes everything,' he murmured. 'How can I not be with you when you are the mother of my child?'

'I want us to be together because we love each other,' I said. 'That's the only thing that's important.'

'You're right,' he said before kissing me in exactly the way I had dreamed of.

'When can I meet Alex?' he asked when we came up for air.

'Debbie's looking after him. We can go straight there.'

On the drive back to Debbie's place, we didn't talk much. I wanted to ask him whether he'd had any relationships during his year away and whether he had intended to get back together with me or not. But I didn't dare ask the questions, because I knew the answers might break me.

Back at Debbie's flat, Alex was asleep in his cot, and I will remember for ever the moment Stuart picked him up. Alex didn't cry when he woke up. He just stared at Stuart as if he knew that this man would love and protect him for the rest of his life. Stuart held Alex in the crook of his arm, his hand supporting our baby's head, and the look on Stuart's face was one of utter adoration. He saw what he wanted to see, and for the past seventeen and three-quarter years, Stuart has been the almost-perfect dad.

After an hour of extreme physical exhaustion on my static bike and running machine, my mind is empty of the past; I am laser-focused on the here and now. Firstly, we need to get a burglar alarm system. We've never bothered before, because crime rates are so low in this area. We get our weekly emails from the Neighbourhood Watch liaison, and on average, there are about two thefts a year in the village, and they're always a quad bike or some piece of farm equipment. Obviously, I can't tell Stuart about the text message, so I will need to imply that the break-in is some random attack, perhaps related to both of our high profiles. I get my story straight in my head before he gets home.

When he walks into the kitchen, I pour him a glass of wine and hand it to him.

'I don't want you to worry, but we had an attempted burglary today. I came home early, and I disturbed some youth who had smashed the downstairs bathroom window. As far as I can tell, nothing has been taken.'

'Bloody hell, Chantal. Have you called the police?'

'What's the point? They're so overstretched; besides, I can't see that a broken window is going to be high up on their list of priorities. But I have got in touch with a local alarm company. They're coming to fit a system this week.'

He runs his fingers through his hair. 'Do you think it's because of my new job? I guess we're a bit of a target now.'

'I don't know. It could be anything. It could be a disgruntled client of mine or just an opportunist who realised no one was at home. It could be your new job, or the fact that I was quoted in the newspapers as being the Lowaskis' solicitor. Honestly, I'm not that worried, but it's definitely better to be safe than sorry.'

'I agree. I hope it hasn't spooked you too much.'

'Don't worry. So long as you and Alex are safe, that's my only concern. Anyway, how was your dinner in London last night?'

'What? Oh yes. Sorry, it seems like an age ago already. Everything's fine. I've just got to get used to the unsociable hours of the new job. How was Alex last night?'

'Talking to me in monosyllables, as normal. Perhaps you can have a heart-to-heart with him at the weekend. It seems that the only person in his good books at the moment is Debbie.'

The next few days are uneventful, and I'm mighty relieved that I don't receive another text message. The alarm is installed, so I can now watch both the interior and exterior of the house through an app on my phone. Alex is thoroughly unimpressed, thinking that it's Big Brother watching stuff. I suppose his real issue is I'm able to tell when he's at home or not, and who he's brought back into the house with him.

On Friday evening, I pick up a couple of duck breasts on my way home, ready to make us a special dinner, but Stuart sends me a text saying he'll be late back. When he eventually gets home, I ask what his plans are for the weekend, hoping that he might forgo his lengthy Saturday golf sessions now that we spend so little time together. But no, he says he's playing a round with a couple of old friends. I suggest that we go out for supper on Saturday evening, but he explains that he wants to maintain his sleep regime so it doesn't get out of kilter for the upcoming week.

At least we managed our regular family Sunday lunch at the local pub. And so here we are on Sunday evening, with Stuart in bed at 9 pm, and I'm left wondering whether we'll ever have sex again. Perhaps it will be on the annual holiday only. It also crosses my mind that he might be using his unsociable hours to keep me at arm's length. Again, I wonder if he's been cheating on me, but over the past fortnight, there's been no evidence to suggest anything is out of the ordinary. Except, of course, Stuart's hours.

Alex has barely been around, too. Luna came over on Saturday, and they spent too long upstairs alone in Alex's bedroom. She slunk into the house behind Alex, and when I asked her how she was, she muttered *okay* without looking me in the eyes. I have to admit I can't understand what Alex sees in her, and wonder if he's chosen her as his girlfriend simply to annoy me.

I'm in the bath when my phone vibrates with an incoming text. I pick it up with trepidation.

I WANT £20K IN CASH. SHOW THIS MESSAGE TO ANYONE AND THE WORLD WILL KNOW THE TRUTH ABOUT ALEX

Shit.
And almost immediately, another message arrives.

BY THE WAY. NICE STRIPED TOP YOU WERE WEARING TODAY.

The phone drops out of my fingers, but fortunately lands on the bathmat, so no damage has been done. What the hell is this about? But worst of all, someone must be watching me. This person knew what I was wearing. It totally freaks me out.

11

One minute I am single, waiting for the love of my life to return, work-focused and coming to terms with the fact that I will probably never have a child of my own. The next minute, I have a two-month-old baby to care for. The reality slaps me hard in the face. Buying all the gear is the easy part, but everything else requires monumental adjustment. The first thing I have to do is quit my job; I'm just so relieved that I've saved up so much money this past year by not socialising. If I keep my spending to the minimum, I reckon I have enough to last me three to four months. I ring up my boss, Lorna Stephenson.

'Lorna, I'm so sorry to do this to you, but I'm going to have to leave Manchester straight away.'

'What's happened?' she asks.

I cross the fingers of my left hand. 'My sister has just been diagnosed with terminal cancer. It's such a shock. Our parents are both dead, so I'm the only relative she has, and I have to be there for her, make sure she's properly looked after.' I hope I'm not putting some curse on Debbie by using her as my excuse.

'That's terrible, Chantal. I'm so sorry to hear that. I can talk to human resources and see if we can give you a couple of months unpaid sabbatical, and you could relocate back to one of the southern offices. Would that work?'

I can't believe how kind and understanding she is, but it won't work, because I'll need longer than that to get sorted, and I don't want any of my existing colleagues to know that I've miraculously had a baby.

'You're so kind, but I simply don't know how long my sister has. I think it's best if I resign and reapply for a job again in the future when our circumstances are more settled.'

'Well, the offer is there,' Lorna says. 'Unfortunately as you're leaving with no notice, I think you'll forfeit any outstanding holiday pay.'

'I totally understand. Would you be willing to give me a reference in the future?'

'Of course, Chantal. And the very best of luck.'

I know how very lucky I am that Lorna is such a nice woman. I can't imagine many people being so forgiving when their assistant walks away with one day's notice.

My second major problem is I have to get hold of some fake ID for Alex. That proves somewhat harder, because being a law-abiding family solicitor, criminal activity is not my area of expertise. I make my way onto the dark web and, depressingly easily, find a man called Misty Morris in Stockport, who is able to produce a fake birth certificate that will turn Noah into Alex. It's not even expensive – just a couple of hundred quid. He wanted to be paid in casino chips, but that takes me too far out of my comfort zone, so we agree on £220 in cash.

I want to leave Manchester as quickly as I can, just in case I run into any of the handful of people I know here and they question what I'm doing with a baby, but first I need to go and meet Misty Morris for the handover. I'm exhausted. Alex still hasn't settled with me; it's like he's missing his mother, which seems a bit ridiculous since she didn't give him any of the love and attention that I'm providing, but I know I just have to give it time.

This morning, I've stuffed my hair into a beanie, put on dark sunglasses, which look ridiculous for this grey day, and Alex is strapped to my chest. He must be able to sense my nerves because he's fidgety and unsettled. I kiss the downy hair on the top of his head, muttering, 'It'll all be fine soon. Mummy will look after you.' Then I pull the hood up of his romper suit and head out towards Stockport.

I've agreed to meet Misty Morris outside a betting shop somewhere in Stockport. I decide not to drive, as I don't want him to know my number plate, and from checking the area online, it looks rough. I take a bus and then walk quickly with my head down, avoiding catching anyone's eyes. Most of the shops are boarded up around here, and it has the air of desperation. I don't feel safe. I'm just thankful that it's eleven in the morning and the only other people wandering around are a couple of winos and an old lady pushing a shopping bag trolley. As I locate the betting shop, I'm not sure what to do. There's no one around; I'm sure I stand out like a sore thumb. There are imposing tower blocks with hundreds of windows. I wonder if anyone is watching, realising that I don't belong here. I walk up to the betting shop window and then jump when the door opens with a little tinkle. A man steps out wearing a black jacket. His grey hair is tied back with an elastic band, and he looks like he hasn't shaven for several days. It's difficult to tell his age, but he's certainly in his fifties or sixties.

'You looking for me?' he asks.

'Misty Morris?'

'Got the dosh?'

'Yes.'

'What's your name?'

'Debs 1234.'

'You need to tighten that one up, lass. Even your newbie hacker will be able to trace you. Anyways, I've got what you want. Give me the money.'

I put my hand down into Alex's sling and take out the envelope with the money.

'Hand it over, then,' he urges.

'How do I know that you're not going to do a runner? I need to see the birth certificate first.'

He laughs at me. A big guffaw, as if it's the funniest thing he's ever heard. Alex wakes up and whimpers.

'We're talking about an effing birth certificate here, not the crown jewels.'

I hand him the envelope, and he studies the notes, holding them up, presumably to check they're not forgeries. He then hands me another envelope.

'It's all as you asked for. Father's name, mother's name and kiddo's name.'

'How do I know you won't tell anyone about this?'

'Oh, lassie, you're really showing your naivety, aren't you? You're small fry; you've got nowt to worry about. Just remember to come to Misty Morris next time you need anything doing. I'm your man, and my lips are sealed.'

He winks at me and strolls back into the betting shop.

My legs are trembling as I walk back towards the bus shop. That was so easy. Too easy perhaps.

When I'm back in the flat and have fed and changed Alex, I pull the birth certificate out of the envelope. It's hard to tell whether it's as good as the real deal, but it certainly looks authentic to me. I smile as I run my fingers over the names. Father: Stuart Heaton, Mother: Chantal Lacey. The only thing that is certain is Alex's birth date. I'll never forget that.

I have acquired a lot more belongings than I arrived with,

due to all the baby equipment I've bought for Alex. So, just a few days in, my savings have gone down scarily quickly. Next, I contact the lettings agent and give her the same spiel as to why I'm vacating early. She tells me that I will still have to pay the outstanding months' rent, and I confirm that I already know that. And then the day comes to leave. I fill up the car with all of our belongings, and as I strap Alex in his car seat into the car, I stroke his head, and he smiles at me. My heart fills with love for this little human.

'Bye-bye, Manchester. Hello to your new and happy life, my baby.'

He blows me a raspberry, and I give him little butterfly kisses, which makes him laugh even more. I know for sure that I have done the right thing. For Alex and for me.

During the drive south, nerves begin to take hold. Can I pull this off? Will Debbie actually believe me? After all, the timing couldn't be more perfect. Yes, I did make love with Stuart before he left for Dubai. No, I haven't seen Debbie during the past ten months, and it's perfectly plausible that I've kept the pregnancy secret from her. She's not the questioning type like I am; my sister takes everything at face value and sees the best in people. Nevertheless, when we pull up outside her flat at 6 pm, my stomach is full of butterflies.

'Right, little one. Let's go and meet your aunty.'

When Debbie opens the door and sees me standing there, she bursts into tears.

'Why didn't you tell me you were coming? I've missed you so much!'

Poor Debbie is looking dreadful. She's put on at least another stone in weight, and her face is pasty and her hair lank. Why she doesn't do a better job in looking after herself is beyond me. It's only after she's thrown her arms around me and stands back that she notices the car seat with baby Alex in it at my feet.

'What are you doing here? Whose baby is that?'

'Are you going to let me in?'

'Yes, sure.' She stands back, and holding Alex in his car seat, I squeeze past her in the narrow hallway and walk into the small living room. I crouch down and unstrap Alex, lifting him up into my arms. I then turn around and hold out his little hand. 'Alex, meet your aunty Debbie. Debbie, meet your nephew.'

'Oh my god!' she exclaims, her hand rushing to cover her mouth. 'I can't believe it! You've had a baby!'

'Yes. Do you want to hold him?'

She nods as fat tears course down her cheeks.

'But why didn't you tell me?'

'Because I wasn't in a great place. I didn't know whether I'd lose the baby, what with my medical history, and I didn't want to get your hopes up. And, to be honest, it's been so overwhelming. I needed some time to myself to process it.'

I hand Alex to her, and she rocks him backwards and forwards and kisses the top of his head.

'I can't believe it! I'm so happy. We have a little boy. Is he Stuart's?'

'Of course he is. I can't believe you've even asked that question.'

'It's just you split up from him. What has he said?'

'I haven't told him yet. That's why I've come back down south. I want to be here for when he returns from Dubai. Can I stay with you for a bit, just until I get myself sorted?'

'Yes, of course you can. Oh my goodness, he's absolutely adorable. I can't believe we've got a baby.'

I bite my tongue to stop myself from saying *I have a baby, not we*. Debbie has one of those faces that is easy to read, and I can tell that she's genuinely delighted. After all, she knows about the endometriosis and the devastating prognosis that the consultant gave me. But at the same time, I can tell that she's peeved I didn't confide in her, and I suppose I'd be hurt if the shoe were on the other foot, although that's a ridiculous notion. Debbie has a pure heart. She'd never do the sort of things that I've done.

After we've unloaded the car and set Alex and me up in her small second bedroom, Debbie makes us some pasta, and we sit down to eat.

'Are you on maternity leave?' she asks.

'No. I took a break. It was all too much. It shouldn't be too hard for me to get a job with another firm down here, but firstly, I need to sort out childcare for Alex. Once that's done, I'll talk to my friend Kathleen. Do you remember her? We were friends from law college.'

'I'll help,' Debbie says, talking with a mouthful. 'I can look after Alex during the school holidays, and then all you need to do is find a nursery for him during term time. There's got to be some advantage to being a primary school teacher myself.'

'Thanks, Debs,' I say, pleased that she has reacted in exactly the way I anticipated. 'That would be such a help. Once I've got myself a new job, I'll find somewhere to live and get out of your hair. How have you been? Any boyfriend?'

Debbie turns beetroot red. She'd make such a lousy lawyer, unable to keep her thoughts from showing on her face. We really are chalk and cheese.

'I have met someone, actually. He's called Martin. I think he might be the one.'

'Oh, Debs, I'm so happy for you! I look forward to meeting him.'

'Me too,' she says quietly.

'What!' I exclaim.

'We haven't actually met yet, but we talk for hours every night, and he's coming over from Canada to stay in six weeks' time.'

I open and close my mouth. Now isn't the time to tell Debbie that she's probably the victim of some horrible scam, that this Martin is most likely some bloke in Nigeria grooming her in the hope that she'll lend him a load of money, just for him to vanish into the ether. Poor Debbie; this is so typical. It's just as well I'm back in Sussex so that we can look after each other. She'll take care of Alex, and I'll make sure that whatever bastard intends to fleece her will get his comeuppance. I feel so sorry for her, especially after her disastrous, short-lived marriage to Jim. Her confidence was totally destroyed. It would be too cruel if this next romance turns out to be a fraud.

'What are you going to do about Stuart? Do you think you two will get back together?' Debbie asks.

'That's the plan,' I say. 'Watch this space.'

12

I'm inside an antiques shop located in a narrow alley in the centre of Horsham, preparing for my second attempt at theft. But this time, I don't have my accomplice and lookout. I'm all alone, and my breaths are coming out short and quickly. I really, really don't want to be doing this. My palms feel sweaty as I pick up the antique watch and examine it. It's a man's watch, chunky and gold, and from the weight of it, I reckon it's the real deal. I glance up at the shopkeeper, who is seated at the counter, reading a newspaper. I wonder if he's the man written about in the article in the local paper a couple of months ago, the guy who got prosecuted for sexually harassing a female employee. He got acquitted, but he's got to be guilty, hasn't he? Otherwise, why would the police have brought charges? I remember Mum and Dad talking about the case in light of all of the 'Me Too' stuff that's been going on. I thought it ironic that Mum thought the shop owner was being ill-treated, 'a media trial based on hearsay' was how she described it, but Dad thought there was no smoke without fire. I'd have thought that Mum would side with the female victim, but she never seems to. Just another thing that's weird about her. But that's the reason I've chosen J. Whittakers Antiquities. That, and because Luna says they haven't got any security cameras.

The shop is sprawling but oppressive. It's a warren of small rooms stuffed full of musty old things, most of which I reckon should have been chucked out with their dead owners. It gives me the creeps in here, but it's one of the few places where they have high-value things out on display. I slip the watch into my pocket and carry on walking around, trying to spot other things that might be valuable and easy to nick.

As Luna said, I've got no choice. The things I took from home didn't make nearly as much as I'd hoped. Luna promised that she'd tried her best, that her fence gave her a good price all considering, but I think we might have been ripped off. I've still got another six hundred quid to find from somewhere so I can make good my promise to Aunt Debbie. It's not fair that she's out of pocket due to me. I can't remember what she said the interest would be on her credit card if she didn't pay it off at the end of the month, but it was some outrageous figure.

And so here I am, stealing again. This shop owner deserves to suffer, not that it makes the actual theft any easier. My heart is thudding, and nerves make my stomach cramp. I sense his eyes on me, even though every time I glance up at him, he's not looking in my direction. When I'm in the furthest room from the till, I notice a small security camera positioned in the ceiling. I swear under my breath. Luna was wrong. I didn't see any in the other rooms, so perhaps they've only got one in here because the shop manager can't see into this room. I hope so.

'Do you need any help, sonny?' The old man appears from nowhere, and he makes me jump. He's wearing a knackered ochre-coloured cardigan that has holes in it, and he stinks of a mixture of body odour and stale cigar smoke.

'No, I'm fine, thanks. Just looking for a birthday present for my dad.'

'How much do you want to spend?' He narrows his eyes at me.

'About twenty quid.'

'Is that so?' he asks, putting his hands on his hips.

'Yes.' I try to hold his gaze, but it's like he's seeing through me, right into the pockets of my anorak. I glance away.

'In which case, why've you got a watch in your jacket that's worth almost a grand?'

I stand stock-still. 'I haven't. I don't know what you're talking about!' I try to brazen it out, but it's obvious he knows exactly what I've stolen. How could I have screwed this up so badly? My only choice is to hand it over and do a runner. I'm about to dart past him when he swings the door shut so that both of us are captive in this small room, surrounded by spooky dark brown furniture and a deer's head on the wall that has beady glass eyes.

'Don't even think about it,' he says, crossing his arms in front of him. 'The cops are on the way, and if you run now, you'll make things a damn sight worse. I've got you captured on the security camera pocketing the watch.'

'I'm so sorry,' I say, wringing my hands. 'I've never done anything like this before, and I was desperate. Can I just give it back to you and say I'm sorry, because I really am?'

'Nope. You can stay in here until the police arrive and then, whatever you've got to say, say it to them. I'm sick to bloody death of having yobs like you come in here and steal things. You're scum, and I hope they lock you up.' He sneers at me and then turns and slams the door shut. It sounds like he's locking me in.

I sink to the floor. What the hell have I done? This is all

because I didn't want Mum and Dad to find out that I'd bashed the car. Now, I think I should have just told them the truth. I feel really, really stupid, because if I had hit a person, it would be all over the news by now, and there's been nothing. It's no crime hitting a deer, but of course, it is a crime driving after smoking spliffs and drinking beer. Would Mum have hit the roof? Probably. She's so on edge at the moment, having meltdowns over much smaller things than bashing my car.

I go back over that evening. Debbie didn't question that I smelled weird; all she was worried about was getting me to the hospital to sort out the cut on my leg. Which reminds me: I need to get the stitches taken out sometime soon. But if it had been Mum, she'd have caught onto me straight away. Knowing her, she'd probably have marched me to the police station herself, just to teach me a lesson, and on the way, she'd have blown my eardrums with her screeching. On reflection, I did the only thing I could. I'll just have to face the consequences.

I send Luna a message saying that I've screwed up and will probably be arrested, but she doesn't reply. About fifteen minutes later, there are voices, and I hear a key in the lock. The shop owner opens the door and tilts his head to one side.

'Get out.'

I stand up and follow him through to the front of the shop, where there are two uniformed police, a man and a woman.

'I'm sorry,' I say. 'I didn't mean any harm.'

I take the watch out of my pocket and place it on the glass counter.

'Mr Corbern wants you to be prosecuted, so we're taking you down to the police station.'

'But I'm really sorry. I shouldn't have done it, and I've never done anything like this before.'

The policewoman asks for my name and address. Then the policeman says, 'We're arresting you for theft under s.1 of the Theft Act 1986. You do not have to say anything. But it may harm your defence if you do not mention when questioned something which you later rely on in court. Anything you do say may be given in evidence.'

'I want my mum,' I say, feeling pathetic.

'How old are you?'

'Seventeen.'

'In which case you're entitled to be accompanied by a parent or a guardian. Please give me your mum's contact details.'

The female constable writes down Mum's name and telephone number while the policeman tells me to come with him, leading me out of the shop in a walk of shame. I keep my head down as I climb into the back seat of the police car, and I feel like sobbing as they drive me across town.

At the police station, they make me empty my pockets, confiscate my mobile phone and put me in a small, windowless room. I'm left there for ages.

Eventually Mum arrives, accompanied by the policewoman.

'They're letting you off with a warning because it's a first-time offence,' Mum says. Her lips look thin, and her jaw is set forwards, as it always is when she's furious. I follow her out of the police station without saying a word. I get into the front seat of her car, and then she turns on me.

'What the hell did you think you were doing? Stealing! Is that what all of our efforts on giving you the best education and every opportunity in life has come to? And do you know the real reason why you got off? Because I'm a lawyer, and I know they couldn't prosecute you. The shopkeeper did everything wrong. Incarcerating you in a room, stopping you before you had left the shop. They would never have got a prosecution, but it doesn't make it any better. You're a thief, Alex, and I have never been so disappointed in you.'

She leans her head back against the headrest of her car seat and briefly closes her eyes. 'As if I haven't got enough stress at the moment,' she mutters. 'How could you do such a thing?'

'I'm sorry,' I say.

She turns towards me, her lips snarling. 'Is that all you can say? Do you know how this looks? Just when your dad has got his dream job, when I'm a solicitor and you're a petty thief. It could be all over the press tomorrow, "Stuart Heaton's son cautioned for shoplifting." Forget the fact that it's just plain wrong; think of the effect it could have on us, your parents, who have done everything in our power to give you a happy, secure childhood. I've spent the past eighteen years making sure that you've had everything you needed. An expensive education, the opportunity to try out any sport or activity you wanted, summer clubs, fancy holidays, lovely clothes. And you chuck it all back in our faces. I suppose it's that girlfriend of yours who put you up to it. Well, enough is enough. You're forbidden from seeing her again.'

'It's nothing to do with Luna.'

'Then what is it? What makes you do such a thing when we've given you so much? I just don't understand you, Alex.' She throws her arms up into the air.

'Everything is about material wealth with you, isn't it?' I say. 'I didn't ask for any of it. I don't want to go to a fancy school with stuck-up, entitled rich kids. I wanted to go to the local sixth-form college, but you weren't having any of it. All you care about is what people think about you, but you're the one who's sold out on your left-wing principles. You're happy to take money from one of the dodgiest business owners on the planet, who pollutes the earth and treats his staff like scum. You're the one who throws the fancy parties for your stuck-up friends to show off Dad's new job. Sure, I shouldn't have nicked that watch, but at least I give a damn. I know what's right or wrong, and I took the watch for a good reason. Not that you'd ever understand that.'

'Enough!' Mum shouts at me. She starts the engine and pulls out of the car park, her fingers gripped so tightly around the steering wheel, her knuckles gleam white. I don't care. I've got nothing else I want to say to her. She can do all she wants to try to make my life a misery, but I'm not going to let her. We'll never understand each other; to hell with her. I don't need her. I remember how she used to be when I was younger, fun and kind and a great mum. But that changed a couple of years ago. We even had a massive row over my A Level subjects. I wanted to study biology, environmental studies and politics. You'd have thought that she would have had a hissy fit over environmental studies, because some people think it's a lightweight subject, but no, she didn't want me to study biology. She just doesn't make sense half the time. She might be my mum, but I sure as hell don't like or respect her.

As soon as she drives into the garage at home and turns the engine off, I'm out of the car and running towards mine, which looks as good as new.

'Alex, stop!' she shouts.

I ignore her.

'Alex, where the hell do you think you're going? You need to stay here, and we need to talk about it!'

What does she think she can do? Actually stop me? It's a joke. I start up my car and reverse out of the garage. She's standing there, her arms on her hips, and I think she's got tears in her eyes. But that isn't my problem; she's brought all of this on herself. I turn the car around and put my foot on the accelerator. I'm going to see Luna.

I met Luna six weeks ago at a demonstration against a

massive housing development that's due to be built that will destroy acres of green fields and ancient woodland on the edge of a small village in the middle of the Sussex countryside. We're both members of Extinction Rebellion and various other eco-protest groups, and I'd seen her around, but we'd never spoken. I just don't get how this current generation of so-called adults thinks it's perfectly okay to destroy swathes of countryside for new homes. Most young people can't afford the homes anyway, and what about global warming and the destruction of natural habitats for wildlife and increased flooding, not to mention all the extra cars on the roads and the fact that we don't have enough hospitals or schools to support the increase in population. It's like our parents don't care about the future of our planet, so it's up to my generation to take a stand.

Most of the demonstrations I've been to have been high-profile with crowds of protestors. But that one was different. I suppose that as planning permission had already been granted, most people thought the fight was already lost. Luna was standing at the gates, her left wrist chained to the wire fencing. A big, burly man wearing a bright yellow tabard and a white hard hat was gesticulating at her. I was really impressed. He was shouting and totally losing his cool, but Luna was composed and quiet and, despite her alternative looks, was articulate.

'Last chance. I'm calling the police!' the man yelled before turning and stomping away, jabbing thick fingers onto his phone.

'Hey, you.' Luna looked at me. I walked up to her. 'You here for the protest?'

'Yes.'

'Can you unlock me? The key is in my jeans pocket.'

I felt a bit awkward rummaging in her tight jeans pocket, but I found the key and unlocked the handcuffs.

'Ready to run?' she whispered.

I nodded.

Just as the construction guy shoved his phone into his pocket and started walking back towards us, fury writ across his face, Luna and I bolted. By the time we reached my car, which I'd parked in the village about three hundred metres away, we were both in hysterics.

'Thanks for that,' she said. 'I have to avoid the police because I'll be arrested next time.'

'It's disgusting,' I said. 'Why should you be arrested for speaking out, for protecting the environment?'

'Yup, quite agree. I'm Luna, by the way. Who are you?'

We sat in the car and talked for ages. Luna's not like anyone I've ever met before. She's twenty, and she left school after her GCSEs, not that she got any. She said she flunked school, because she wanted to be an activist, and what good would exams be for that? I shrugged. I'd never thought of that before. She said she lived with her mum in a one-bedroom council flat, and she was on benefits. She spent her time campaigning for the environment and making the world a better place for everyone. I really liked Luna; I still do. She doesn't have the qualifications or any of the things that my parents and school friends think are important, but she's the most authentic and passionate person I've ever met.

After leaving home, I drive to where Luna lives. I've dropped her off here lots of times, but I've never been inside. I think she's ashamed, especially as she knows we live in such grandeur, but I couldn't care less. I wish she'd believe me. It's a low-rise block of flats, red brick and really not so bad. I walk up to the front door of the block and slip inside just as someone is leaving. There's a load of letter boxes on the wall in the entrance lobby, and I find one marked Williams, Luna's surname. She's in flat 3C.

I climb the stairs and find flat 3C. There's no doorbell, so I rap on the blue door. There's the rattling of a chain, and then the door is opened. The woman isn't at all what I expected. For starters, she is a black lady, and she's wearing smart clothes, navy trousers with a crease down the front of each leg, and a white blouse. Luna is mixed race, but for some stupid reason, I assumed her dad was black. Sometimes I worry that I'm as bad as Mum in my preconceptions.

'Yes?' the lady says.

'Um, I'm a friend of Luna's. Is she home?'

'Are you Alex?'

I nod. 'You'd better come in, then. It's good to meet you. I'm Mel Williams.' She shakes my hand and throws me a warm smile, such a contrast to Mum's reaction towards Luna.

'Luna, love, your boyfriend is here.'

I know it's silly, but my heart swells knowing that Luna has told her mum about me and calls me her boyfriend. I thought she might want to keep me under wraps, what with me being nearly three years younger than her. I walk into the small living room, which is neat and tidy even if the furniture looks a bit knackered.

'What are you doing here?' Luna asks. She seems flustered.

'I needed to see you.'

'You could have called.'

I shrug my shoulders.

'Hey, young lady, you be nice to the lad.'

'Stay out of it, Mum,' Luna says. 'Haven't you got to go to work?' But her tone of voice is light, and I can see the affection the two have for each other.

'That I have. Now be well behaved in my absence. See you later, darling.' She blows Luna a kiss.

'What's up?' Luna asks, curling up on the sofa.

I sit down next to her. 'I got caught shoplifting, and the police came. They cautioned me. I didn't manage to steal anything, and my mum is being a total bitch. I want to leave home.'

'Where will you go?'

'Dunno. Was wondering if I could come here for a bit.'

'We've got no space,' Luna says. 'I have the bedroom, and Mum sleeps on the sofa.'

'You're right, stupid idea.'

'Don't look so down,' she says, squeezing my hand. 'I'll help you plot a way out of your gilded cage, and we'll work out how we can totally screw over your parents, yeah?'

13

CHANTAL – NOW

I feel so hopeless watching Alex speed away when he should be punished and grounded. Most of all, I am utterly disappointed. I thought we'd brought him up with morals, but it appears we've failed as parents.

I've managed to put the texts to the back of my mind for the past twenty-four hours, but now I can't help but think about them. It really feels like things are disintegrating, becoming outside of my control, and that's a feeling I hate. Although the text demanded £20K in cash, I haven't heard any more, and for now I'm hoping it's an empty threat. If the blackmailer was serious, surely they'd send me a date, time and location for the drop-off?

Although I can't mention the threatening texts to Stuart, I have every intention of getting him to side with me regarding Alex so we present a united parental front. For a change, he is home in good time, and I'm ready and waiting.

'We need to talk,' I say as soon as Stuart walks in through the front door. He pales and puts his briefcase down on the ground. 'It's about Alex.'

He lets out a puff of air. I wonder if he thought I wanted to talk about our marriage or my accusations that he's having an affair.

'What's up?' He follows me into the kitchen and loosens his tie as he sinks into a chair. I stand with my back against the curve in the island unit.

'Alex got caught shoplifting today and received a police caution. If I hadn't turned up, they might have charged him.'

'Bloody hell.'

'Exactly. How bad will it be for you if it gets out? I can't guarantee the police won't accidentally on purpose leak the fact that Stuart Heaton's son got done for shoplifting.'

He groans. 'It certainly won't look good, especially as I'm just getting my feet under the table. I'm interviewing both the Home Secretary and the Metropolitan Police Commissioner this week. Is there anything we can do to stop the local police from talking?'

'No, we'll just have to keep our fingers crossed. They may not have worked out that Alex is your son.'

'I'll talk to Alex. Is he home?'

'No. He sped off in his car. I think we might need to confiscate it.'

Stuart rolls his eyes, which infuriates me. We've always taken a different approach to parenting. I think that bad behaviour should be punished – not physically, of course – but certainly with actions commensurate with the crime. Withholding pocket money, stopping the child from attending a party, or something else that makes them stop and think. Stuart is much more touchy-feely and takes the carrot approach, preferring to talk the issues through. That can work in some circumstances, but in an instance like this, the crime is too great.

'What are you doing?' I ask as Stuart's finger jabs his phone.

'Calling him and telling him to come home.'

'Good luck with that,' I mutter.

To my surprise, fifteen minutes later Alex's red Fiat pulls up in front of the house.

'Alex is home,' I shout up the stairs to Stuart.

A few seconds later, Stuart bounds downstairs, and they're talking in the hallway. I stand just out of sight, but so I can hear them.

'What on earth were you doing, son?' Stuart says.

'I'm sorry. Shouldn't have done it.'

'Things are different now. You're nearly an adult, and you need to think through the consequence of your actions – not just for yourself, but how it's going to affect us, your family. We're high-profile now.'

'I didn't ask for that,' Alex says.

I can't bear to hear and not see them, so I walk out into the corridor. Alex is standing there, his arms hanging limply down his sides, his eyes fixed on the floor.

'You might not have asked for it, but our jobs are what pay for your lifestyle: your car, your education, this house.'

'I don't want any of that. I don't want your money! I don't want to be part of this family!'

I gasp. I can't help it. Alex looks up and throws me daggers. How is it possible to love and hate someone at the same time? If only he knew how hard I have fought for him.

'I want to move out,' Alex says. 'I'll go and stay with Aunt Debbie.'

'No,' I say.

'Actually, love.' Stuart places a hand on my arm. 'It might not be such a bad idea. It'll give Alex the chance to calm down, and you know what a good influence Debbie is on him. Just for a few days.'

I turn away from them and stride back into the kitchen, hugging my arms around myself, trying hard not to burst into tears. I'm furious. It's always Debbie who comes to the rescue;

big, bubbly Debbie, who seems to know how to mother better than I do, yet she's never been an actual mother.

'Hey,' Stuart says, walking up behind me and giving me a hug. 'I know it's tough, but Alex has just been stupid. It's not like he's hurt anyone, and I'm sure that it's given him the jolt that's needed. He's a good boy at heart, and he's said he's sorry.'

I nod because I can't answer. I wonder if he really is a good boy at heart. I step away from Stuart's grasp and wipe my eyes with the back of my hand. 'You're right. A few days apart might be a good thing. I'll give Debbie a call.'

I can hear Stuart and Alex chatting on the stairs, but I ignore them and ring Debbie.

'Is it okay for Alex to come and stay with you again for a couple of nights?'

'Of course it is. You know I love having him over, even if he eats me out of house and home.'

'We'll give you money to cover his food.'

'I was only joking, Chantal. I don't want your money.'

'No, I insist.'

'And I won't have him to stay if you're going to insult me by paying me for the privilege. I love that boy, and it's a pleasure to have him over.'

'He got caught shoplifting.'

There's a long silence, and I wonder if the line has dropped.

'Are you still there?'

'I heard you. Right, I'll talk to the boy. Leave it with me.' And then she hangs up.

The next morning, I'm early into the office, because there is little point lingering at home when neither Stuart nor Alex are there. I'm sitting at my desk, staring into space, when Kathleen looks through the glass wall panel and raps on it. She opens the door.

'You look like you have the weight of the world on your shoulders. Want to talk about it?'

I glance at my watch. It's only 8.45 am. 'Fancy a quick coffee?' I suggest.

'Sure.'

Kathleen and I met at Law College, where we were both doing conversion courses to become solicitors. She was quirky and funny and not at all like the other students, who, on the whole, were serious and focused on work to the exclusion of all else. Kathleen was one of the people behind the scenes who fought tirelessly for same-sex marriage. When I arrived back in Sussex with a baby and no job, she was one of the first people I called. She had done her articles – her solicitor training – with Egerton Brook Steading and was an associate solicitor in the family law department. Even back then, it was one of the leading firms in the southeast of England. We met for a coffee one Saturday morning in my favourite little coffee shop set in a dark-timbered building in Horsham that sadly no longer exists. These days, it's a phone shop.

'I'm so happy you're home,' she said as she stirred two sugars into her latte.

'I've had a baby.'

She dropped her spoon. 'You what? Oh my god, are you serious?'

'Yes, and I had to quit work, but Debbie's going to help out with childcare, so I'm looking for another job down here.'

'Wait, wait! You had a baby, but you didn't tell me?'

I can see she's hurt, and I'm ready for this. 'I couldn't risk telling anyone, Kath. You know how unlikely it was for me to get pregnant let alone carry a baby to full term. I wanted to tell you, really I did, but I thought it might jinx things. And anyway, it's rather fun that Alex is a happy surprise.'

'For sure he is! Is Stuart the dad?'

I laugh. 'That's what Debbie asked me. Yes, Alex is Stuart's, but I haven't told him yet. I'm going to wait until he's back in the UK. In the meantime, I was wondering if Egerton Brook Steading have any vacancies in the matrimonial department?'

'I don't know, but I can certainly ask and put in a good word for you.'

'Thanks, that would be awesome.'

Kathleen did exactly that, and barely a month later, I was an employed solicitor working in the same department as my friend. But life isn't fair, and I've risen through the ranks faster than her. I am convinced it's all down to prejudice. Kathleen is openly gay, she has married a woman, and although all the other partners would deny it, I am convinced that I was made an equity partner over Kathleen because I fit the conventional mould and she doesn't. I've tried to talk about it with Kathleen, but she just shrugs it off. Life isn't fair.

Our friendship has stayed strong over the years, especially after Trisha gave birth to twins, but we're both so busy we rarely have time for a social chat.

'You look like you've got the weight of the world on your shoulders,' she says as we walk around the corner to Starbucks.

'We've had some problems with Alex. You saw how he was at Stuart's party ... well, yesterday he got caught shoplifting.'

'Oh no,' she says. 'I'm sure it's just pushing the boundaries and being a silly teenager.'

There's no one in the queue, so Kathleen orders a skinny latte without sugar (rather different to what she used to order), and I order a mint tea. We carry our drinks to an empty table near the back wall and sit down.

'Alex is perpetually angry with me, and he resents Stuart's new job.'

'Have you thought about therapy?' she suggests. 'We're always suggesting it to our clients.'

'For Alex?'

'Yes. Maybe he just needs an outsider to vent to, to help him put the difficult teenage years into perspective.'

Kathleen might be right, but I'm not the sort of person to let someone else solve my problems. I'd rather sort Alex's issues out myself. I'm also deeply disappointed. It's ironic really how I'm so good at resolving other people's family problems, but I can't sort out my own.

'You've got all of this to come,' I say, but somehow I doubt she will. Trisha is a stay-at-home mum, and although Kathleen isn't genetically related to her children, they chose their sperm donor, selecting him from a large database of contenders, a bit like shopping from an Argus catalogue. Both women are besotted with their girls. We chat a bit about the Lowaskis' case and a couple of tricky divorces that Kathleen is working on, and then stroll back to the office for a meeting Kathleen has at 9.30 a.m.

We're just at the front door to the office when my phone pings again. I take it out of my pocket, and my heart sinks.

YOU'VE GOT TWO DAYS TO GET ME THE £20K IN CASH. IF YOU DON'T, THE WORLD WILL KNOW THAT ALEX ISN'T YOUR SON. I'LL LET YOU KNOW WHERE AND WHEN.

'Chantal, are you alright?'

I realise I've stopped still, and Kathleen is standing there holding the door open for me.

'Hey, what's going on?' Kathleen asks as I shove the phone back into my pocket.

'Just some more home shit.'

'It sounds like you could do with that evening out with

Trisha and me. Why don't you come over for supper tomorrow after work?'

'I'm not sure,' I say.

Kathleen places a hand on my forearm. 'I'm not taking no for an answer.'

14

I t's not the money that's the issue. Of course it's a large sum, but I have it. That's the beauty of my job: I earn well and have plenty stashed away and invested for a rainy day. It's more the issue of who knows the truth, and why are they blackmailing me now? I think through the consequences of the truth coming out; it would be horrific. Stuart would never forgive me. Without a doubt, we would get divorced. Any trust that Alex had in me would dissipate, and most likely, he would never talk to me again.

And then there are the wider implications. How could my firm continue to employ me as a partner when I obtained my baby illegally? I would lose my job – most probably my license to practice as a solicitor – and my reputation would be destroyed. As if all of that wasn't enough, there is a very strong chance I would be prosecuted, and prison could be my new home. Whatever this person knows, or thinks they know, I cannot take the risk. Yet I did it all for the right reason. Alex has had a wonderful childhood, with every opportunity open to him. Yes, I might have been a helicopter mum, ferrying him from football to rugby to piano lessons and judo and chess clubs and archery. I wanted him to try everything, to help him find a passion in life. Looking back, I wouldn't have done anything differently. Control is my middle name, and I'm damned good at it.

As soon as I'm back in my office, behind the closed door, I call the number the text message has come from, but it goes straight to voicemail. I don't leave a message, but I do send a reply.

Who are you?

I get no response, and there remains a single tick next to the message, which suggests the phone is off and it hasn't been read. I check it every hour through the rest of the day and into the evening. For once, I'm glad that Stuart is in bed so early, as I don't have to pretend that everything is fine. I wait and I wait, but the single tick remains next to the message and my phone doesn't ring. Eventually, around 2 am, I fall into a fitful sleep.

I'm awake at 6 a.m. The first thing I do is check my phone. I have another message. This time it's in sentence case rather than the aggressive capitals.

Put the money in a padded envelope and leave it behind the dumper bin on Delphus Street. Making it easy for you, choosing your home town. Drop it off at 9 pm tomorrow evening. I am watching you all the time. If you tell anyone or involve the police, you know what will happen ...

It's the words 'making it easy for you' that confuses me. The suggestion is that the blackmailer could have asked me to go somewhere further from home. I can't help my mind flipping back to Manchester. That's where this all began. Getting into semantics isn't going to solve anything, though. I need to focus on the practicalities. I want to get this over and done with, but of course, I'm worried that if I capitulate now, the blackmailer will be back for more in the future. I pace up and down the kitchen and then go for a run on the running machine, but my normal fast-paced exercise doesn't ease my confusion and unease. I feel like I need to run a full marathon to banish the agitation. I take a cold shower and decide. I'm going to give the blackmailer the money, and if they come back for more, then I will have no choice but to go to the police.

After getting dressed, I grab my phone from the bedside table. Then I scroll back to look at the previous messages from the blackmailer, but to my confusion they've gone. How the hell is that possible? I thought messages couldn't be deleted. I double-check in Messenger and WhatsApp and in my text messages, but they're not there. I can only see the last message, the one with the explicit instructions.

Instead of going into the office, I drive into town and am at the bank when the doors open. The cashier is a young woman in her twenties.

'I'd like to take twenty thousand out in cash,' I say.

Her eyes widen. 'We normally need notice of that much.'

'Please, can I speak to your manager.' I try to be polite and smile at her, but I feel unusually anxious and tap my fingers on the counter.

She disappears around the back and returns a couple of minutes later. 'Please, can you take a seat? My manager will be out to see you as soon as he can.'

I have learned patience over the years, but it doesn't come naturally to me. To be a lawyer means you have to be patient; you're following procedures and bureaucracy and systems; due process always takes time. But this, I just want to get it over and done with.

'Mrs Heaton,' the man says as he walks towards me. He's

about my age, wearing a navy suit that is too tight, and he has the red nose of someone who drinks to excess. He's wearing extremely strong aftershave that might be pleasant in a lesser quantity. 'Please follow me.'

We walk into a tiny room, just big enough for a desk and two chairs.

'I understand from my colleague that you wish to take out twenty thousand pounds.'

'Yes, is that a problem?'

'No, but we need to double-check that you aren't being coerced in any way. We owe a duty of care to our customers.'

The temptation is to laugh out loud, but I restrain myself. 'As you'll see, I have plenty of funds in my account.'

'May I have one of your bank cards?'

I fumble in my wallet and remove a debit card. He types into the keyboard on the desk and looks through various pages on his monitor, which I can't see, as it's angled away from me.

'May I ask what this money is for?'

'No,' I say.

'Unfortunately, we need to know for security purposes.'

I sigh and think of the first thing that comes into my head. 'I'm buying a watch for my husband's birthday, and if I put it on a card, he will see what I've bought. Hence I need cash. To put your mind at ease, I am a solicitor.'

'Quite, thank you very much, Mrs Heaton. I'll be back with the cash as quickly as I can.'

And so I settle in for another wait.

I've never seen more than five hundred pounds in cash. Who carries around large sums of money these days? So I'm a bit surprised when he returns with an A4 padded envelope. He takes the money out and counts the fifty-pound notes and hands it to me. I take the envelope, thank him and put it in my briefcase.

Back in the office, Kathleen reminds me that I'm due at their house for supper this evening. It's the last thing I feel like, but perhaps the distraction will do me good. It certainly will be better than spending a miserable evening at home with Stuart asleep and Alex either at Debbie's or not talking to me.

Kathleen and Trisha live in a new build house in a small enclave of houses three miles outside Horsham. Although we've been friends for so many years, I always feel that our friendship is fragile due to the uncomfortable reality that Kathleen and I are colleagues and sometimes competitors. I rather wish that we hadn't both stayed at Egerton Brook Steading. It might have made things easier for us, enabling us to open up more and be truly supportive of each other. My admission that Alex was arrested for shoplifting is the most personal thing I've shared with her in a long time, not because I don't trust her, but because I am very wary of mixing work with home life.

Kathleen married Trisha just five years ago, although they have been a couple for well over a decade. They chose a sperm donor, and eighteen months ago, Trisha gave birth to twin girls. I've seen the babies only once, and they're adorable.

Kathleen and I leave work at the same time, and I follow her home, conscious that my car seems very flashy next to her sensible Toyota. Their home is a red-brick house with a picket fence around the garden, lending it an American feel. They have hanging baskets on either side of the front door, and two little plastic tricycles are neatly parked in their front garden. I follow Kathleen into the house.

'Hello!' she shouts up the stairs.

'Hiya, darling. I'm just about to put the girls in the bath. Could you take over the food for me?'

'Okay,' she says. Trisha is a fine cook, and Kathleen murmurs to me, 'I hope I don't spoil it.'

'I'm sure you won't,' I say.

She takes my coat from me and hangs it up on a wooden coat stand in the hallway, and I follow her into their kitchen. It's a stark white design with white quartz countertops and white tiles on the floor. I imagine it'll be a nightmare to keep clean as their little girls grow up.

'Can I help?' I ask as Kathleen peers inside the oven.

'Actually, why don't you go upstairs and help Trisha? Then she can nip down to give me instructions. I'll send her back up with a glass of white wine for you.'

'Thanks, Kath. That would be great.'

I remove my shoes, conscious of their spotless beige carpet, and pad up the staircase in stockinged feet.

'You've got me as a helper,' I shout to Trisha. I haven't been upstairs in their house before, so I'm not sure which way to go.

She pokes her head out of a doorway to the right of the staircase. 'In here!'

The children's bathroom has a white bath and pale blue tiles on the walls. The two little girls are splashing around in the water, surrounded by bubbles and floating yellow ducks. They are both chubby with dark brown curls and look utterly adorable. Just seeing them there eases the stresses of my day; I can't help but smile.

Trisha is kneeling on a fluffy white bathmat, and she shifts as if to get up when I walk into the room.

'Don't move,' I say, sitting on the plastic-covered stool. 'You've grown so much,' I say to the girls, who ignore me.

'Ivy and Alice, this is Mummy's friend Chantal. Say hello.'

'Hello,' they say in high-pitched voices, immediately returning to splashing.

'Kath says could you nip down and show her what to do with the cooking whilst I keep an eye on the girls?'

Trisha rolls her eyes at me and tuts. 'She's quite capable of checking if the potatoes are cooked. Anyway, how are you after your lovely party?'

I groan. 'Alex made quite the fool of himself.'

'He's just a typical teenage boy; it was quite funny, really. I guess we've got all of that to come.'

The little girls are babbling away to each other, and I get up and kneel next to Trisha on the bathmat. I push my sleeves up and start playing with them.

'You're quite the natural with children,' Trisha says after a couple of minutes, smiling at me. 'Did you only want the one?'

I pause. 'Um, no. I'd have loved to have more, but it just wasn't to be.'

She throws me a compassionate look. 'I guess it meant you could focus on your work and rise to the top. It would have been harder if you'd had more children.'

'But Kath has done well too,' I say.

'Not as successful as you. She was gutted she wasn't made an equity partner, but I'm sure you know that.'

I'm quiet because I didn't know that. Kathleen has never spoken about the fact that I became her superior even though we are the same age and, for much of our time at the firm, we rose up the ranks together.

'It doesn't mean she's not a brilliant lawyer,' I say.

'That's what I tell her, and besides, she might not have wanted to become a mum if she'd had all the extra responsibilities. You're lucky that you started young, but it's harder for Kath, being in her forties, with the sleepless nights and everything that comes with having twin babies.'

Trisha leans into the bath and takes out the bath plug.

'Right, you two, time for rubbing down and bed.' She hands me a towel. 'Can you do Alice?'

We're drying the little girls when Kathleen comes upstairs with a glass of wine in her hand for me. She places it on the windowsill and then bends down and takes Alice from me, cooing and throwing her up into the air.

'I'll take over the girls now,' she says, giving Trisha a quick peck on the cheek and then tickling Ivy.

Trisha puts Ivy on the ground, and the toddler grabs Kathleen's hand.

'Chantal, let's go downstairs, and I'll finish off supper, and you can have a relaxing glass of wine,' Trisha says.

The rest of the evening is pleasant, and there's much banter between the three of us, but that little giveaway of Trisha's – that Kathleen is jealous of my position at work – niggles at the back of my mind.

That night I lie in bed, trying to suppress my fury towards the nameless, faceless blackmailer. If they think I'm just going to leave the money and let them get away with it, they've severely underestimated me. Over the next twenty-four hours, I formulate my own little plan. I intend to catch them in the process.

For once, I'm glad that my husband has gone to bed at 9 pm and my son is fully engrossed with something on his computer; neither of them will notice that I've gone out. I put on a pair of black jeans, a dark anorak and a black beanie that I discover in the back of Stuart's wardrobe, which I'm pretty sure he's never worn. I stuff my phone in my pocket and put the envelope with the notes in a Tesco's carrier bag. I feel anonymous and powerful dressed in an outfit I would never normally wear. I drive to the multistorey car park by the cinema in town, choosing it because it has CCTV and automatic number plate recognition, scanning cars' number plates as one drives in. Just in case anything untoward happens, I want the authorities to know where I've been.

I walk from there, clutching the carrier bag to my chest, marching with my head down. My footsteps echo as I stride along the quiet shopping streets. It's dark already, and being a small market town, the only people out and about are folk emerging from restaurants and pubs.

Like most people, I have no idea where big dumper bins are in the centre of town, but I'm sure my blackmailer has done his or her research and scouted town for a suitable drop-off place. I've memorised where Delphus Street is and taken a look at it via Google Earth, but whenever those images were captured, there weren't any bins on the street at that time. I turn off East Street into Delphus Street, passing a charity shop and a takeaway kebab shop that is closed. Two doors down, I see one large black dumper bin. It's wedged up against a wall that's about waist height and placed between a woman's clothing shop where I bought a cut-price cashmere sweater last month, and a coffee shop. Both, of course, are closed. It's also dark here, with just one streetlamp throwing a weak orange glow a bit further down the street. Whoever has chosen this spot has done their homework. It's quiet, with no one passing by, as nothing is open at this time of night, yet there's access from both ends of the street. There must be flats above the shops, because I can see a light on in an upstairs window. I wonder if there's someone up there watching me. If I were the blackmailer, that's what I would do. Rent a room and watch.

I stand still for a few long moments, straining to hear anything. The only sounds are a siren in the far distance and a low hum of music – from where, I don't know. I walk up to the black dumper bin and take a deep breath. Perhaps my blackmailer is hiding inside it. I lift the lid, but other than a nauseating stench, there's nothing inside it. I let the lid clatter back down. Next, I inspect the wall behind the bin. I have to use the light on my phone to see anything, not that there's much to see. There is nothing on the ground or on the wall, but I can see it's a perfect place for leaving the envelope; no one is going to peer down here. Once again I glance around me, but there's no one to be seen. I shove the Tesco bag with the money inside it behind the dumpster bin; I then stand up and walk away decisively in the direction I came from, making sure my footsteps are heavy and loud. At the end of the street, I look over my shoulder but can't see anyone, so I double back on myself and stand in the doorway to the clothing shop. I have a clear view of both ends of the street, but I'm largely in the shadows. I intend to wait.

I'm good at waiting; I'll stay here all night if needs be. I'm wearing warm clothes, and I have a chocolate bar in my pocket for sustenance. Half an hour later, I hear footsteps. My heart starts racing. Two young men walk past me, chatting away, but they pass the dumpster bin without a sidewards glance. It's not them. A few minutes later, just as I'm getting pins and needles in my left foot, the headlights of a car light up the street. The car is driving very slowly and, to my dismay, pulls up just a few feet from where I'm standing. The car idles for a couple of long minutes, but I don't dare peek my head out of the doorway to look. What if this is the blackmailer? What if he's got a gun? Am I about to be killed? I stand as far back as I can against the shop's glass door, my heart thumping. And then a car door slams, and I hear footsteps coming towards me. I hold my breath and try to stop my knees from buckling.

'Excuse me, ma'am, but what are you doing?'

It's a policeman, standing there in uniform, his head tilted to one side.

'Um, nothing.'

'You've been loitering here for some time. Do you need any help?'

'No, no, it's fine. I was just about to leave. I was waiting for someone who hasn't turned up.'

He tilts his head as if he doesn't believe me, but one thing is for sure, I don't want to be questioned by the police. That would be awkward in the extreme.

'Thanks for looking out for me,' I say, and I hurry away. I'm livid. Was it chance that a member of the public reported me, someone who lives up in those flats above the shops perhaps? Or has the blackmailer played a clever game?

I don't sleep much and am awake when Stuart's chauffeur arrives at the crack of dawn to take him to the studios. I get up, throw on some old clothes and drive back into Horsham. This time, I head straight for Delphus Street and pull up on the opposite side of the street to the bin just as the rubbish lorry pulls away from the kerb next to the dumpster. I wait, my hand clasping my neck. Could it be one of the rubbish collectors who has been tasked to take the envelope? It seems a bit unlikely. I wonder if I should follow the lorry but decide first to check if the envelope is still there. I don't intend to hang around for more than a few seconds, so I park the car with the nearside wheels up on the pavement and put the hazard lights on. I cross the road and walk behind the bin.

As I assumed, the envelope has gone. I drag the bin forwards to check around it and, holding my breath, open the lid. It's empty, and it still stinks. I run my hands through my hair. I missed a trick; I should have installed a hidden camera to watch. I'm sure such things exist that run on batteries. If, god forbid, this happens again, I'll be smarter next time.

I run back to the car and drive in the direction the rubbish lorry went. It's stopped again on the next street. Abandoning my car on a single yellow line, I run towards the man, who is wheeling another dumpster bin towards the beeping lorry.

'Excuse me,' I say breathlessly. 'The bin you just emptied on Delphus Street, did you see a padded envelope next to it?'

He stares at me and frowns. 'No. The bin was empty. That one often is, so we didn't touch it.' He shakes his head at me and hauls himself up into the passenger seat of the lorry, which pulls away before he's even closed the door. It drives off, turning left at the junction in the distance.

I'm annoyed, and as there's nothing else to do, I head homewards. I'm damned if I'm going to let the blackmailer get away with this, but the only way I'm going to get ahead of him is to recall those days nearly eighteen years ago that I would rather forget. I think of the few people who might have been able to piece together the truth. Jade. Melody. Tammy. Misty Morris. Lorna, my lovely boss, and my work colleagues. But they couldn't have known the truth. Of course, I've known for years that there was the risk that the truth might come out. Alex has had a wonderful childhood, and we've gone nearly eighteen years without a hint of a problem. But for it to come out now ... well, the timing couldn't be worse, with Stuart's dream-come-true job and the most lucrative divorce case I'll have ever handled. And that may well be the problem; Stuart and I are both in the limelight, ripe to be taken advantage of.

The only solution is to find out who is blackmailing me. I'm a damned good lawyer, though I say it myself, and if anyone can root out the truth, it's me. When I'm back home, I take my laptop and sit at the kitchen table, sipping a large cup of black coffee. Unsurprisingly, I haven't been on the dark web since my one experience nearly eighteen years ago, and I'd rather not go there now. I realise that there's little hope of finding Misty Morris with his blatant pseudonym, but I put his name into Google nevertheless. Unsurprisingly, I find nothing related to a man in Manchester or even in the UK. For all I know, he could be dead or locked up in jail, or he could have expanded his illegal operation and be living the high life in Malaga.

And then I wonder. Would he have kept records of all the work he did? And if so, perhaps he's in trouble and is blackmailing the people he helped over the years. It would be ridiculously easy to find me, and even though I gave him a pseudonym, he could have kept a copy of Alex's fake birth certificate, and then all it would take is for him to look up Alex and then work out who his parents are. I remember him telling me that I was small fry, but I'm not anymore. Stuart and I are sitting ducks with our fame and wealth and influence. I suppose I was just hopelessly naive to think that the past wouldn't catch up with me.

And then I think about Jade. I've tried so hard not to think about her over the years. In my dreams, she's alive and hunting me down, and sometimes I think I see her lurking in doorways, walking ahead of me at a train station. I knew from early on that I needed to forget about her, however harsh that may seem.

15

How could anyone ignore a baby's cries? His wails rip right through me, burning the insides of my ears, making my heart break with sorrow for this little mite who has a mother who simply doesn't care. Jade is leaning her head back against the ripped car headrest, her eyes closed, drawing deeply on the spliff in between her lips. Every so often she blows the smoke out of the small opening where she has wound down her side window.

'Jade,' I say. She ignores me.

'Jade, Noah needs you.'

She keeps her eyes closed, and her jaw is slack now. The spliff is between the index and middle finger of her right hand, and ash falls off into the footwell. The smell is almost rancid.

'Jade.' My voice is insistent.

'Fuck off,' she says, but her words are drawn out as if she can't quite control her voice.

'This is your baby! You should be looking after him, not smoking dope. It's disgusting!' Yes, I know I sound sanctimonious, but it's nothing to do with my education or values or class. It's just the primeval urge to be a mother talking, totally at a loss as to how someone could treat their child with such little care.

'Come on, Jade. Chuck that thing away and feed your baby. He's probably hungry.'

'Do it yourself,' she drawls.

'He's your baby boy, Jade. Come on.'

She ignores me, and with her eyes still shut, she takes another long inhale of weed and then opens her eyes, turns her head and blows it straight out of the window into my face. How dare she! I'm trying to do right by her and her child, yet she doesn't care.

I put my left hand on the roof of the car, which is warm now from the sun, and with my right hand, I'm about to open the car door to force her to get out, but the car shifts slightly. I lean on the car again, and it moves forwards another inch.

I realise that she hasn't put the handbrake on. I stand up and take a step backwards. And then Jade shouts out of the window: 'Noah's ruined my effing life, so the least you can bloody do is leave me to have a smoke in peace!'

I step away, horrified. She might think that privately, and I'm not too naive to realise that the adjustment to mother-hood is utterly overwhelming for many women, but to artic-ulate it fills me with fury. She doesn't deserve to be a mother. Poor baby Noah, he's really drawn the short straw in the lottery of life. What chance does he have of growing up into a strong, healthy boy who might have a positive impact on the human race with a mother who doesn't care? Zero. Jade may have no education, no money, no home, but none of that is important if there is love. Yet Jade has made it quite clear that she doesn't love this poor little mite, that he's got in the way of her life, that she couldn't care less what happens to him. And I am infused with anger towards her. How dare she treat him with such disregard when there are people out there – people like me – utterly desperate to be a mother?

I stride around to the rear of the car, and when I'm standing behind it, I place both hands on the boot, and I push. It really doesn't take much effort at all for me to make the car edge forwards. It rolls downwards maybe a couple of metres, and then, for a split second, it hovers right on the edge of the white chalk cliff, the front half of the car suspended above air. Jade's screams pierce the solitude, and she moves, probably trying to open her door, but that movement propels the car forwards. I watch it as if in slow motion as the knackered little silver car tumbles over and over itself like a toy before landing with a gigantic splash in the middle of the beautiful, toxic lake.

And then there is silence.

Even baby Noah stops crying, as if he knows that something truly terrible has just happened. I run over to him and quickly unstrap him from his car seat, placing little kisses on his soft downy head and his little cheeks, and I jiggle him up and down on my hip as I stare at the lake. My heart is pounding as I wait for the car to bob up to the surface, for Jade to emerge, coughing and spluttering. But there isn't even a ripple. No air bubbles. Absolute silence, just broken by a little gurgle by Noah and a red hawk that swoops through the sky in front of us and then disappears over the horizon.

I wait for five minutes, and then I start pacing up and down. Jade is gone, and I made that happen. Noah reaches for my hair and tugs it, and then he smiles at me. He actually *smiles*, and my heart melts.

'It's alright, sweetheart. You don't need to worry ever again. I'm your mummy now, and I'm going to give you a wonderful life. I'm going to get you some milk, and then I'm going to change your nappy. Let's pretend you were born today.'

If I had a boy, I was going to call him Alex, and a girl, Melissa. When Debbie and I were little, we used to name our dolls, and we discussed what we would call our future children. I had told Stuart my preferred names, and he was happy with both of them. But that was before my diagnosis, before my dreams were destroyed.

'Welcome to the world, Alex,' I say, and he smiles goofily back at me, making my heart melt.

16

I really want to leave home. Dad is never there. Mum is so self-absorbed, and I don't share either of their values. I guess the problem is I don't respect them. Yes, they've done well for themselves with 'good' jobs and material wealth, but none of that is important. What really matters is the legacy that we leave, the difference we have made to our fellow human beings and our planet.

That's why I like Luna so much. We think the same. She said she's going to introduce me to some people who live in a squat in Brighton, and I might be able to live with them. I could move back to Aunt Debbie's, but although she gives me more freedom than Mum and Dad, it's so claustrophobic the way she still treats me like a little kid. Thinking of Aunt Debbie, I'm worried that I still don't have enough money to pay her back for the car repairs. But this evening I haven't got time to think about that, because Luna and I are on our way to a meeting of environmental activists.

Luna has never been to this particular meeting before, because without a car she couldn't get there. The public transport around here is terrible – another thing that needs sorting if we're going to stop people from polluting with their cars. The directions have been sent on an ultra-secure messaging system that I've never heard of, but Luna says it's the only safe way of communicating so the cops and the PIs that the large companies employ can't disrupt our plans.

We're on the outskirts of Shoreham, and Luna is giving me directions.

'It's there on the left,' she says. We're in a big industrial estate, but not one of those modern ones. This one is creepy, with large derelict warehouses and old bits of machinery dumped in front of imposing corrugated iron buildings. 'Park around the back of that building,' she says, pointing to a single-storey brick office that has a rust-covered boat standing in front of it.

'This place is due to be redeveloped,' Luna says as I switch off the car engine. 'But surprise, surprise, rather than putting up affordable eco-houses, it's going to be some swanky estate for multimillionaires. People like your parents.'

I bristle because she's right. There are lots of cars already parked up, and to my surprise, some of them are fancy, like expensive Teslas and even a hybrid Jaguar. I was worried that I might need to downplay my privileged background, but perhaps I don't need to be ashamed of it. It's my beliefs, and the actions that I take personally, that matter.

'You need to speak up,' Luna says as she pushes up the sleeves of her tattered jumper. 'If you want to be taken seriously, you have to come up with your own ideas and agree to put in the legwork. Sign up for stuff, okay?'

There's a security guard standing at the door, and it seems more like we're attending a rave than a protest group meeting. Luna gives our names, and when we're checked off the list, he lets us in. We walk straight into a cavernous space with a concrete floor and exposed breeze-block walls. There are lots of dark green plastic chairs set out in several rows of big semicircles. At a guess, there must be about fifty people here, talking together in small groups, and there are people from every walk of life and every age. Luna waves at a couple of younger people, a girl and a boy – both with dreadlocks – but most people you would walk past on the street without giving them a second glance.

'Hello, everyone!' A man wearing jeans and a white T-shirt claps his hands and then hollers again. 'Let's begin.'

Luna leads me to the front row.

'Shouldn't we sit near the back?' I ask, feeling uncomfortable.

'That's for wimps.'

We sit down, and a woman takes the seat on my left, nodding at me as she does so. She could be one of Mum's friends; she's certainly the right age, wearing smart navy trousers and little kitten heels.

'Good evening, everyone, and thank you for joining us. My name is Ian Coley, and I'm the organiser of E-Protest Sussex, where our *E* stands for environment and not electronic. The agenda this evening is to start off welcoming our new members, of which there are a few. We will then talk through all of the planned protests for the next month, and then I will ask you for your input. So let's start with our new supporters. Please raise your hands if this is the first time you have been to one of our meetings.'

I put my arm in the air.

'Young man here in the front row. Please introduce yourself.'

I feel my cheeks flaming. I'm not an exhibitionist like my parents; the very worst thing I had to do at school was Show and Tell. Luna nudges me in the ribs, and I clear my throat. 'My name is Alex. I'm doing my A levels, and I'm passionate about the environment.'

'Good for you, and welcome, Alex. We need more people of your age group, as you are our future.'

Six or seven other people introduce themselves, and then Ian reads out a list of protests that are planned for the next month. People volunteer to take on different roles, whether that's writing press releases or getting banners printed and put up, or fund-raising or attending rallies. Luna offers to take part in a protest for a new housing development in a green field site between Horsham and Crawley, and I follow her lead. About half an hour later, Ian opens up the floor to questions and suggestions, as he calls it.

'Tell them about LALO Clothing,' Luna whispers to me.

'And say what?' I ask.

'All the crap things you've found out about them. If we don't take a stance against them, who will?'

Before I can stop her, she puts her arm up in the air.

'Yes, Luna,' Ian says, smiling warmly at her.

'Alex, my boyfriend here, has some inside information and strong thoughts on LALO Clothing.'

Once again, my cheeks are aflame.

'LALO Clothing is very much on our watch list. What are your thoughts, Alex?' Ian asks.

I'm furious with Luna for dumping me in it, as I can feel everyone's eyes on me. I clear my throat again and then start talking. 'As a UK-based fast-fashion company, they're one of the worst polluters in the world, yet they seem to wriggle out of their environmental responsibilities time and time again. It's not just in their clothes production process, where they use obscene amounts of water and then pump untreated water back into the systems, particularly in Bangladesh, where they do most of their manufacturing, but it's the conditions they keep their staff in. They're paid a pittance, and their working conditions are terrible. Look, I can't claim I've been there to see it myself, but how else can they afford to sell a pair of cotton trousers for ten quid? The fashion industry alone pumps 1.2 billion tonnes of carbon into the atmosphere. It's just got to change.

'And what sickens me the most is that LALO have refused to join the global coalition, the Fashion Pact, yet they're this country's biggest seller of cheap clothing. And then there's the waste. By 2030, it's thought that people around the world will be discarding more than 134 million tonnes of textiles per year. But 95 per cent of these textiles could be reused and recycled. LALO make their clothes cheaply, and they fall apart – I know that because I bought some trousers just to see what they're like – and that's what they want. To encourage people to buy, chuck out and buy again. In my opinion, this needs a two-pronged attack. Education about the effects their clothing have on the environment, particularly educating kids my age who buy from LALO, and taking a stance against them. LALO's headquarters are right here in Sussex. It's up to us to speak out and take action.'

There's a pause when I stop talking, and in that split second, I think that I've made a terrible fool of myself. It's not like I'm speaking from real experience. Most of my facts come from articles I've read on the web. But then Ian starts clapping, and before I know it, everyone is clapping, and if I thought my face was red before, it's crimson now.

'Thank you, Alex. You are a credit to your generation and totally right. LALO has been on our radar for some time, but perhaps it's time to do something about it. Alex, do you have any thoughts for first steps?'

I shrug, because now I'm really out of my comfort zone. It's one thing being an armchair environmentalist, quite another planning a protest.

'Aren't the founders going through a messy divorce?' a woman from a row behind me asks.

There's some chatter about the Lowaskis' hypocrisy and ostentatious living, and then Ian takes control again.

'What do we want our outcome to be?'

People shout out answers, such as raising awareness of how much they're polluting the environment and how it stinks that they haven't signed up to the Fashion Pact. Ian writes down the objectives on a big flipchart. A few minutes later, the group has created a plan of action to raise awareness about LALO's poor business practices, and Ian has asked Luna and me to organise a protest outside their gates to stop their lorries from going in and out.

I come out of that meeting on a greater high than I've ever got from drink or drugs. Lots of strangers shake my hand or pat my back and mutter that I might be the next Greta Thunberg. The only problem is Luna, who refuses to meet my eyes. I think she's pissed off that I got all the attention. Her foul mood continues all the way back to Horsham.

'Hey,' I say as I pull up outside her block of flats. 'Don't be angry with me. You're the one who has made all of this happen, and there's no way I'm doing that protest without you.'

'You're right,' she says, immediately snapping out of her mood. She pulls my face towards hers. 'Can you sneak me into your house after the demo? I'll do some stuff to you that will blow your mind.'

'Can't say no to that, can I?' I laugh.

The protest is planned for Thursday, because apparently that's the day most lorries leave LALO Clothing's premises, stocking up shops and distribution warehouses for the weekend. I'm nervous, but I tell myself it's because I've never done anything like this before. But I'm also worried because Mum is going to go apeshit if she finds out, Dad too, probably, and I'm having to skive off college again. Luna says I shouldn't care what Mum thinks because she brings it on herself, and Dad is a pompous git. She's probably right.

When I arrive, Luna is already there with about six or seven of her mates, wearing grunge clothes; most of them are covered in piercings and tattoos, with their hair in dread-locks. As I walk towards them, I worry they may think I'm not cool enough.

'Hi,' Luna says, giving me a full-on snog in front of all the others. She then takes my hand and introduces me, and it seems that because I'm Luna's boyfriend, they're going to accept me.

'This is the first protest that Alex has organised, and he's done a great job, hasn't he?' she says. In fact, I've done practically nothing other than send out a couple of group emails and liaising with a chap called Vince to get the banners printed.

LALO Clothing is a stand-alone industrial unit, with vast warehouses as far as the eye can see. How they got planning permission to build in a green field site is beyond me. One of the guys reckons they bribed the planners. There are tall metal gates surrounding the whole site, and at the entrance-way, there's a massive grey gate that is open. The sides of the road down to the main buildings are neatly manicured with yellow flowers that match their logo. As we're standing there, one of LALO's lorries chugs past us. Its sides are covered in photos of young women modelling skimpy outfits; all of them have yellow flowers in their hair or strategically positioned on their bodies. The LALO logo is bright yellow, loud and gaudy, but I suppose some people think it's fun.

After the lorry has turned left and disappeared, Luna hands out a bunch of handcuffs. 'Let's pull the gates closed and then handcuff ourselves to them so no one can get in or out.'

Vince has turned up and is fixing huge banners to the

railings. They read 'LALO is killing the world. Polluters. Slave drivers. SAY NO TO LALO.'

'Hold out your hand,' Luna says. I do as I'm told, and she clamps on a handcuff around my wrist and then tugs me to the gate, locking the other end to the railings.

'Oi, what are you doing?' A security guard appears on the other side of the gate. 'You're trespassing. You need to leave now.'

Luna laughs at him. I'm impressed by her bravery. 'What are you going to do about it, matey?' she asks.

'Are we expecting the press?' one of the female protesters asks.

'Ian said he was notifying a few journalists. Depends if there's something bigger happening elsewhere.'

I really hope the TV crews turn up. That would be hilarious and give Dad a run for his money.

But they don't.

A LALO lorry appears. The portly driver gets down from his cab. 'What the hell are you lot doing?'

'Did you know what harm LALO is doing to the environment?' Luna asks.

'They pay my effing bills, and I won't get paid unless you let me in. Stop being a bunch of jerks.'

I follow the lead of the others and just stand there impassively while the lorry driver climbs back into his cab and puts his hand on his horn. It's loud and hurts my ears, but with my hands cuffed to the railings, there's little we can do. Next time, I'll go through Dad's address book and contact some of the media myself. That's what we need.

Two security guards arrive on the inside of the gates, and they talk in muffled, low voices into walkie-talkies. More lorries join the queue, and now I reckon there must be six or seven backed up onto the main road. Luna grins at me, and I smile back. This is working a treat.

But then I hear sirens that get louder and louder. Two police cars pull up to the side of the lorries, and four policemen in uniform stride towards us.

My heart sinks.

We're arrested, all of us; they have to send for more police cars in order to get us to the station. I'm shoved into the back of a police car with a friend of Luna's, and this time I don't mind that I'm on my way to the police station. When I stole that watch from the shop, I knew it was wrong, but this is something different altogether. We're bringing attention to a cause that the world needs to know about, and frankly, if I get charged for an offence relating to that, then so be it.

Of course, Mum doesn't see it like that. It's a few hours until she arrives at the police station, and I don't think I've ever seen her look quite so angry. She's pale, and she won't meet my eyes, and when I ask if we can give Luna a lift home, she literally spits out the word *no*. I'm not charged with aggravated trespass, but they tell me that if I do it again, the police will prosecute. I guess I will be charged sooner or later, because I will do it again, and I'll let the world know that my mum works for LALO and my dad sways with the wind.

When we get home, Dad is there, and Mum goes apeshit.

'I can't believe you're such a selfish fool!' she shouts at me. 'Have you given a second's thought as to the implications of your actions. You are so lucky they didn't charge you. If you carry on like this, you'll have a criminal record, you won't be able to get a decent job, you won't be allowed to travel to America. And what about us? Did it ever cross your mind what the implications are to us? LALO is my client, the biggest, most high-profile divorce case I've ever handled. And your dad, he's just got the job of his dreams, and you've let that little snake of a girlfriend influence you so much, you could ruin everything!'

She picks up a mug that's drying on the drainer next to

the sink and hurls it at the wall. It smashes into smithereens onto the stone floor. All three of us just stare at it. I've never seen her go totally mental like that, and even Dad is speechless for several long seconds. I can't decide if it's scary or funny.

'Chantal, what the hell?' Dad breaks the silence.

'I'm sorry, but I've never been so furious,' she says through gritted teeth. She's literally trembling.

'You're totally overreacting. At least Alex is passionate about something; he's not sitting at his computer all day, watching god knows what.'

'It's the implications,' she hisses.

'He's been a bit stupid. The theft was far worse, and I do accept that Luna is a bad influence, but fighting for something he believes in ... well, that can't be wrong.'

I feel like waving my hands and saying, *I'm here, right in front of you. Stop talking as if I'm out of the room.*

'I think we should support Alex's passion for environmental conservation.' Dad turns to look at me. 'Perhaps we can get you on the show to discuss environmental activism and how it's affecting your generation.'

'That would be cool,' I say.

'You cannot condone such irresponsible behaviour! I forbid you!' Mum says.

And then they start ripping into each other, shouting and hurling insults, and I just have to get the hell out of the room. I run upstairs to my bedroom, but whilst I can't hear what they're saying to each other, the raised voices and Mum's shrieks pierce through the walls and the ceilings of the house. I don't understand why she's being so pathetic about it. Dad's right; they should be pleased that I'm doing something positive. But as normal, it's all about them; it's all about how I reflect on them. They can go to hell.

I put my earbuds in, and just as I'm switching on my

music, the front door slams so hard the house quivers. I see Dad stomp across the driveway, open the garage and reverse his car out. He drives fast as he pulls away. It sure as hell isn't me who's acting like the child around here. Mum is psycho, and Dad is weak. I've just got to get out of here.

17

S tuart doesn't come home.

We screamed at each other last night in what was definitely our worst ever row in the twenty-six years we have been together. Of course, we argue like all couples, but the next morning it's normally all forgotten. I shouldn't have thrown that mug at the wall, but something inside me snapped. I have done everything I can for Alex. I've given him an amazing life, opportunities that would never have come his way if he had stayed with his birth mother. I have taught him morals and led by example, but it seems like he's trying to destroy everything. Not just himself, but us too. Stuart told me that I was overreacting, that I had lost all sense of rationality and he barely recognised me these days. And then he left.

I assumed he'd be out for a drive for an hour or so, perhaps pop into a mate's house or even go to the pub, and then he'd be home, and we'd make up as we normally do. I left the lights on in the hall downstairs and lay in bed, listening for footsteps that never came. He didn't answer his phone or respond to my text messages. I vacillated between being angry and worried. What if he'd had an accident? I don't think I'd ever forgive myself if he'd driven his car off the road.

On the dot of 6 am, I switch on the television, and there he is, looking perfectly normal, as if he'd had a good night's sleep and there was nothing wrong in his world. I suppose the makeup artist could have concealed any rings under his eyes, and being the consummate actor and presenter that Stuart is, any personal pain would be well hidden. I take small solace in the fact that he's alive, but I can't stop wondering where he spent the night.

By the time I get into work, I'm exhausted. Alex slunk out of the house without saying a word to me. I was relieved, as I'm not sure I can look him in the eyes at the moment. I'm trying to concentrate on some paperwork when I get a phone call from Trevor Steading's secretary. He is one of the founding partners of the law firm and currently our managing partner, which means he's ultimately responsible for the running of the firm. Other than attending partners meetings with him, we have little to do with each other on a day-to-day basis. I have no idea what he wants.

I stand up, smooth down my skirt and pick up a notepad and pen from my desk. I walk along the corridor and take the stairs to the next level up. His door is shut, so I knock on it.

Trevor has an office twice the size of the other partners and a view onto the high street. He is a corpulent man with a bald head and a penchant for bright ties, which he matches with equally bright socks. He is blind in one eye as a result of a golfing accident about ten years ago, although the injury hasn't appeared to have much of an effect on his life or ability to do his job. He smiles at me as I enter.

'Chantal, have a seat.

'I understand that congratulations are in order for your husband's promotion. I don't watch breakfast television myself, but my wife tells me that he's been appointed lead anchor.'

'Yes,' I say, shifting in my chair as I wonder what this is the preamble to.

He clears his voice. 'I had a phone call this morning from André Lowaski, the owner of LALO Clothing.'

I edge further forwards, my nerves pinging while Trevor leans backwards.

'As you know, the Lowaskis are one of our biggest clients, and if the divorce case goes well, Mr Lowaski has promised us more work on the commercial side of things. Unfortunately, he has got wind of a demonstration against the company, a small rather ineffectual protest, I understand, but unfortunate in light of recent negative press. He says that your son was involved in this. Is that correct?'

I sigh and nod my head. 'Unfortunately, yes.'

'Mr Lowaski is concerned about you representing him in his divorce. Understandably, he is worried about a conflict of interest and any personal information that might be leaked out – inadvertently, of course – should your son get access to any of your papers.'

'But I would never–'

Trevor holds out his hand to stop me from talking.

'If the client is concerned about your involvement, then we need to take action.'

'Are you going to remove me from the case?'

'No. You are our best divorce lawyer. I have told Mr Lowaski that he can be assured of complete confidentiality, and that you never take any client information out of the office. Furthermore, you will take control of your son, who is young and foolish, and make sure that this never happens again.' He pauses and takes a sip of coffee from a small cup on his desk. 'I assume I said the right thing, Chantal?'

'Yes,' I say. 'Thank you. Please be rest assured of my discretion, and I have already had a firm talking to my son.'

'I'm glad to hear it. The foolishness of youth, hey? I'm sure your boy will see sense soon enough, coming from such a fine gene pool as you and your husband.'

I stand up to swallow the scream that is in danger of exploding out of me.

'Keep me posted on the progress of the divorce. To land LALO Clothing as a commercial client for the firm would be huge, although I don't need to tell you that.'

When I leave Trevor's office, I go straight to the ladies' toilets, hiding myself in the cubicle. Trevor could have so easily removed me from the case. If he'd done that, it would be the ultimate humiliation. The fact of the matter is that all my current problems relate to one person: Alex.

And then, as I'm sitting on that toilet seat, wondering what the hell I should do to control our son, my phone vibrates with another incoming message.

YOU GOT OFF TOO LIGHTLY. I KNOW YOU WERE WATCHING OUT FOR ME, BUT THAT BACKFIRED BECAUSE I CALLED THE POLICE. I WANT ANOTHER £10K.

I bury my face in my hands. I suppose I was naive to think I could hang around all night and wait for someone to pick up the money I'd left behind the bin. It was a clever move for my blackmailer to call the police out to say I was loitering with intent. But another ten grand? It's been two days since the last lot. This could go on indefinitely. How the hell am I going to stop it?

I try to think rationally. Who else's body would have been pulled from a car out of Jongleur Hill Reservoir? Of course, it must have been Jade. I've always known she died there, because there weren't even any air bubbles after the car sunk. Obviously Jade didn't own that car. She'd probably stolen it; otherwise the police would have identified her from the vehicle. I have no idea where Misty Morris is, so he is number one on my list to track down. I only met Jade's two flatmates briefly, but they certainly knew she was pregnant and surely would have been concerned about what happened to her. Melody and Tammy. How the hell am I going to find them all these years later? One thing I know for sure: I need to go to Manchester.

The London train passes through Stockport, so I decide to stop off and go and find the betting shop where I met Misty Morris all those years ago. I can visualise it so clearly in my mind's eye, yet when I get to the area I think it was in, I doubt myself. Assuming it's the same street, it still looks run-down, and if anything, there are even more shops with shuttered fronts or boarded up. The only shops that are open are two charity clothing shops, a phone repair shop and a newsagent. I pass a William Hill betting shop, but I'm almost sure this isn't the right one, because I think I would have remembered if it had been a nationally recognised name.

When I walk inside, three pairs of eyes turn to stare at me. The two men in the shop and the woman behind the counter eye me with suspicion, and I wonder if they think I'm a cop, dressed in smart clothes, carrying a small case. I walk up to the grey-haired woman, and she raises an eyebrow.

'This is a bit of a long shot, but I'm looking for a man who went by the name of Misty Morris twenty years ago. He used to spend quite a bit of time in betting shops.'

She stares at me as if she hasn't understood what I said, but just when I think I'll need to repeat myself, she shouts over to the two men, 'Heard of a Misty Morris?'

They both shrug their shoulders and shake their heads.

'Sorry, love,' she says. 'Can't help.'

'Thanks anyway,' I say, and leave the shop. There is a pub on the other side of the road, the exterior painted in dark grey, which gives it an ominous feeling. It's not much better on the inside, with low dark ceilings, smelling of stale beer; the 1980s pop music blaring through the space is at odds with the people and the place.

Once again, I'm stared at by nearly everyone. There's a sixty-something man behind the bar, sipping a Coke, reading the *Metro*.

'Excuse me,' I say, repeating what I said to the woman in the betting shop.

'This place changed hands ten years ago. Never heard of him, but people come and go in places like this. What are you, a private investigator?'

'No,' I say. 'Just someone he used to know.'

'We don't get many people like you in here.'

I smile awkwardly, thank him and hurry back outside. This is hopeless. Misty Morris could be anywhere: in prison, in another country, or dead, for all I know. I walk back to the train station and hop onto a train heading into Manchester's Piccadilly Station.

The city has changed dramatically in the two decades since I was last here, with the centre of Manchester turning decidedly posh. The skyline is full of shiny glass and metal high-rise buildings. There are trendy bars everywhere and restaurants serving fancy cuisine. I check into the Hilton Hotel, where my room on the twentieth floor provides me with dizzy-making views of the city and the hills of the Peak District in the distance. I have absolutely no idea where to start looking for Melody and Tammy; it's not helped that I don't even know their surnames. All the information I have is the address where they used to live and that Tammy had a job in Selfridges – I assume as a shop assistant – and Melody was an aspiring model. I decide to try their home first, and tomorrow I will go to Selfridges.

I can't remember the house number of Jade and the girls' flat, but my sense of direction has always been good, and I'm hopeful I will recognise the street. There is a row of taxis waiting in front of the Hilton, and as I exit the door, the hotel porter waves the next taxi forwards. It's a black cab, like the ones in London, driven by a bearded Pakistani man who smiles at me engagingly.

'Where to, love?' he asks.

'This is a bit of a strange request. Could you take me to Lemonsby Street, Cheetham Hill? I'm not sure of the number, but hopefully I'll recognise it. And then if you could wait for me and bring me back here, that would be great.'

'Yes, of course. Hop in,' he says, with a broad grin. 'I live up that way.'

If the traffic was bad twenty years ago, it's even worse now. I watch the taxi metre go up and up, but I don't care. I just need to find Melody or Tammy.

'Here we go, Lemonsby Street,' he says.

The problem is, everywhere has been gentrified. I used to recognise her house as being the scruffiest on the street, but they all look the same now. I rack my brains. I think it was number two, or perhaps it was number twenty. I ask the taxi driver to go very slowly.

'I don't remember exactly which house my friend used to live in,' I say.

'How long ago was he here?'

'It's a she, and it was nearly twenty years ago.'

He sucks in air between his teeth. 'An age. My auntie lives on the next street, and she's been here since 1990, the kind of woman who knows everyone and everything. If you get stuck, I can ask her.'

'Thanks,' I say. 'I'll knock on the door to number two, and let's take it from there.'

Most of these houses look like they're single homes now, although twenty years ago the majority were divided up into flats. Number two has a black shiny door and just one doorbell. I ring it.

A woman wearing a beautiful turquoise sari shot with gold opens the door; she keeps the chain on between the door and the frame.

'Hello, I'm sorry to disturb you,' I say. 'I'm looking to trace two girls who lived here eighteen years ago. Their names were Melody and Tammy.'

She looks at me suspiciously. 'I don't know anyone with those names. We moved in here in 2010. My husband might remember the person we bought the house from, but other than that, I'm afraid I can't help you.'

'That might be useful.' I hand her one of my business cards.

She glances at it and narrows her eyes. 'You're a solicitor.'

'Yes,' I say. 'But I'm here on personal business.'

'Because we don't want trouble.'

'Rest assured, I just want to track down an old friend.'

She clearly doesn't believe me, but she takes my business card anyway. I thank her, turn around and walk back to the taxi. My driver is on the phone, talking rapidly in Urdu.

He switches to English when I get in the cab. 'Yes, Auntie. Yes, yes, yes. I need to go now.' He rolls his eyes at me in the mirror and puts his phone back into the holder on the dashboard. 'She can't stop talking, my aunt Zainab. What she said was a lot of the houses on this street were owned by Bilal Ali. He slowly developed them and sold them for a lot of money. Mr Ali moved to Cheshire five years ago and now lives in a mansion in Wilmslow. That's where all the posh people live.'

I smile. 'Do you think your aunt Zainab could get me the contact details for Mr Ali?'

'Auntie knows everyone. I'm sure she could.'

'In the meantime, can we try house number twenty, please?'

'Of course, ma'am.' He drives a bit further up the street and double parks to let me out, but I'm sure it's not this house. Number twenty is in the middle of the street, and I'm sure that their house was towards the beginning.

'It's not this one. Would you mind taking me back to the hotel?'

'Of course, ma'am.'

When we're back at the Hilton, I tip the driver well.

'If you leave me your number, I'll get Bilal Ali's details for you. How long are you staying here?'

'Hopefully just a day or two. If I can't track Melody or Tammy, then I'll be heading back down south.' I hand him a business card.

'If I'd known you were a lawyer, I might not have been so helpful!' he says, with a twinkle in his eye. 'Only joking. I'll call you.'

'Thank you so much for your help. I really appreciate it.'

I have an early dinner in the hotel and try calling Alex and Stuart, neither of whom answers my call. I'm clearly still in both of their bad books. I do a search for a model called Melody, but I don't know her surname, and I've no idea if she actually made it as a model. It's a futile search, so instead I decide to focus on Tammy.

The next morning, I have to wait until 10 am for Selfridges to open. I approach a shop assistant and ask to speak to someone in their human resources department, handing over my business card, in the hope that the fact I'm a lawyer might encourage them to talk to me. The shop assistant looks a bit startled, but she hurries away, asking me to wait.

I wander around the handbags section for nearly ten minutes until a woman my age, wearing a beige fitted dress that makes her pale complexion even paler, strides towards me.

'How can I help you?'

'I'm looking for a young woman called Tammy who used to work here twenty years ago. I realise this is an unorthodox request.'

'I need to stop you there,' she says, holding out her hand. 'Firstly, I don't have access to records going back that far, and secondly, due to data protection, there is no way I can give you any information unless you have a warrant. I'm sure you know that better than anyone.'

'I do,' I say, trying not to bristle. 'I was just hoping.'

She nods at me. 'Good luck.' And then she turns on her heel and strides away.

I'm at a loss as to what to do now. Perhaps I'll need to employ a private detective. I wander around the shop, fingering expensive items of clothing, and then I see a shop assistant who, unlike many of the others, looks as if she's in her late thirties or early forties.

'Excuse me,' I say. 'Forgive me for asking, but how long have you worked here?'

'Why?' she says, understandably suspicious.

'I'm trying to track down a friend who worked here almost twenty years ago.'

'The only person I know who has worked here that long is Kerry Jones. She's the manager of the shoe department. I can go and get her.'

'That would be kind of you. Thank you.' I am very impressed how everyone I meet is so willing to help.

About five minutes later, the first woman appears with another woman and points at me. The manager of shoes is a black lady with close-cropped hair and bright red lips. She is wearing a pair of magnificent boots, high-heeled in red suede, that come up over her knees. They are a statement piece that might verge on tarty on someone less statuesque, but she carries them off perfectly. Her name badge says 'Mae'.

'How can I help you?' she asks.

'This is a long shot, but do you remember a young woman called Tammy who used to work here about twenty years ago? She is a black girl, she was attractive with a good figure, but I'm afraid I don't know her surname.' I realise I sound ridiculous.

'Why are you asking?'

'Her roommate was called Jade Sykes, and she went missing. I'm trying to track Tammy down because there are some new leads regarding Jade.'

Mae tilts her head and stares at me. I can sense that she knows something, but is trying to weigh me up.

'I'm a solicitor,' I say, showing her a business card. 'It's possible that Tammy might be entitled to some money.'

'Yes, I know her,' she says eventually. 'She's the daughter of my mum's best friend. I got her the job here, but she blew it. She stole a pair of Louboutins and got fired. Tammy doesn't deserve any money, but her long-suffering mum does.'

'Do you know how I could get hold of Tammy?'

'I don't have her number, but I've heard on the grapevine that she's a pot washer at the Nashville Diner.'

'Where's that?'

'Just off the far end of Deansgate, beyond the Hilton Hotel. Hold on to your wallet if you track her down,' she says. And then Mae is distracted by a tangerine-skinned, strident-voiced customer who wants to try on a pair of Jimmy Choos. I slip away.

I walk briskly down the full length of Deansgate, past the

entrance to the Hilton Hotel, and on until I see the Nashville Diner on the opposite side of the road. It's lunchtime now, not that I feel like eating a gigantic burger. The place is quiet, but I decide not to ask the waitress about Tammy. If she gets wind that someone is looking for her, I reckon she might be the type of person to do a runner. Instead, I nibble at my burger and fries, answer a few emails on my phone and while away the next hour. When I've finished my burger, which was surprisingly good, I leave the restaurant by the front door but wander down a side alley to the trades entrance.

And there she is, leaning against the wall, smoking a cigarette with one hand and looking at her phone in the other, a stained blue-and-white striped apron wrapped around her middle. Tammy hasn't aged well. She looks tired, and her previously neatly cropped hair is now a huge frizz.

'Tammy?' I ask.

She glances up at me and frowns. 'Who's asking?'

'You probably don't remember me, as we met very briefly, but I'm an old friend of Jade.'

'Jade? Jade Sykes?'

I nod.

She doesn't say anything and just narrows her eyes at me.

'What do yeh want?'

'To have a chat with you over a cup of coffee.'

'No thanks.'

'There could be some money involved,' I say hurriedly.

She looks me up and down before talking. 'My shift finishes at 4. Need to pick the kids up at 5. I'll see you here at 4 pm, okay?'

'Yes. Thank you.'

I can feel her eyes on my back as I walk away. I think about what Mae said and how Tammy seems a shadow of the girl I met all too briefly many years ago. The pieces of my jigsaw are coming together. I would bet a lot of money on the fact that Tammy is my blackmailer. If she is, then she's chosen the wrong victim.

Two hours later, I'm sitting in a small greasy spoon cafe opposite Tammy. She can't sit still. She's either shuffling in her chair or biting her chipped nails or tugging at her hair. I've bought her a cup of tea, and she's added three lumps of white sugar.

'Did you ever hear from Jade?' I ask.

'Nope. She disappeared. After the baby was born, she left our flat and lived in a squat for a while.'

'And then?'

'Nothing. Disappeared one day, and no one has seen her since. Well, if they have, I don't know about it.'

'Does anyone know what happened to her?'

Tammy shrugs. 'The others think that Jade did a runner with the baby. She was forever talking about going to Australia, but she didn't have the money for a bus pass, let alone a flight to the other side of the world.'

'Are you still in touch with Melody?'

'Nah. Melody got together with some white geezer a lot older than her. She moved down south, no idea where. We sent each other messages for a couple of years, but then lost touch.'

'What do you think happened to Jade?'

'Look, she was my mate. We didn't see so much of each other after the baby was born, but we went back a long way. If she'd done a runner, she'd have got in touch with me at some point. I'm sure she would. But I never heard from her again. Even after I got banged up by my ex and had my babies, and he was harassing me and I needed to get a new phone number, I kept the old one just in case Jade reached out to me. She never did.'

'What do you think happened to her?'

'She's dead.'

'That's terrible,' I say, shuddering slightly. 'Why would you think that?'

'She was into drugs. We all were back then, so she might have taken an overdose, or some bastard killed her and got rid of her body. I dunno.'

'That's awful,' I say. 'Did you share your suspicions with the police?'

Tammy's laugh is bitter. 'Nah, that's not my style.'

'Do you know who I am?' I ask, quickly changing the subject to see how she reacts.

She holds my gaze, and I think I see a flicker of recognition, or is that fear in her eyes? Does she know that I've rumbled her? I consider asking outright whether she is blackmailing me, but I need to have more facts. I'll let her think that I don't know for a while until I tease out the truth.

'Jade used to clean for you. I went to your flat one time when you weren't there.'

I shudder. I feel ridiculously violated at the thought that they were using my flat and perhaps going through my things all those years ago.

'Why are you looking for her now?' Tammy asks.

'Because I have something of hers that I'd like to give back,' I say.

'What's that, then?'

'It's between me and Jade. But thanks for your time anyway, and if you do hear from her, will you let me know?' I hand over a business card.

Tammy looks at it and eyes me suspiciously. 'What's in it for me?'

'I'll make sure you're well rewarded if you come forward with any information.'

I see the flicker of a smile edge at Tammy's lips. *Bingo,* I think as I stand up. She thinks she's so clever blackmailing me, but she's in for a big shock. I didn't get to be this wealthy and successful without having a hard edge. Tammy has massively miscalculated.

'It's good to see you again, Tammy,' I say, shrugging on my coat. I leave a couple of pounds on the table as a tip, which I expect she'll pocket, and stride out of the cafe.

I am sure that it's Tammy behind the blackmail. She needs the money, she's shifty, but she's totally miscalculated her enemy. I never act impulsively. Well, that's not totally true; I was impulsive that one time. But this time, I will gather all the facts, and then I will seek revenge. Poor, poor Tammy. She has no idea what she's up against.

18

I'm relieved that Mum has gone to Manchester for a couple of days for work. It's been peaceful at home without her; Dad and I watched the footie without her interrupting and telling us what we should or shouldn't do.

I've got a lot of revision to do for my A Levels, so after school, I come home and do some studying, but after a while I feel like sleeping, so I lie on the bed, listen to music and doze off.

I wake with a start. Mum is standing next to my bed, her hands on her hips.

'Alex,' she says, 'it's 6.30 pm.'

I scowl at her. 'What is it?'

'We need to talk.'

I rub my eyes and sit up. I've been dreading this, the scolding talk. 'Only if you promise not to go apeshit.'

I can see that she's trying to control herself. She does that thing of digging her red-painted fingernails into the palms of her hands.

'Did you choose to protest against LALO because they're my client?' she asks.

I wrap my arms around my knees. 'You see, that's your problem, Mum. You always think everything's about you, and it's not. LALO Clothing need to be taught a lesson. They're polluters and don't give a toss about the environment.'

'Fair enough, but being involved in an illegal protest is not the way to go about making your voice heard. You've been cautioned by the police twice in one week, and I don't see that you're the slightest bit remorseful.'

I can't help but roll my eyes. 'Because I'm not remorseful. Yeah, I am about nicking the watch, but about protesting against LALO, I'll do that again and again, because the world needs to know the truth about them. Why don't you get it?'

She sighs and paces up and down my room, throwing a glance of disgust at a heap of dirty clothes I've left on the floor. She crosses her arms. 'There's a right and a wrong way to go about everything. If you want your voice to be heard, then come up with a legal way of shouting about it. But if you could keep quiet until the Lowaskis' divorce is completed, then I would be grateful. You're massively undermining me and my firm. Frankly, I could lose my job because of your actions.'

'Again, it's all about you, isn't it?' I thought Mum had principles; I thought she cared about the environment. I mean, she's good at composting, and she'll repair clothes or give them away to charity, and she's looking into getting an electric car ... but I suppose that's all superficial, easy stuff to do when you're loaded. If she really believes in saving the environment, she wouldn't take on a polluting client like LALO Clothing.

She puts her hands on her hips and stands at the end of the bed. 'I've given a lot of thought as to what an appropriate punishment for your behaviour would be.'

'For god's sake, Mum, I'm not five!'

'You're not going to Nepal during your gap year.'

'What! No way.' I jump off the bed. 'No, you can't stop me from doing that!'

'I can and I will. I'm withdrawing you from the programme.'

I honestly feel as if I've been punched in the gut. I've been dreaming about going on the environmental educational programme to Nepal for the past two years. I've fundraised for it, and I know it's one of the reasons I've been offered a place to read environmental studies at Exeter University the year after next. Mum can't do that to me. It's just not fair.

'It's for my future. Exeter uni might not take me without the experience; the lecturer who interviewed me was really impressed that I was going. You could be ruining everything.' I'm trying to stop myself from bursting into tears. I can't remember the last time I did that, but this really feels like the end of the world.

'I've organised for you to do a six-month stint working in a solicitor's firm in Crawley.'

'But I don't want to be a lawyer! I'm not interested in that.'

'Perhaps not, but it's obvious you need to understand the difference between right and wrong. They do predominantly criminal cases, so you can attend court and do some prison visits. It'll be good for you.'

'No!' I say, but Mum has turned away and walked out of the room. *Bitch!* I want to shout after her, but I don't. I just pummel my fists into the mattress and bury my face in my pillow and scream as loudly as I can.

After I've calmed down a little, I ring Dad.

'Hi, son, what's up?'

'What time are you coming home? I need to talk to you.'

'Sorry, Alex, but I'm not coming back tonight. Something's come up, and I've got to stay in town. Is everything alright?'

'No. Mum's being a complete bitch.'

He sighs. 'Don't call your mother that.' But I can tell there's no conviction in his voice, that he thinks she's a bitch too.

'Look, we'll talk tomorrow evening, okay? A man-to-man down at the pub.'

'Cool.' It's the first time Dad has invited me out for a drink, but I've only got a few weeks to go until I'm eighteen.

'Keep a lid on things until I'm back,' he says, and hangs up.

I can't stay in this house, not whilst I'm alone with Mum. I sneak downstairs, and I can hear her in the home gym, running like a maniac on the machine. I'm getting out of here whilst I can. She hasn't started making supper yet, so there's nothing to grab from the fridge. I hurry out to the car and drive to Aunt Debbie's.

She's my only relative who is always happy to see me, and this evening is no different. When I ring her doorbell, she smiles at me, and standing on tiptoes to give me a peck on the cheek, she asks, 'To what do I owe the pleasure this time?'

'Any chance I could have supper with you? Mum's being a total psycho again.'

She stands back to let me in. 'It'll have to be a simple pasta, because I don't have any of your special food.'

'That's fine,' I say. 'Mum won't let me go to Nepal on my gap year.'

'She's what?' Aunt Debbie stops still and frowns. 'I thought she was all for it, what with you helping out kids and raising the money to go and doing all that eco stuff you're so keen on.'

'I don't have nearly enough to fund it myself. I need another two grand, and if she won't pay, there's nothing I can do. Besides, I still owe you money for the car repairs.'

Aunt Debbie pulls out a chair for me at the kitchen table. There's a large half-eaten piece of chocolate cake next to the pile of exercise books that Debbie always has scattered around her house.

'Oh, Alex, I'm so sorry. I know how much you were looking forward to it. What's made her change her mind?'

'I got taken in by the police again. Me and a bunch of others were protesting outside LALO Clothing's main office. I was let go with a caution, but Mum went apeshit.'

'Not surprising really, Alex. I mean, it's embarrassing for her being a solicitor and having to rescue her son from the police station twice in a week.'

'Did she tell you about the theft?'

'Yes.' Debbie looks sad.

'I did it for you.'

'I know, love. And I really appreciate it, but you can't go breaking the law even if you mean well. Theft is theft.'

'I'm sorry I did it. Luna said she knows someone who would buy the stuff off us, and then I would be able to repay you.'

'I'm not sure this Luna is a great influence on you.'

I throw my head backwards and groan. 'Not you too. Please don't talk like Mum.'

'Oh, Alex, love, give me a hug.'

Aunt Debbie squeezes me tightly. She's so different to Mum, who never gives hugs or kisses unless I'm ill or something.

'If I had the money, I'd pay for you to go for Nepal.'

'I know you would,' I say. 'Could you speak to Dad about it for me? I haven't had the chance to discuss it with him yet, but he'd probably listen to you, as you're a teacher.'

'Of course I will, love. And I'll see if I can change your mum's mind, too. She's angry at the moment, but perhaps she'll see sense when she's calmed down a bit.'

'Can I stay here tonight?'

'Have you got everything you need for school tomorrow?'

'Yes,' I say, although I'll probably have to borrow some of Josh's books. I left in a hurry without thinking about tomorrow's schedule.

'Of course you can. The room's made up. Just make sure you tell your mum where you are. We don't want to make her any angrier than she already is.'

Aunt Debbie and I watch a film together on Netflix. It's a silly romcom, which I think is lame, but Aunt Debbie laughs and cries in all the right places; then she's embarrassed and tells me to ignore her and that she's a silly old aunt. She sends me upstairs to take a shower first, and half an hour later, I'm lying under the Thomas the Tank duvet, sexting Luna, but weirdly, it feels wrong doing that here at Aunt Debbie's, so I turn the phone off and fall straight to sleep.

THE NEXT AFTERNOON, I'm in with the nurse at our doctor's practice.

'Didn't you get the message?' the nurse asks me, a look of disapproval on her face.

'Sorry, yes. I didn't get around to it.'

'Well, let's whip those stitches out now. It looks like the wound has healed well.'

I don't look, but all I feel is a slight tickle.

'All done,' she says, returning to look at a folder on her desk. 'Now Doc would like a quick word with you whilst you're here. He's going to fit you in between appointments.'

'Why?' I ask, wondering whether he knows something about the accident and is going to tell the world what I've done.

'I'm not sure. He'll tell you. Take a seat in the waiting room. He won't be a mo.'

Luna has sent me another message about organising a new protest outside LALO Clothing again, but I've got cold feet about it now. I still want them to change their practices, but I'm not sure it's a good thing to anger Mum. It's more important to me for her to see the light and let me go to Nepal. If she gets wind of another protest, they'll be no chance of that. I'm just writing a reply to Luna when a voice comes over the loudspeaker. 'Alex Heaton to room one, please.'

Dr Thompson is a young man wearing a short-sleeved shirt and chinos. He looks up from reading notes on his computer screen when I walk in, and smiles. I've never met him before, but then again I can't remember the last time I needed to see a doctor. Probably when I was twelve and had a mild bout of mumps.

'How's the wound on your leg healed?' he asks.

'It's good. The stitches have come out.'

'Excellent.' And then he glances away from me and rubs his hands together, and I get a sinking feeling.

'Is there something the matter?' I ask.

'When you were in the hospital and your leg wouldn't stop bleeding, the A&E doctor suspected you might have a clotting issue. He took some blood for analysis, and it's come back indicating that you have something called von Willebrand's disease. Have you had any clotting issues in the past?'

I shake my head. 'I suppose if I cut myself, I bleed quite a bit, but nothing particularly abnormal. What is this disease? Is it serious?'

'No, you don't need to worry about it. It's quite a common clotting disorder, nowhere near as serious as haemophilia. Do you get long-lasting nose bleeds and bruise quite easily?'

'Yeah, I suppose I do,' I say. 'I've never really given it that much thought. It's just the way I am.'

'People with von Willebrand's disease, or VWD as we call it, have a low level of von Willebrand factor in their blood, and that's what's needed to help blood cells stick together or clot when you bleed. If someone hasn't got enough of it, it takes longer for bleeding to stop. It's an inherited condition, so the chances are either your mum or dad have it, too. You're blood group O, which is the group most commonly affected by VWD. Have your parents ever mentioned it?'

I shake my head.

'I suggest you have a chat with your parents, and if they're concerned, we can organise to get their blood taken.'

'What does this mean?' I ask.

'There is no treatment or cure, and it really shouldn't make any difference to you leading a normal life. The only thing is, you need to tell a doctor that you have VWD if you have an operation, or tell your dentist if you have any teeth removed, for example. Otherwise, there's nothing to worry about.'

'Okay. Will you tell Mum and Dad that I've got this VWD?'

'Not if you don't want us to, but I strongly recommend that you discuss it with them.'

'Alright,' I say, standing up from the chair.

'And try not to cut yourself!' Dr Thompson chuckles.

When I get home, I'm relieved that Dad is back and Mum isn't.

'Can we go to the pub?' I ask as I dump my school bag.

Dad glances at his watch. 'It's a bit early.'

'I want to talk to you, and you promised.'

He sighs. 'Alright, but don't tell Mum.'

Our local is just two miles down the road, but Dad drives. We're quiet on the way there, and I'm trying to work out how best to convince him to change Mum's mind about Nepal. Dad has always been more laid-back about everything. It's definitely Mum who wields the whip in our household.

The pub is on the outskirts of the village. It's got low ceilings and serves food in a conservatory at the back. It's not the sort of place me and my mates would come to. At weekends, it's full of local families, and although we don't visit often, they know who we are. The ceiling beams are low, and I have to duck my head as we walk in. Dad's fine because he's always been a bit of a shorty.

'Mr Heaton!' the barman says. 'Our local celebrity.'

Dad tries to brush it off. 'What would you like, Alex? A Coke?'

'A beer.'

Dad laughs. 'I seem to recall you've got another two months to go until your eighteenth. A Coke for him and a half pint of Sussex Draught for me, please.'

'Coming right up.'

'Go get us a seat, Alex,' Dad says.

I find a table near a window, and Dad comes over with our drinks. A few people turn around and stare at him, and it makes me feel really uncomfortable.

When we're settled in, I say, 'Mum's trying to stop me from going to Nepal.'

'Probably because you got arrested twice in the space of a week.'

'I know, but this is my future we're talking about. If I don't go to Nepal, I might lose my place at uni. And I was going to be doing good out there, really making a difference. You've got to make her see sense, Dad.'

'I'll talk to her, but can't make any promises. And I don't think you need to worry about your uni place. That's just conditional on your grades.'

'Maybe, but I really want to go and do something worthwhile in my gap year, not working in a boring solicitor's office in Crawley.'

Dad chuckles.

'There's something else; please don't tell Mum. I've got

some weird disease called von Willebrand's. It stops your blood from clotting properly.'

Dad pales. 'Is it serious?'

'No, the doc was really relaxed about it. I just need to tell the dentist if I get any teeth taken out.'

'How did you find that out?'

'I had a silly skateboarding accident and cut my leg. Nothing major, but it took a while to stop bleeding, so the school nurse sent me to the hospital. Really, it wasn't a big deal. But it's hereditary, apparently, and most common with people with O blood type. The doctor said he's going to call you and Mum, in case you've got it too.'

'I certainly haven't, and I'm pretty sure Mum doesn't either. I'm blood group AB and your mum is type B.'

'How do you even know that?' I ask.

Dad hesitates for a moment. 'We had a few issues getting pregnant before you were born, so Mum and I both had check-ups.'

'So that's why I'm an only.'

'Yup, but your mum never wants to talk about it. It was a difficult time for her.' He takes a sip of beer. 'Tell me more about your ideas on environmental conservation,' Dad says.

And then I'm away, and if we were a more emotionally demonstrative family, I'd give Dad a hug because he seems really interested, not just 'oh, let's humour our son because he's young and hasn't got a clue what he's talking about.' He asks some really pertinent questions about timber sustainability and global warming, and about how I think kids should be educated in the future.

It isn't until much later, when I'm back in my room finishing off a biology essay, that the implications hit me. If Dad is AB and Mum is B, there's no way that I can be an O. I've studied genetics and know how blood types work. My throat constricts. I go onto Google and look at the charts. I'm right. Holy crap.

I think back to our conversation in the pub, and there's no way that Dad was hiding anything. I lean back in my chair and swallow bile. Dad can't be my real dad. Mum must have cheated on him, and to this day, he doesn't know.

19

CHANTAL – NOW

I'm working late, partly because I have a lot of work to do and I want to prove to Trevor that I'm doing a great job, but also because I don't want to go home. I know that Alex will have bent his father's ear about me stopping him from going to Nepal, but I'm going to stand steadfast on this one. He needs a punishment commensurate with his crimes.

Kathleen pops her head around my door. 'You should go home. You look tired.'

'Got too much to do.'

'Are you sure you're not overdoing it?'

I hesitate before answering because I'm suspicious of her now, but her face is open, and I think that's a look of genuine concern.

'I'm fine, thanks, Kath. I'll be leaving shortly.'

It's hardly surprising I look rubbish when my son is behaving so badly and I'm being blackmailed and I have to keep a lid on everything. I vacillate between being pumped up with energy and then to feeling strangely lethargic, but I'm not one to give into tiredness. I force myself through it, every day throwing myself into work in the office followed by a tough workout in the gym as soon as I get home.

Tonight it's 8 pm by the time I switch off the light in my office. Everyone else went home hours ago. I pack my bags and walk through the silent office block and downstairs. It's dark outside now, and although all of us partners have private parking spaces, the lot isn't directly behind our offices. I have to turn left out of the building, walk past another low-rise office block and then left again. My silver Mercedes Cabriolet looks lonely in the empty car park. There's a streetlamp that throws an orange glow, and as I walk towards the car, my heels echo on the tarmac. It isn't until I press the remote key fob and open the doors that I realise. The soft top of my car has been slashed, as have all four of the tyres.

I grasp onto the top of the car to steady myself. Who the hell would do this? I glance around, fear prickling the back of my neck. Is someone watching me? Are they about to pounce and use the knife on me? There are no windows overlooking this parking lot, and if I scream, I'm not sure that anyone will hear me. It's a bustling metropolis during the working day, but at night, it's like a morgue. I fumble in my handbag for my phone and dial 999.

'What's your emergency?'

'Police, please.'

I give the call handler my name and address. She says, 'Hold the line whilst I put you through.'

'Someone has slashed my tyres and the roof of my car. I'm in the centre of Horsham, in the private parking lot behind Roundstone Street,' I explain.

'Are you in imminent danger?' the call handler asks.

'No, I don't think so, but I don't want to wait out here. I'll go back to my offices.' I give the office address.

'I'll get a squad car to you as soon as possible. It shouldn't be too long. I'll pass your telephone number to the officers, and they will call you when they're on their way.'

I walk briskly back to the offices, glancing over my shoulder, all my senses on hyper alert. When I walk in through the front door, I lean against the wall and briefly close my eyes. I need to get a grip. And then my mobile phone pings with an incoming text.

IF YOU DON'T PAY UP, IT WON'T JUST BE YOUR TYRES NEXT TIME …

I try calling the number, but as before, the phone is switched off and doesn't accept messages. Who the hell is doing this? Could it be Tammy? Could she have followed me down to Sussex and worked out where I park my car? It seems more likely that it's that dreadful girlfriend of Alex's. She's seen that we're well off, and perhaps Alex has put her up to it, livid that I've ruined his gap-year plans. I feel like I'm getting paranoid, suspecting everyone around me. Or it could just be a random attack, some miserable youth with nothing better to do, seeing my fancy car standing all alone in the parking lot.

About ten minutes later, I hear a siren getting closer, and I step outside the building as the squad car pulls up. A policewoman climbs out of the car.

'Are you Chantal Heaton?' she asks.

'Yes.'

'I understand your car has been vandalised. Are you safe otherwise?'

'Yes, I'm fine. I haven't seen a soul, but someone has taken a knife to my car.'

'Let's go and have a look.'

Her colleague gets out of the driver's seat, and we walk together to the car park.

'Do you have any idea who might have done this?' the policewoman asks as her colleague paces around the car, inspecting the damage.

'No.'

'Do you have any enemies?'

I laugh. 'I'm a solicitor, so of course there are people who don't like me. It goes with the job.'

She smiles wanly. 'So you reckon this was more likely a random attack of vandalism?'

I really don't, but I can't tell her that. 'I honestly don't know. Will you be able to check out if there are any CCTV cameras overlooking the parking lot?'

'Yes, we can certainly do that.'

'But I assume that's all you'll do?' I know better than most how overstretched police resources are, and a vandalised car is going to be very low down on their list of investigations. But I have to report it as a crime in order to claim on my insurance.

The policewomen walk around the car again, shining a torch, and then they do a quick scout of the parking lot, no doubt looking for the offending knife, but nothing glistens in the dark.

'I suggest you leave your car here tonight and deal with this tomorrow. Have you got anyone who can give you a lift home?'

'I'll get a taxi. I don't live too far away.'

They take down all of my contact details, and I return to the office to call for a cab.

By the time I'm back home, Stuart is fast asleep in bed, and I have a monumental headache. I pour myself a large glass of wine and take a couple of paracetamols. I need to get a grip and discover who is behind this horrible campaign of terror. Alex lopes into the kitchen, but I'm really not in the mood to talk to him this evening. We've barely spoken since I've banned him from going to Nepal.

'Can we talk, Mum?'

'I've had the day from hell, so if you don't mind, I'd rather wait until tomorrow.'

He stands in the doorway for a moment and crosses his arms, jutting out his chin. 'Please, Mum.'

'What is it?'

'Will you reconsider about me going to Nepal?'

'I've already told you, your behaviour at the moment is unacceptable, getting into trouble with the police, and no doubt you'll flunk your exams too. It seems like you've been totally derailed by that girl.'

'You mean Luna?'

'Yes, of course.'

'Luna may not be white and privileged like us, but she's got a loving mum, and she's got principles. You've made judgements without knowing anything about her. Her mum has brought her up as a single mother, and unlike you, she's actually supportive of Luna's work as an activist. Mel's a social worker who does good in the world. She's not interested in money; she just wants to help people and make the earth a better place.'

I stand up straighter. 'What's her name?'

'Who?'

'Luna's mother.'

'Mel Williams, why?'

I swallow hard. 'What's Mel short for?'

'Dunno. Melanie probably. Why?'

I turn away from Alex. The pieces of the jigsaw are coming together now. Could Luna be Melody's daughter, and she's hitched onto Alex to come after me? My silly, naïve son has been targeted, and I feel like I've been violated. That girl has spent time in our house, used my son and made him into a love-struck puppy, while she and her mother have fleeced me for cash.

'Mum, what's the matter?'

'Nothing, Alex. I have too much on my plate at the moment.'

He mutters something inaudible under his breath, a profanity probably, turns on his heel and leaves the kitchen. I listen to his loud, thudding footsteps as he takes the stairs two at a time.

Our family dynamics seem upside down at the moment. Stuart and I don't get a moment to talk, and Alex is a seething ball of fury, making terrible decisions and in danger of self-destructing. Even worse than that, he might be under those women's spell. Even if Mel isn't Melody, the sooner I get Alex away from Luna, the better. I reckon a holiday would be a good idea, straight after Alex's last exam. I'll talk to Stuart tomorrow to find out when he can take a few days off, and perhaps we can jet off to the South of France for a long weekend. But first, I need to fathom what I'm going to do about Mel and Luna.

At 8 am the next morning, I call the garage and arrange for them to collect my car on a low loader. I then call my insurers and arrange to collect a courtesy car from a rentals place in town. By the time I'm in the office around nine thirty, it seems that my car is the talk of the workplace.

'Jeez,' Kathleen says as she perches on the edge of my desk. 'Your car is rather flashy and a bit of an obvious target. Nevertheless, I didn't think things like that happened around here.'

Kathleen has just shown her hand, calling my car flashy. I let the bitchy comment go. 'The police said there's been a spate of vandalising cars,' I lie.

'Thank goodness you weren't there when they did it.'

'Quite. Although I think I can give as good as I get.'

'Not when you're faced with a knife, Chantal. Anyway, if you need a lift home later, just shout.'

'Thanks for the offer, but the garage has given me a courtesy car.'

'How are things with Alex? Has he calmed down?'

'Yes, he's alright.'

She opens her mouth and closes it, as if she's going to say something, but then changes her mind.

'Spill it,' I say.

'I heard that Alex got arrested outside LALO Clothing's offices.'

I sigh. 'Does the whole office know?'

She nods.

'Trevor called me in and told me that I need to keep Alex under control. Talk about the ultimate humiliation.'

Kathleen grimaces. 'Awkward, but at least he hasn't taken you off the case.'

I don't say anything, but I wonder if that's what Kathleen would like. Fortunately, she gets a phone call and is called away. I'm relieved the conversation is over.

The rest of the day is uneventful, and by the time I go home, I'm in a more buoyant mood. That is, until I indicate right to turn into our drive. There is a woman loitering there, wearing a pink anorak, jeans and biker boots with a brown crossbody bag over her front. I stop the car and wind down my window. I am horrified.

'What are you doing here?' I say curtly.

'We need to talk,' Tammy says, narrowing her eyes.

'Not here. Get in the car, and we'll have coffee somewhere.'

'Don't want me to see inside your fancy house? Is that it?'

She's right, but for the wrong reason. I don't want her anywhere near my husband or, especially, my son. We only see what we want to see, and whereas Stuart thinks Alex has his ears and his smile, I see Jade's nose and eyes. Tammy might, too. Tammy walks around to the passenger door and gets inside.

'Did you come all the way from Manchester to see me?'

'Yes.'

'Why?'

'Because we need to talk, you and me. I got curious. I hadn't thought about Jade in years, but you got me thinking. I may just be a pot washer in a crappy restaurant, but I'm not stupid, you know. I went to the library and did some digging, and you know what I found? Of the seventy-seven bodies found in Manchester's canals, the vast majority were men, and none of the women fitted Jade's description. So I then searched further afield and found an article in the *Manchester Evening News* from 2017 about an unidentified body found in Jongleur Hill reservoir. I think that body was Jade, and you think that too, don't you? That's why you came to see me.'

I slam my foot on the brake and pull the car up to the side of the road, so the passenger's side wheels are on the pavement. She may think she's clever, but Tammy has just shown her true colours. So it was her who slashed my tyres and is trying to blackmail me, and she's not even pretending it isn't. I wonder if I'm safe in the car with her.

'You need to leave me alone, do you understand?' I say through gritted teeth. 'I'll give you the money, but then it's all over. Finished. If you come back for any more, I'll tell the police everything, and who do you think they'll believe? Me, an upstanding solicitor, or you, the pot washer from Manchester? You need to get out of my life. Come back the day after tomorrow and I'll give you the money, and then piss off back to Manchester and stay there forever. Do you understand?'

'But–'

'There's no but. Kindly get out of my car.'

'What, here?'

'Just get out!'

And she does. I leave her there, standing on the pavement in a small village in the middle of the Sussex countryside, where there are two buses a week and no other means of public transport. I wonder how she worked out which was my car in the parking lot. Had she followed me and waited there until there was no one around, and then slashed my tyres? Did she know that Jade was meeting me at Jongleur Reservoir? If so, why didn't she say anything to the police when Jade didn't return? Tammy is a chancer, but she's picked on the wrong woman. Now I just have to work out how I'm going to make sure that she's out of my life so that the blackmailing stops forever. I'm still going to check out Mel and Luna Williams, but those two can wait a day or so.

The next morning, there's a note on my desk, asking me to go and see Trevor Steading as soon as I get into the office. This can only mean one thing, and it's not good. I try to steel myself as I walk up the stairs, trying to get the arguments clear in my head. I knock on Trevor's door.

'Ah, Chantal, come in,' he says, more in the manner of a kindly uncle than an executioner. 'Have a seat.'

He gets straight to the point. 'I'm afraid that Mr Lowaski has asked that you be removed from his divorce case. Kathleen will be taking over as the lead.'

'No! Why? Only a couple of days ago you said everything would be fine.'

'And at that point, I assumed it would be. Unfortunately, the press have got wind of your son, Alex, being instrumental in organising the protest against them, and there is a new campaign on social media denouncing their business practices that they believe Alex may be involved in.'

'Alex is seventeen! He's not instrumental in anything.

Look, I can control Alex. He won't be doing any more stupid demonstrations.'

'I'm sorry, Chantal, but the decision has been made. As you'll be aware, this case is very important to the firm, and we can't risk any external influences upsetting things. I'm sure when you've thought it through, you'll see this is the only solution. There will be other cases, I'm sure.'

As I walk out of Trevor's office, I feel a rage boiling inside me. How can one stupid action by my idiot son cause me to lose the biggest case of my career? All of my problems are about Alex now, and it's untenable. I walk into my office and slam my door so hard, the glass splinters in the partition wall. It's safety glass, so it doesn't shatter, but there's a big cobweb-shaped splinter. I look up at the staff sitting in the open plan office beyond, and they're all staring at me, slack-jawed. I scowl at them, and they hurriedly look away, returning to their screens, heads down.

I want to scream, but I can't, not here. Instead I take a sheet of paper and tear it into smaller and smaller pieces, letting them float to the floor. I understand that Lowaski might have identified Alex from the protest because he was taken to the police station, but how on earth could he know whether Alex had anything further to do with the campaign? Unless, that is, they've hacked into whatever email system the protest group is using, or Alex has defied me and done something stupid again.

There's a knock on the door. I don't answer and turn my back to it.

'Chantal?' I glance over my shoulder. It's Kathleen. 'What's going on?'

'Hasn't Trevor told you? He's taking me off the Lowaski case and making you the lead.'

'Oh yes, I'm sorry. I knew you'd be upset, but it isn't anything personal against you.'

I swivel around to face her. 'Yes, it is. They don't believe I can control my own son.'

'Oh, come on, Chantal. It's not like that. It's obvious they can't risk any conflict of interest. I'll keep you in the loop whatever happens.'

I'm not sure what good that's going to do me.

I know it sounds rude, but I say, 'Please can you just leave me alone, Kathleen? I've got a lot of work to be getting on with.'

She takes a step backwards. In all the years we've known each other, she has never seen this side of me, the angry snake that I keep firmly coiled inside my belly. And I wonder about Kathleen. My friend knew that I had endometriosis and that it was a miracle I had Alex, plus her partner has admitted that she's been jealous of me for years. I can't imagine she's had anything to do with the blackmailing, but I wonder if she let slip about Alex's behaviour to Trevor. Perhaps this is her way of ousting me from the top job in the Family Law department. Perhaps my friend is in fact my enemy, a wolf in sheep's clothing.

When she's gone, I sit down at my desk and stare at my computer screen. When there is another knock on my door, I'm shocked to see that an hour has passed, and I've done absolutely no work. It's Rebecca from HR. She walks in and sits down on the chair opposite my desk.

'I understand you've been under considerable stress recently,' she says. 'I think it would be a good idea if you took a couple of weeks off to sort out your family issues.'

'What family issues?'

'I've been told that you've been taken off a big divorce case due to your son, and a couple of people have reported that you seem a bit distracted and stressed. There is also the matter of the broken wall panel.' She glances at the glass, but immediately returns her gaze to me. 'I checked your file and see that you still have a lot of holiday allowance.'

'You've got to be bloody joking! Are you telling me I need to use my holiday allowance?'

'No, I think it might be a good idea to have a break, and you can be signed off by your doctor for stress. If you need a little longer, then you can use your holiday allowance.'

'I can't believe this!' I say, rubbing my eyes. 'I've sweated blood and tears for this firm.'

'Yes, and that has been recognised. But you smashed your partition wall this morning; that is untenable behaviour and could be construed as criminal damage. The last thing we want to do is go down the disciplinary route for an equity partner. I'm sure you understand that.'

'So it's go home and shut up for a while, or otherwise you'll force me out of my job?'

'I didn't say that, you did,' Rebecca says. 'It's for your own well-being. Take some time off, relax, and come back here fully refreshed, and we'll make sure that the staff know that there is a pressure problem with the glass in your wall and that it was an accident.'

I nod, because I've been backed into a corner and clearly have to go along with her suggestion. For now, anyway.

It isn't until Rebecca has left that I think this through. Kathleen walks past my office, absorbed in conversation with another solicitor. It's her; it must be. Kathleen must have betrayed my confidence and told Trevor about Alex. She must have rung downstairs and spoken to HR and told them that she's worried about me, and that I splintered the glass. She may be a friend, but this has been a long time coming. I have been Kathleen's senior for years, but now she has the chance to stab me in the back, push me aside and rise to the top. My so-called friend has betrayed me.

20

I try everything to calm down. I drive around for a while and scream in the car so much that my throat is raw and sore. I go home and push myself hard in our gym so that every muscle hurts. I take a burning hot shower followed by an icy cold one. I drink a glass of neat vodka and uncork a bottle of white wine. But I am still infuriated: by Alex, by Tammy the blackmailer, by Kathleen, by my errant husband Stuart, and the fact that things seem to be slipping out of my control. And most of all, Alex. Alex and I haven't spoken properly since he stormed out of the house when I told him he couldn't go to Nepal. Well, he certainly isn't going now.

When I see his car pull up into the garage and he climbs out of it, I don't feel that normal deep warmth towards him. Instead, I recognise that nature may be stronger than nurture. Perhaps I never stood a chance. Perhaps he was always destined to be like his birth mother. He saunters into the house and dumps his bag in the hallway, loping into the kitchen and opening the fridge.

He starts when he hears me walk in behind him.

'Oh, Mum, there's something I need to discuss with you.'

'And there's something much more important that I need to talk to you about. Due to your irresponsible, pig-headed behaviour, I have lost the biggest case of my life.'

'That seems a bit far-fetched.'

I explode. 'You are so naive! Every action has a consequence, and if you don't think through those consequences, the results can be devastating. Don't you have an iota of remorse? Look what we've given you! This perfect life, everything you could possibly want, and you chuck it back in our faces. I am so disappointed in you, Alex. Not only are you not going to Nepal, I'm stopping your pocket money and confiscating your car.'

'But–'

'No buts to me! You need to do some serious thinking. Go to your room.'

'I am not a child! You don't get to push me around like some minion. If you've lost your client, it's because of you and nothing to do with me. Why do you always blame me for stuff?'

'Because in this instance, it is one hundred per cent your fault.'

'What's going on here?'

I didn't hear Stuart walk in. Both Alex and I start talking at the same time.

'Stop, both of you!' he shouts, flinging his arms out wide. 'Alex, go to your room. I need to talk to your mother.'

Alex scarpers, and that angers me even more. He listens to Stuart, but totally ignores me. I hear Alex's bedroom door slam.

'What's going on?' Stuart asks, crossing his arms. He's looking handsome in a white open-necked shirt, his tie stuffed into his jacket pocket. There is a little patch of foundation that he's missed removing when he took off his studio makeup.

'Thanks to that boy, I've lost the biggest case of my career, and our firm might lose the client.'

'Surely you're exaggerating. I don't think you're being fair to Alex. Punishing him by stopping him from going to Nepal is not the way forwards.'

'I totally disagree!'

'Hear me out, Chantal. He's passionate about the environment, and that is a good thing. Yes, he's been a bit stupid, but not enough for you to throw all your toys out of your basket.'

'That's not fair!' I interrupt. 'Our managing partner has said that the client has demanded I be taken off the case due to Alex's behaviour. He needs to be punished for that. His behaviour is completely reprehensible, and there is no excuse.'

'Do you even know what's going on in your son's life?'

'What?' I ask, frowning.

'The thing with you, Chantal, is you only take an interest if it suits your personal agenda. Did you even know that he's been diagnosed with a blood disease?'

'What?' I take a step backwards and lean against the kitchen counter to steady myself. 'What blood disease?'

'He's got something called von Willebrand's.'

'What does it mean? Is it serious?'

'No, but he just needs to be careful.'

'How come you know and I don't?'

'Because he told me and he didn't tell you.'

'So if he doesn't tell me, how am I supposed to know?'

'Because you're his mother, and you should be there for him and try to understand why he's behaving in the manner he is. But your work is more important, isn't it? So poor Alex has to go off to Debbie's because he feels more welcome there than in his own home.'

'And what about you? You're either not here or off to bed at 9 pm; it's hardly like you're a great father or husband. Besides, you're having an affair, aren't you? Why else the guilt-trip flowers and being late coming home when your shift at the studios finish at midday?'

I hold my breath. I can't believe I actually accused him out loud. This is not my style.

He inhales deeply, and I wait for him to deny it. He briefly closes his eyes and then speaks very quietly. 'You're right. I'm sorry, Chantal, but I'm in love with someone else. I didn't want to tell you like this in an argument, but perhaps now is as good a time as any.'

'What?' I whisper. I feel dizzy, as if everything I know as real is crumbling to dust in front of my eyes.

'I'm planning on leaving you. We haven't been happy for a very long time, and I didn't go looking for anyone else, but these things just happen. As soon as I'm sorted in our new house, Alex can come and live with me, and you can concentrate on your career or whatever it is that makes you happy.'

'You can't leave me,' I say, my voice cracking.

'I know it'll be hard. It's inevitable there'll be publicity, but I'll try to keep a lid on things. Hopefully we can do this as amicably as possible.'

'No!' I scream. 'You're not leaving! You don't get to decide that all by yourself.'

'Actually, I do,' Stuart says. I can see the vein in his temple hammering.

'Who is she, then? Some little bimbo who has fallen for your new-found fame?'

'No. She's just a kind, normal person.'

'Who? You've got to tell me!'

He sighs. 'She's a schoolteacher.'

My fury is loud and visceral. He is more controlled, but I know he's about to explode. I hope he does. I pick up a glass from the drainer and hurl it at him. It misses, but he doesn't hang around; he darts out of the room. I sink onto the kitchen floor, my head in my hands, too shocked even to cry. I hear Stuart upstairs, flinging open cupboards, and then he stomps back downstairs, and I rush out into the hallway.

'Stop, Stuart! Please.'

But he ignores me, throwing open the front door and slamming it shut just as I make a dash for it. I bend over as if my stomach is cramping, the pain in my gut making my legs buckle. I listen to his car start up and drive away, and I know that my whole world has just disintegrated around me.

And it's all Alex's fault.

I stagger around the kitchen, doubled over, because it feels as if a knife has been plunged into my stomach. Stuart is my everything, the love of my life. Yes, I know things have got a bit stale between us of late, but there's nothing that can't be sorted. I'll forgive him for his fling, because it's just a mid-life crisis. His ego has got too big now he's a celebrity, and he's probably picked up some young bimbo who is great in bed and makes him feel even more important than he already does. I am the poster girl for marriage; there is no way I can get divorced.

A scream rises from my stomach, and I know I have to suppress it because Alex is still in the house, and despite everything, I can't let him see or hear me like this. I run into my small study next to the gym, a room I barely use because I prefer to work at the kitchen table in the heart of the house. I lock myself in and give in to the screams and the sobs and the anger and the self-pity and that feeling that my life is all over.

21

I can't believe it. I just can't believe that Mum has pretended that Dad is my real father for the whole of my life. I wonder if that's why she didn't want me to study biology. I thought it so weird at the time because it's a great academic subject, something for Mum to be proud of, because that's the only thing that matters to her, what other people think. But now it makes sense. She would have realised I would study genetics and blood types and might uncover the truth about my heritage. It is impossible for AB and B blood types to conceive a child with group O blood type. Totally and completely impossible. If Mum is B, then my father, whoever he might be, must have had B or O blood. Mum has been lying both to me and Dad for the past eighteen years.

I can't think straight. This is the sort of screw-up that you read about online, crazy stories where a child is lied to for his whole life, and now I realise that it's not just fiction. I am that story. I know for sure that Dad hasn't worked it out. He wouldn't have had that conversation with me about blood types so calmly. Besides, he's not like Mum. Dad would tell me the truth. Or perhaps he wouldn't. It's so confusing.

Mum and Dad screamed at each other. I've never heard them shout like that, and it was horrible. I buried my head underneath my pillow like a little kid so I didn't have to listen, but then the front door slammed, and the reverberations shook me. I watched as Dad strode across the driveway, carrying two big cases, got in his car and sped away. And now Mum's gone totally berserk, screaming and crying and throwing things around, and frankly I'm freaked out and even a bit scared. I try calling Dad, but his phone is turned off. I leave a message asking him to call me. I don't blame him for leaving Mum, but he might have thought about me. Why didn't he take me with him? Perhaps neither of them give a shit about me.

I open my bedroom door and tiptoe downstairs. It's only when I'm in the downstairs hall that I hear Mum. She's in her little study next to the gym. She's hardly ever in there; she uses it to store books and files and other crap. The door is shut, and it sounds like she's going totally mental, sobbing and chucking things around the room. I hear thuds against the wall and the shattering of glass, and now I'm totally freaking. I knock on the door and say, 'Mum,' but she doesn't hear me, or if she does, she's ignoring me. Mum is normally so controlled – uptight if anything – and I've never seen her like this. I run back upstairs, taking the steps two at a time, and call Aunt Debbie.

'Hello, Alex. How are you doing?'

'You need to come over. Mum has totally lost the plot, and she's wrecking her study, sobbing, chucking stuff around. Dad has left carrying suitcases, and I don't know what to do. I think she might hurt herself. I'm really worried.'

'Stay right there, in your room. I'm coming immediately.'

'Thanks, Aunt Debbie. Thank you.'

I stand at my bedroom window, counting down the minutes until Aunt Debbie arrives. I can't hear Mum anymore, and that makes me even more nervous. I wonder if I should call for an ambulance or something, but that would be super embarrassing for her, and I'm not sure there'd be any coming back from it. What if they carted her off to a psychiatric ward? She'd never forgive me. The brother of a friend from school took his own life last year, and it was totally out of the blue. I don't think Mum would do anything like that, but who knows? All the worst scenarios swirl around my head, and when, exactly twelve minutes later, Aunt Debbie's red car pulls into our driveway, I let out a sigh of relief. She leaves it at a skew-whiff angle in the driveway and climbs out. I run downstairs to let her in.

'Oh, sweetheart, what's happened?' Aunt Debbie must have been in the middle of cooking something, because she's still wearing an apron, and there are brown chocolate marks where she's wiped her hands on it.

'I think Dad has walked out, and Mum has gone apeshit.'

'Where is she?'

'In her study. Down the corridor, the room she hardly ever uses next to the gym.'

'I'll go and have a word, but best you nip upstairs and stay out of the way until I call you.'

I walk up the stairs, but have no intention of staying there. I want to hear what Mum tells Aunt Debbie. I wait a few seconds and then tiptoe back downstairs. I hear Aunt Debbie knock on the door.

'Chantal, love, it's me, Debbie. Alex is really worried about you, and he asked me to come over. Can I come in?'

I can't make out what Mum is saying, but Aunt Debbie pushes open the door. I tiptoe closer, and I can hear Mum sobbing. They've left the door slightly ajar.

'Oh, darling, give me a hug.'

There's some shuffling sounds, and Aunt Debbie says, 'There, there. Would you like a drink? I can make you a cuppa.'

I hold my breath, because if either of them come out now, they're going to see me loitering in the corridor.

'No, I'm alright, Debs. It's just such a shock.' Mum's voice sounds hiccupy.

'You know I'm here for you, come what may. I've got to be honest and say you've seemed very stressed the past few weeks.'

'There's been a lot of stuff going on. What's worse is I suspected Stuart of having an affair. All the telltale signs were there, bringing me gifts and flowers, coming home much later than he should have, and I asked him to his face. He lied to me, Debs.' She sniffs. 'He looked me in the eyes and lied to me. Now, just a couple of weeks later, he's saying it's true.'

'Most men are bastards, aren't they?' Aunt Debbie says, and I bristle. That's not fair, and I hope it's just Aunt Debbie trying to be nice to Mum, and that's not what she really thinks.

'I'm a divorce lawyer. I should know the signs, know what to look out for. I feel like such a fool,' Mum says.

'You're not. It's just easier to pretend everything's okay, isn't it? To be honest, I've thought you seemed unhappy for a long time. Perhaps it's for the best. You can have a clean start and find someone new. You're slim and pretty, not like me, so I'm sure you'll be hooked up in no time.'

'I don't want to be hooked up. I want to be with Stuart.'

'I know, love, and it's a terrible shock, but you can't make him stay, not if he's fallen for someone else.'

'How do you know?'

There's silence for a moment.

'Oh my god! He said he's with a schoolteacher. Do you know her?'

'I'm sorry–'

Mum cuts her off. 'You've known my husband was cheating, yet you didn't say anything to me? What sort of a sister are you? Were you gloating in my misery, is that why you kept quiet?'

'No, it's nothing like that. I didn't tell you because I wasn't sure, and it's not my job to stir up trouble.'

'What's she like?' Mum spits out the words.

Aunt Debbie's quiet.

'For god's sake, Debbie, whose side are you on? Don't tell me; she's in her twenties, blonde, big tits ... the stereotype.'

'No, actually.' Debbie talks more quietly now, and I have to strain to hear. 'She's in her forties, she's got two children in their early teens, and she's been divorced about five years.'

'I can't believe you knew, but you didn't tell me!' Mum wails. 'That makes it even worse. He could at least have left me for a younger, prettier, more intelligent version of myself.' She's crying again now, and her voice comes out muffled. 'What's her name?'

'I'm not sure ... I think it's best if Stuart tells you.'

'You're my sister, my own flesh and blood. I'm asking you, no, I'm begging you. What's her name? You owe me that, Debbie.'

'She's called Jill Pendleton,' Debbie says softly.

'I can't believe you knew but you kept it from me. Why didn't you tell me?'

'I love you, Chantal, but it's not my position to interfere in your marriage.'

'Does she work at the same school as you?'

'No,' Aunt Debbie says. 'She's a geography teacher at the senior school.'

'Did Stuart meet her through you?'

'Of course not. I don't know her well, but we've got friends in common.'

'I'm going to be the laughing stock of the town and the office. I'm meant to be the poster girl for marriage, not divorce.'

'That's not true. You know what gossip is like; it'll be forgotten in a week or so. Anyway, won't it make you seem more empathetic to your clients if they know you've been through the same thing?'

'Are you trying to say my marriage breakdown is a good thing? Because it isn't. It's utterly devastating. It feels like my world has collapsed.' Mum sobs again.

'I know, love. I've been there.'

'Oh, come on, Debbie. You were married for a matter of weeks. Stuart and I have been together the whole of our adult lives. There's no comparison.'

She's quiet for a while, and I can sense Debbie's hurt through the walls. I suppose she's rubbing Mum's back and trying to work out what to say next, but then Mum speaks again.

'It's all bloody Alex's fault. He's been behaving like a belligerent, spoiled kid the last few weeks, led astray by that hideous girlfriend. It's like he's chucking everything in my face on purpose.'

'That's not fair, Chantal. The boy will be picking up on the bad atmosphere between you and Stuart. He's a good kid with a kind heart. You should be proud of him.'

'He lost me the biggest case of my career. Did you know that? I'm in danger of losing my job and my husband and everything I've slogged my guts out for the past twenty years. Sometimes I wish–'

She doesn't finish the sentence, and I'm glad because I'm ready to put my fist through the wall. It's not my fault she's failed at her job and her marriage. She's the liar around here.

'How long have you known about the affair?' Mum asks.

'I've known for a while that Stuart was having a liaison.'

'A liaison!' I can hear the scorn in her voice. 'He's been screwing another woman and lying to us all. How long has it been going on?'

'Five or six months.'

'What, months? Oh my God! How could you not have told me? You've totally betrayed me. You're meant to be on my side, Debbie, my sister, looking out for me. How could you do that to me? You're as much of a liar as he is.' Mum is wailing now, that horrible keening noise that you hear on the news, from the relatives of people killed in a bomb or terrorist attack.

'Get out! Get out of my house.'

There's the sound of a scraping chair on the wooden floor. I run in my socks back along the corridor and up the stairs.

'Just get out!' I hear Mum yell. And then the front door slams yet again.

I see Aunt Debbie stumble towards her car. She looks pale and close to crying herself. Mum really is such a bitch. All Aunt Debbie was doing was trying to help out, to offer some sympathy, to be there for her sister. But, as per normal, Mum's pushed her away too. I watch Aunt Debbie get into her car. She just sits there for a moment; then she fumbles in the handbag that she left on the front seat and takes out her phone. My mobile rings.

'Hello, love,' she says. 'I've just been with your mum, but she's asked me to leave. Would you like to come back to my place?'

I hesitate. I'd much rather be at Aunt Debbie's, but what if Mum does something really stupid and I wasn't here to keep an eye on her? I wouldn't be able to forgive myself.

'What if Mum hurts herself?'

'I don't think she will, love. She's just in shock at the moment.'

'Yeah, but even so, I think I'd better stay here, just in case she needs me.'

'You're a good lad,' Aunt Debbie says. 'Your mum is lucky to have you. Well, you know where I am if you want to come over. There's always a bed for you in my home.'

'Thanks,' I say. 'And thank you for coming. Even if Mum was horrible to you, I'm grateful.'

'You're a lovely young man,' Aunt Debbie says. 'Don't let anyone tell you otherwise.'

I do some homework, then watch a movie on Prime. I ring Luna, but she's at a demo that she didn't tell me about; there's loads of shouting in the background. She yells down the phone at me, saying that I should come and join them, that they're in Coventry and that it's really exciting. That's the last thing I'm going to do. I pretend I can't hear what she's saying and hang up on her. I want to tell her about Dad, but it'll have to wait, because she's too distracted now.

I try ringing Dad every hour, but his phone is permanently off. It's making me uptight. I'm worried that Mum might have told him that he's not my father, and maybe that's one of the reasons that he's pissed off and isn't taking my calls. I'm not sure what I'd do if that's the case. Would Dad really walk away from me if he's found out the truth? I've no idea.

By 8 pm, I'm hungry, and I walk back downstairs. Mum isn't in the kitchen; I suppose she's still cooped up in her little study. I knock on the door, but there's no answer. I try opening it, but she's locked it from the inside.

'Mum,' I say, 'are you okay?'

'Go away, Alex.'

'Just want to check up on you.'

'Fuck off and leave me alone!'

I'm shocked. Mum has never spoken to me like that before; in fact, she hardly ever swears. Well, screw her. I only wanted to check up on her. She's too self-centred to hurt herself. There, I was worrying about nothing. I stomp back to the kitchen, but there's nothing that takes my fancy in the fridge, and I'm not in the mood for cooking. I'll take up Aunt Debbie's offer and go to stay with her. My immediate problem is that Mum confiscated my car keys. Hopefully she hasn't got them locked up with her in her study. She's dumped her handbag on a kitchen chair, and I have a rummage inside. My car keys are zipped inside a pocket. At least that's one positive thing.

I rush upstairs and throw some clothes and my washbag into an old duffel bag and put my laptop and books into my school rucksack. I've got enough stuff to last me two or three days, at least. I send Aunt Debbie a text message to say I'm coming over and ask if she can make me some pasta. I add a couple of heart emojis because I know she'll appreciate them.

I then carry the bags downstairs. When I open the door, I'm startled to see a woman standing there, about to put her finger on the buzzer. She's a black lady about Mum's age, wearing a pink anorak and old jeans.

'Can I help you?' I ask.

She takes a step backwards and appears to wobble, grabbing onto the wooden pillar of the front porch.

'Are you okay?' I ask.

'Yes, sorry. I'm fine. It's just you really remind me of someone.'

'Are you after Mum or Dad?'

'Your mother. She's expecting me.'

'Good luck with that,' I mutter under my breath. I leave the stranger standing on the doorstep and hotfoot it to my car. I need to get out of here before Mum comes to the front door and tries to stop me from leaving.

22

CHANTAL – NOW

Every day I see how people's lives are decimated through betrayal or deceit, or they are forced to take a different life path through the duplicity or selfishness of their partner. From my own experience, I know that in the face of adversity we have two options: to be crushed or to pick oneself up and carry on. I have never been the type of person to dwell on the past, wallowing in regrets, wondering about the *shoulds* and *if onlys*. As much as possible, I like to live in the moment, and that's why I tend to scream and shout and have a complete hissy fit, letting out all of my negative emotions. Personally, I consider that to be much healthier – not, of course, that that was a conscious consideration when Stuart walked out on me. The dismay and betrayal and hurt cut through me, and the anger towards Alex for being the root cause of all of my current problems is so visceral it meant I was totally at the mercy of my emotions.

But sometimes we need to be jolted or even shocked out of our own self-pity. When I hear Alex leave the house – to go to saint Debbie's, no doubt, or that freak of a girlfriend – I feel like destroying the house. To make it a visible reflection of how broken I feel inside. But as I fling my study door open and stride towards the kitchen (because where better to start the destruction than the very heart of the home?), the door-bell rings.

I stop dead in my tracks. Is it Debbie coming back? Or perhaps it's Alex, who has forgotten that I confiscated his car keys? I tiptoe towards the door and peer through the peep-hole. Seeing Tammy standing there flips a switch inside my head. As Alex might say, I have to get my shit together.

'What are you doing here?' I open the door a few centimetres.

'You told me to come back. You said something about money.'

'Yes, yes, sorry. I forgot. Come in.' I hold the door open and watch her eyes widen as she sees our big hallway. I lead her into the kitchen and tell her to sit down.

'Tea or coffee?' I ask.

'Tea, milk and two sugars,' she says, without saying *please*.

Putting the kettle on and making a cup of tea gives me a couple of precious minutes of thinking time, and time to compose myself. Do I ask her outright if she's the black-mailer, or do I skirt around the subject and wait for her to trip herself up?

I hand her a mug of tea and sit down opposite her at the kitchen table.

'Why did you come looking for me?' she asks, without acknowledging the tea.

'I'm the one asking the questions,' I say, keeping my eyes firmly on hers. As I assumed, she doesn't like my confronta-tional gaze, and she wriggles in her seat, glancing everywhere except at me. 'Why do you think I'm going to carry on paying you off?'

'What?'

'I assume you think I've got hundreds of thousands in the bank and that you can bleed me dry.'

'What are you talking about?'

I throw my arms out to the sides. 'Stop with the pretence, Tammy. You're a dreadful liar.'

She stands up then and wags her index finger in my face. 'I haven't got the foggiest what you're on about. Look, I spent money I haven't got on a train fare and left the kids with their gran to come all the way down here to talk about Jade. I've got a bad feeling about her, that it might be her body that they fished out of that lake, so stop accusing me of shit and tell me what you know.'

I narrow my eyes at her, but keep my lips firmly sealed. There's a long pause as I consider what to say, but Tammy just rolls her eyes at me and starts striding towards the kitchen door. She's got more gumption than I assumed.

'You're right, Tammy. We need to have an honest conversation. I'll tell you what I know, and then you can do the same.'

She stops, turns around and chews the side of her lip.

'Yeah, alright.' She walks back to the kitchen table, takes off her pink anorak and places it on the back of the chair and sits back down again. 'It seems like you and me are the only two who give a toss about what happened to Jade.'

I clear my throat. 'You're right about that.'

'Are you being blackmailed?' she asks.

'Yes.'

'And it's got something to do with Jade?'

'No, I never said that. You came to that erroneous assumption.'

'So what does the blackmailer want, and why did you think it was me? Because I swear on my kids' lives it's not.'

I stare at her, and this time she holds my gaze.

'I'll help you find out who it is, though, if you want,' she says.

I smile. It appears that Tammy and I might be able to come to an understanding after all.

It's the next morning, and considering the events of yesterday, I sleep surprisingly well and wake up with renewed vigour and total clarity on what I have to do: pretend to the world that all is normal, and work incredibly hard behind the scenes to win Stuart back. I select my favourite kick-ass outfit from my wardrobe, a pillar-box red jacket with sharp shoulders, almost 1980s style, over a crisp white blouse worn together with a tightly fitting black pencil skirt and high-heeled black shoes, the outfit I often wear in court. I wish my car were back from the garage because driving the courtesy car, a white Ford Fiesta, doesn't provide me with the same armour as my Mercedes Cabriolet, but needs must. I'm at my desk by 8 am, the first person in the office.

Fortunately, Alicia hasn't handed the Lowaski files to Kathleen yet, so all the paperwork is still in my filing cupboard next to my desk. There are a number of forms that require completing and some emails from the forensic accountant and Mrs Lowaski's solicitor that need responses, so I have plenty of work to do. I see that the maintenance team has taped over the cracks in my glass wall; that suits me, because it makes looking into my office harder. I've lost track of time when there's a knock on my door. It opens before I can respond.

'Chantal, what are you doing here?' Kathleen asks, her eyebrows knotted together.

'What does it look like I'm doing?' I don't look up but carry on typing.

'I thought HR told you to take some time off. I was coming to collect the Lowaski files.'

'There won't be any need for that. I'm working through them.' I have to stop myself from smirking. I glance at her, and Kathleen looks utterly crestfallen. She's making no pretence of her wish to step into my position and scoop up all of the best clients.

'Look, I know you meant well, Kath, but I'm fine. I lost my cool yesterday, which as you know isn't my style at all; however, last night I went home and had a composed and rational conversation with my husband and son. Alex understands the implications of his behaviour and has promised to calm down and quit his activism. I totally get why André Lowaski and Trevor wanted to take me off the case, but I can guarantee that there won't be any more embarrassing scenes. Stuart is fully supportive of me, and any petty disagreements we had have been ironed out. There really is no need for you or anyone else to worry about me.'

Kathleen shuffles awkwardly. That's why she couldn't be head of department, she's too easy to read. Disappointment, dismay and jealousy are writ all over her face.

'But if he's asked to take you off the case–'

'I won't front it anymore; you will. But I know this case inside out and back to front. I'll do most of the work, and you can get the glory.' I smile at her, and she knows I've backed her into a corner. I'll be the one who will earn the money because I'll be the person billing the chargeable hours, while she'll take the rap if things go wrong, and I've a feeling that they will. Despite André Lowaski's desire to get full custody of his children, I don't believe for one moment that his wife is an alcoholic and that the judge will accept that she is an unfit mother. Good luck to Kathleen.

'Also, I've had an enquiry from a billionaire Russian

looking to divorce his wife. If that comes to fruition, you can have the case,' I say.

'Really?' she asks, her eyes widening. She is so very gullible. As if I'd willingly hand over such a lucrative, high-profile case. 'So you'll keep me posted on the Lowaski case and shout if you need any help?'

'Of course. You can have access to everything. I'll send you the passwords.'

'Thanks, Chantal, and I'm glad you're okay. You freaked me out yesterday.'

'You and me both,' I say. 'I don't know what came over me. I haven't been sleeping well worrying about Alex, and I guess it all got too much. Rest assured, that won't happen again.'

She backs out of my room. I think I've appeased her for now, but no doubt she's hotfooting it up to the HR department to tell them that I've ignored the order to stay at home. The problem is, Kathleen has disturbed my flow, and I can't stop thinking about Stuart. I click onto Google and bring up live TV. And there he is, looking relaxed and dapper, interviewing some gushing opposition MP who is talking a load of bullshit. I peer closer at Stuart. He looks totally normal, refreshed and alert, but perhaps that's the studio makeup.

And then I notice his tie. The bastard is wearing the navy silk tie with the pale and yellow polka dots and the bespoke embroidery with his initials on the back that I gave him for Christmas. How dare he wear that when he's fled to be with his mistress! I suppose she can't afford to give him expensive designer ties. Or perhaps he's doing it on purpose, flaunting what he's wearing to make me feel even worse than I already do. I click away the tab and turn the photograph of Stuart, Alex and me taken three years ago on a holiday to Greece upside down on my desk. I can't think about him right now. The only way forwards for me is to focus. First I will do my work, and then I will plot how to get Stuart back.

Whenever I walk out of my office to get a drink or go to the toilet, I'm very aware that no one wants to meet my eye. Even Alicia seems to be working harder than normal, fully engrossed in typing with headphones clamped over her ears, and I could never call her a slacker. Yes, my little scene of smashing the window was unbecoming, but this shunning is rather pathetic. Shortly after midday, there's another knock on my door, the one I've been expecting: Rebecca from HR.

She walks inside, closes the door behind her and takes a seat opposite me.

'I'm surprised to see you here, Chantal,' she says, placing her elbows on her knees and leaning forwards, a warm smile on her face. But I know all about body language and neurolinguistic programming, and despite her overt friendliness, I don't trust her.

'I am feeling perfectly well today. My family situation is under control, I slept well, and whilst I accept full liability for the breaking of the glass, that is no need to banish me from work.'

'I thought we agreed that the Lowaski case–'

I interrupt her. 'I have already spoken to my colleague Kathleen Robertson about that, and she will be doing all client-facing work. It's under control.'

'Trevor said–'

'I know what Trevor said, Rebecca. Do you want me to go and talk to him?'

She blanches slightly. I can imagine what Trevor thinks of HR – pretty much the same as what he thinks of marketing. An unnecessary drain on the firm's resources that has to be tolerated, but is really a right pain in the butt. He's old school and thinks that a solicitors' firm should be run by the solicitors for the solicitors and any other appendages are totally unnecessary. I don't agree with him, of course, but in this instance his view serves to my advantage.

'No, that's fine. I will inform him,' she says. 'Don't forget you're covered by medical insurance, though.'

I don't like the implication, so I lift up the lid on my laptop. 'If there's nothing else, I have a lot of urgent work to do to protect my client's interests.'

She hesitates, then stands up. 'I'm only looking out for you,' she says.

'That's very kind of you,' I say, but I know she can hear the sarcasm in my voice.

After she leaves, my concentration wavers. I need to work on my plan to get Stuart back. Firstly, I need to find out about the bitch he's planning on replacing me with. I call my favourite private investigator, the one I've commissioned to work on the Lowaskis' case.

'Chantal,' Ian Shustack says, 'I hope you're not chasing me?'

'Absolutely not. I have another job for you. Are you up for that?'

'So long as I'm paid, I'll work.'

'Good. She's a secondary school teacher, and she's called Jill Pendleton. I want to know everything about her. She's divorced. I want to know about her ex, her children, how much she's worth, what her interests are, her medical record and anything else you can get hold of.' I swallow. 'You don't need to tell me who she's sleeping with.'

There's a pause before Ian replies, 'Is this a personal job?'

'Possibly,' I say. That's why I like Ian. He gets me, but he's also the epitome of discretion.

'I'll do my best. What's the timescale?'

'Yesterday.'

'You'll have something by the end of the week.'

I would like to plan my strategy to get Stuart back, but until I know my adversary, there's little point. Besides, I'm happy to go quiet on Stuart for a few days, let him wonder whether I'm okay.

I leave work at 4.30 pm, walking out of the office purposefully, with my eyes straight ahead. I walk quickly towards the car park, thinking about the workout that I will do when I get home, wondering whether Alex will be back. As I approach the courtesy car, I can see something flapping under the windscreen wiper. I hope it's a flyer promoting a local pizza service, but as I glance around, none of the other cars have a note on them. My heart is pounding as I lift the wiper up and slide out the little note. It's typed in capital letters, exactly the same as the text messages.

IF YOU DON'T GIVE ME THAT ADDITIONAL £10K, YOUR LIFE IS AT STAKE.

It slips out of my fingers and floats down onto the tarmac.

What the hell? This can't be possible. I grab the roof of the car and lean forwards, gulping in air to try to stop the nausea. The blackmailer can't be Tammy, so who the hell is it? Who is behind all of this? Has she got a partner in crime, Melody perhaps? Or could it be Alex – or more likely, his nasty little girlfriend, Luna? I remember now that Alex says Luna's mother is called Mel. Is she Melody? Are Luna and Melody in this together? Or is it Misty Morris after all? Perhaps it's him I need Ian to be tracking down, but it's one thing asking for professional help to find out information about my husband's mistress, quite another to enlist his help to track down information about a criminal I hired all of those years ago. I simply can't risk it.

I grab the piece of paper and crumple it up into a tiny ball, dropping it into my handbag. As I get into the rental car, I try to breathe deeply, to stop the nerves from gripping the inside of my stomach. I have to think logically; that's what I'm so good at. The most obvious answer is that Tammy is in cahoots with someone else, and the most likely person is Melody. It is now absolutely imperative that I focus on finding her before she finds me, bearing in mind it is almost certain that she knows exactly where I live, where I work and, quite possibly, what I've done. I need to find Luna's mother, Mel Williams the social worker.

I get in the horrible rental car and sit there for a few long moments to take stock. It's twenty to five, and I need to get a move on if I'm going to track Mel down today. I do a quick search of the telephone directory on 192.com and am disappointed that there are lots of M. Williams in Horsham, but no Melody Williams. I shouldn't be surprised. If she's a social worker, she's not going to make it easy for people to discover her full name and address, but that isn't going to stop me. In my role of family lawyer, I know a couple of the children's social workers, and if necessary, I'll contact her through them. In the first instance, I ring the telephone number listed online for people who are known to Social Care and want to talk to their social worker.

'Good afternoon. Please, can I speak to Mel Williams?'

'Who's calling, please?'

'My name is Jade Sykes. I'm a solicitor.' I grin. That should shake things up a bit.

'Does she know you?'

'Yes, but we haven't been in touch for nearly twenty years.'

'If you hold the line, I'll see if she's available.'

I bounce my leg up and down with excitement. It's a bit like being in court, not knowing what you're going to be asked next and having to prepare your argument on the fly.

'I'm sorry, but Ms Williams is in a meeting. Can I take a message?'

My shoulders sink with disappointment. 'Do you know what time she'll be finished?'

'No, sorry. It's a departmental meeting, and sometimes they go on for quite a while.'

'No problem. I'll call another time.'

On reflection, perhaps it's better this way. I know she's in the office, and that means I can stalk her. I start the car and drive towards the Council buildings. I find a parking space on the street behind and walk towards the offices. Two can play at this game.

I slip into the car park and stand underneath some trees that edge the park behind. There are some kids playing tennis on the courts beyond the trees; they're shrieking every time the ball goes out. The noise goes straight through me. Fortunately, I don't have to wait too long listening to the screams. On the dot of 5 pm, people start emerging from the offices. Cars start up and leave. Then I see an elegant black lady with a canvas bag flung over her shoulder; the bag is promoting a local health food store. She's talking to a skinny man, mid-twenties at a guess, with a red, bushy beard. After a couple of minutes, he steps away, and she waves at him, turning around and walking towards the main road. I run after her.

When I'm within touching distance of her navy anorak, which is a smarter version of Tammy's pink one, I reach out and tap her shoulder. She stops and jumps slightly before swivelling around.

'Mel?' I ask.

'Yes,' she says with a frown.

'I'm sorry to accost you,' I say, with a broad smile on my face. 'It's me, Jade Sykes.'

She frowns at me, and I know immediately that she's not the Melody I'm looking for. For starters, although she's a good-looking woman, she is not striking with model looks in the way Jade's friend was, and no one would have changed that much in the past two decades. And clearly the name Jade Sykes means absolutely nothing to her.

'I'm sorry,' I say, taking a step backwards. 'I thought you were someone else.'

'But you called me Mel,' she says.

'I've got a friend called Melody, and from behind, you look really similar. I'm so sorry to have disturbed you.' I step backwards, but then she tilts her head ever so slightly and it's as if there's a spark of recognition behind her eyes. The breath catches in my throat.

'I think we do know each other,' she says, narrowing her eyes slightly. 'Even though we haven't been introduced. You're Alex Heaton's mum, the divorce lawyer, aren't you?'

Now she has me on the back foot, and that's not somewhere I like to be. I can either deny it, which would likely be futile, because my photo is plastered on Egerton Brook Steading's website, or run with it. In that split second, I decide.

'Oh – my – goodness, you're absolutely right! I'm Chantal Heaton, and I've heard so much about you from your delightful daughter, Luna.' I step forwards and place a hand on her arm.

'What did you call yourself just now?'

I laugh and hope that it doesn't sound as forced to her as it does to me. I need move the conversation on, and quickly. 'I cannot tell you how thrilled I am to meet you, Mel. My husband and I were only just talking about how we need to get you over for lunch one weekend. They're quite the little couple, are Luna and Alex.'

She rolls her eyes. 'They adore each other, do those two. We even refer to you and your husband as "the in-laws" as a bit of a joke at home. I thought it would wind Luna up, but she's that serious about Alex; she doesn't seem to mind.'

I feel like spitting on the pavement. As if I would ever countenance Luna becoming a member of my family.

'Are you free to go for a coffee?' Mel asks, glancing at her watch.

'Unfortunately, I have a prior engagement, but we must do meet up another time.'

'That would be lovely. Luna's at one of those demonstrations that she's so into and should be back this evening. I keep on thinking it's a phase, all of this environmental protesting, but it seems that she and Alex are seriously committed activists. I suppose we should be grateful for kids like them, standing up for what is right and fighting to protect our earth for future generations.'

'You're absolutely right,' I say, making sure the fake smile stays plastered on my face. 'What is she protesting about now?'

'She's on her way home from something in Coventry, and then they're trying to stop a fracking site somewhere at the foot of the Downs.' Mel glances at her watch. 'I'm hoping she'll be home for tea.'

'Thank goodness for the young,' I say. 'It was lovely to meet you, and you must come over for a coffee soon,' I say. 'What's your phone number?'

She recites her mobile number, which I type into my phone. 'Just out of curiosity, Mel, what's it short for?'

'Melissa,' she says. 'But I never thought I suited the name, so I've always been Mel. Anyway, it was lovely to meet you, Chantal.'

I do an awkward flutter of my fingers and stroll away in the opposite direction.

I am ninety-nine per cent sure that Mel is not my Melody, but I am one hundred per cent sure that her daughter, Luna, is up to no good, and it's time that I confront her.

24

ALEX

I wake up in Aunt Debbie's narrow single bed, and my heart sinks as I remember why I'm here. I grab my phone, hoping to see missed calls and text messages from Dad, but there are none. No messages from Luna and nothing from Dad. I get that he wouldn't want to talk to Mum, but what about me? Has he pissed off to be with this new woman and discarded me along the way?

I chuck the phone onto the bed and then pick it up again, wondering why I haven't heard from Luna. Yesterday she was all excited about the demo she attended in Coventry, and how she had to run away from the police, and that it wasn't the sort of demo she was comfortable with because some people set fire to a car and then rammed a shop window. I'm glad I wasn't there. I'm all for peaceful environmental protests, but that's a step too far. I want to tell her that I've discovered Dad can't be my real father. I know she'll understand, because her mum only told her who her dad was when she turned twelve. She has always been so angry about that, blaming her mum for stopping her from having a relationship with her father. But when she tracked her dad down, she was so disappointed. He didn't want to know her. He is married with three kids, living in a house as posh as ours, apparently, and as far as he was concerned, there was no place for the little mixed-race girl in his life.

Yes, Luna will understand. She'll advise me on what I should do and how best to handle Dad. She should have been home last night before heading off to another demo today. It's a bit early for Luna, as it's just before 8 am, but I try calling her anyway. Her phone goes straight to voicemail. I send her a message, asking her to call me when she's awake.

I can hear Aunt Debbie clattering around downstairs, preparing the breakfast things. I have a horrible thought that something awful might have happened to Dad. What if Mum went really mental and did something terrible to Dad? I go online onto the live breakfast show, and there he is, looking perfectly normal, talking to the weather woman about the rain that's forecast over the next few days.

'Why haven't you rung me, Dad?' I ask out loud.

I'm really worried that he knows the truth and that's why he's rejected me as well as Mum. Perhaps he'll legally adopt that woman's two children and I'll be discarded. I stomp to the bathroom and take a cursory shower. I know that I was born before Mum and Dad got married. They never tried to hide that from me, so it's possible that he's known the truth all along, but why would he have pretended to be surprised about our blood groups? No, the more I think about it, the more I'm sure he doesn't know the truth. I'm so pissed off with him, but I love Dad. He's always been the fun dad, on my side, rolling his eyes whenever Mum was too strict with me. I honestly think that Dad loved me, but does he still? I really can't bear the thought of him rejecting me.

I walk downstairs, and Aunt Debbie greets me with a full English breakfast, a vegan version, obviously. I don't have the heart to tell her it's the last thing I feel like when she has gone to so much trouble, so I eat it, every little morsel.

'What's in store for you at college today?' she asks.

'Revision. Boring stuff.'

'I bet you can't wait to leave.'

'I thought I couldn't, but Mum still wants me to work in a solicitor's firm rather than going to Nepal, so perhaps I shouldn't defer my uni place.'

'Look, love,' she says, placing her hand over mine. 'Your mum's not in a good place at the moment. Let things settle down at home, and then we'll have another chat with her. My suggestion is not to do anything hasty.'

'Suppose you're right.' I stand up and then give her a kiss on the cheek. I honestly don't know what I'd do without Aunt Debbie.

'You're growing up into a very fine man,' she says. 'I'm proud of you.'

Aunt Debbie wouldn't be so proud of me if she knew where I was going today. I can't sit through revision classes and pretend everything is alright when my parents hate each other and I've just discovered I've no idea who my real dad is. I can't talk to Mum, so I decide to talk to Dad. I leave my car in the station car park and catch the next train to London.

I went to Dad's television studios about five years ago, shortly after he joined as a normal news presenter. He showed us around, and to be honest, I was rather disappointed. It looks so big and imposing on television, but in real life, it's quite a small space with high-definition screens on the back walls and automated cameras and a glass desk with a screen built in. I suppose his new studio is more relaxed and bigger as he moves from the large comfy, plush blue sofa to the glass desk where he reads the news. And five years on, I guess it's even more high tech, but I'm not going there for a tour. I want to talk to Dad and find out the truth.

After getting off the train at Victoria Station, I have to juggle with tubes and buses, and at one point, I get on the district line and go the wrong way. I feel like a complete idiot, and it makes me realise how much more comfortable I am in the countryside. Each to their own. It's gone 11 am by the time I arrive at the studios, and I hope Dad is still there. I walk in through the big glass doors and up to the reception desk, my trainers squeaking on the marble floor. The entrance is cavernous with security that looks as tight as at an airport, with burly uniformed guards standing next to security gates. There are two men and a woman sitting at the main desk. One of the men looks up, and I shuffle forwards.

'Hello, I'd like to talk to my father, Stuart Heaton.'

He frowns at me, throwing me a look as if I'm a deluded fan. Perhaps he thinks that I'm pretending the famous presenter is my father.

'Mr Heaton is currently on air. It won't be possible for you to talk to him.'

'I'll wait until he's finished, but can you get a message to him?'

'I'm sorry. Mr Heaton won't see or speak to anyone unless it's been pre-booked.'

'I'm his son. My name is Alex. He's got his phone switched off and has done since yesterday afternoon. Of course he'll want to see me.'

'In which case, Alex, I suggest you leave your dad a message and wait until he's off air.' The man's tone of voice makes it perfectly obvious that he doesn't believe me.

'Which entrance does he come out of?'

'I'm afraid that if you make a nuisance of yourself, the security guards will escort you off the premises.'

'He's my dad. Do you want me to show you a photo of us together, because I've got plenty on my phone.' I take my phone out of my pocket and start scrolling through my pics.

'That won't be necessary,' he says. 'If you take a seat over there, I'm sure he'll see you when he leaves the premises.'

'But–'

The receptionist is looking over my shoulder, and I turn around. A woman strides forwards, and I am forced to step to one side, as I've clearly been dismissed. I walk towards a bank of chairs lined up against the glass wall of the building and sit down. Hopefully Dad will leave via this main entrance hall, and I'll be able to catch him. Up above the reception desk is a bank of big television screens, and in the centre one, there is Dad talking to someone who is getting hot under the collar. I can't hear any sound, but it's quite funny to watch. And then that guest is off screen, and the camera pans to Dad and his co-host, a woman called Brittany, who my mates think is hot, though I don't. Dad and Brittany are laughing at something, and then it's the weather forecast. I take my phone out and google what time breakfast television finishes. 11.30 am. Not long to go.

Dad doesn't emerge until 12.15. He's wearing his overcoat and looking at his phone. As he walks through the security gates, he looks up and smiles at the guards, then waves at the receptionists. I'm annoyed that the male receptionist I spoke to doesn't even point to me, so I get up and wave my arms in front of him.

'Alex!' he exclaims, his eyes widening with surprise. 'What are you doing here?' And then his face clouds with worry, and he places a hand on my shoulder. 'Is everything alright?'

'Yeah, it's okay, but I need to talk to you, and you haven't replied to any of my messages.'

'I'm sorry, son. I've had that phone off.' He puts the phone in his hand in his right pocket and removes another phone from his left pocket.

'Why have you got two phones?'

He flushes slightly. 'One's for work, and the other is for home.'

I know he's lying.

'Have you skived off school?'

'Yeah, because we need to talk.'

He nods. 'You're right, Alex. I've got some explaining to do, and I'm really sorry I've kept my phone switched off.' He glances at his watch. 'Let's go out for lunch. There's a pizza place around the corner.'

We walk in silence, but every so often I glance at Dad, and he's clenching his jaw in the way he does whenever he's annoyed or uptight. He stops outside a restaurant called Amore Italiano, which has a green-and-white awning over the front door and fake plants in the window. Dad pushes the door open and lets me go in first.

'Signor Heaton, how are we today?' The head waiter greets him in what sounds like a fake, or certainly exaggerated, Italian accent.

'Thank you, I'm well, Mario. This is my son, Alex.'

'It's a pleasure to meet you, young man,' Mario says.

I wonder how often Dad comes in here to eat and whether he brings *her* here.

We sit down at a table near the back of the restaurant. Dad puts his menu on the table and leans forwards towards me, speaking in a low voice.

'It was unforgivable of me to walk out without giving you an explanation,' he says. 'I'm really sorry, Alex. Things between me and your mum have been difficult for a long time, and I'm afraid I've fallen in love with someone else.'

'I overheard you.'

He winces slightly. 'I'm sorry, son. I really didn't want to hurt you, and I'll always love you. I hope you know that.'

'Did you marry Mum because she was pregnant?'

His eyes widen. 'No, absolutely not. I was in love with your mother long before she had you, and even if she hadn't fallen pregnant, I would have married her. You were just a beautiful bonus. We were very young when we got together, but we've had many happy years. You simply turned us from a couple into a family, and that was the best thing that ever happened.'

'So why have you cheated on Mum?'

He sighs deeply. 'Things have been hard for a long time now. Your mum and I don't see eye to eye on a lot of things, and that love has just dissipated. I didn't mean to fall for someone else, and I feel a cad for cheating on her. I certainly didn't want to hurt your mum.'

'Who is she, the new woman?'

'She's called Jill Pendleton, and she's a warm-hearted, gentle lady with a beautiful soul. I hope that you'll love her too one day. She'll never try to be your mum, because you've already got one, but hopefully she can be your friend. She's got two boys, a bit younger than you, and we're hoping to buy a house together, big enough for all of us. It'll be your choice whether you want to stay living with Mum or whether you want to move in with us. Just know that you'll always be my first priority, and I want to do right by you. I know it's been tough, what with my new job and your mum getting angry with you.'

'I've been a bit of a dick towards you.'

Dad laughs. 'You're not doing anything that I wouldn't have done at your age. I'm proud of you, Alex. Proud that you're passionate about the environment and making a difference. Perhaps you might choose a bit more carefully which demonstrations you get involved in, though.'

'Can you get Mum to change her mind about me going to Nepal?'

'I'll see what I can do, but you'll need to give me some

time. Your mother and I are not exactly on speaking terms at the moment. Anyway, let's order some food.'

From the way Dad is talking, it's obvious that he has no idea that I'm not his real son. I could tell him, but if I do, will that change his feelings towards me? He might prefer to be with this Jill's sons, and then I'll be nothing to him. I want to stay in Dad's life, I love him, and he's the only person who can make Mum see sense. If I tell him now, that could totally blow my chances.

'So what do you want to eat?' he asks, breaking my train of thought.

'I'll have the capricciosa, please,' I say, just picking the first pizza on the list.

'Good choice.'

'Are you going to get divorced?' I ask once Mario has taken our order.

'I want to. Your mother might contest it, and let's face it, I'm unlikely to do well out of this, considering she's such a good divorce lawyer. But it's not about the money or the assets. She can keep the house and have half of everything else. I don't want her to suffer, nor you. I'm sorry it's come to this, and I'll do everything I can to minimise the upheaval to you.'

There's little I can say. Dad seems genuine. Besides, it's only a short time until I'll be on my gap year and then off to uni.

'How is your Mum?'

'She went apeshit after you left. Aunt Debbie came over to try to calm her down, but she sent her packing. I stayed last night at Aunt Debbie's.'

'I'm sorry,' Dad says softly. 'You're such a good lad, and you don't deserve any of this. I'll pay for your trip to Nepal and anything else you need. Don't worry.'

If I was undecided about telling Dad the truth before, I'm

mighty relieved I didn't. It's the right decision. For now, anyway.

Back at Aunt Debbie's, I do a couple of hours of revision and then decide to make Aunt Debbie and me some supper. Luna still hasn't called me, and I'm annoyed because I've got so much to tell her. I lose myself in cooking, and by the time Aunt Debbie gets home, I've got a bean stew bubbling away on the stove.

'Something smells good. How was college?' she asks, dumping a large canvas bag of exercise books on the floor and putting the kettle on.

I look at her warm and open face and decide I need to tell her the truth. Debbie is the only person who has never judged me, who has stood by me, come what may. Besides, perhaps she knows the truth about my birth father, as she and Mum have always been close.

'I skipped revision classes and went to see Dad.'

'Oh,' she says, plopping down on the chair next to me.

'He explained how he didn't mean to hurt me or Mum and how he's going to do right by us.'

'I'm glad to hear that. Your dad isn't a bad person, Alex. Sometimes people just fall out of love.'

'I know that. Look, there's something I want to tell you, and I need you to promise you won't tell a soul.'

She frowns. 'Of course I'll keep your confidence. What is it?'

'I've discovered that Dad isn't my real father.'

Debbie goes so pale I wonder if she's going to faint. 'What?'

'Dad told me that he's group AB blood type, and Mum is B. I'm O, so it's impossible for Dad to be my genetic father. It explains why I'm four inches taller than him.'

She goes very still for a moment, and her jaw drops open. 'Oh my goodness, Alex. Oh, my darling, are you sure?'

'Totally,' I say.

She reaches across to me and pulls me towards her large bosom, but after a moment, I wriggle free.

'What has Chantal said?' Aunt Debbie asks.

'Nothing. I haven't told her I know, and I don't think Dad knows either.'

'What a terrible shock for you,' she says. 'How are you feeling?'

'Did you know? Did Mum ever say anything to you?'

'Of course she didn't,' Aunt Debbie says, levering herself out of the chair. 'Is there any possibility you might be mistaken?'

'The only way I could be mistaken is if Dad gave me the wrong information about his and Mum's blood types, but he seemed very certain about them. So no, I don't think I'm wrong. The trouble is, I don't know what to do about it.'

I have no idea what to do about the note. It feels like I can't think straight, as if my head has been tangled in a massive spider's web and my brain is being fried. Everything that is happening leads back to Alex. My whole adult life has been dedicated to doing the best for him, giving him opportunities, supporting him, showing him what's right and wrong and being a loving mother. Yet I've failed. And worse than that, all my good deeds are being chucked back into my face. I have to accept the simple truth: he has bad blood, and there's literally nothing I could have done to stop that surfacing at some point.

The more I think about it, the more sure I am that Alex is the blackmailer, most probably encouraged by his hippy girlfriend, Luna. If, somehow or another, he's found out that he's adopted, then this makes sense. He'll want to punish me for the betrayal, for keeping his true identity a secret for the whole of his life. My immediate concern is whether he's already told Stuart. If he does that, I am facing total ruin. It would be a disaster; literally the whole world will turn against me. I'm not sure whom I should tackle first, Alex or Stuart? I decide it has to be my husband.

My immediate problem is, I've no idea where Stuart is, whether he's staying with his mistress or dossing down in a hotel. And until Ian reports back to me, I'm not sure how to find him. Stuart's phone has been switched off since he left home, which means I can't even track him via the app Find My Friend. He will have left the studios by now, so I decide it will have to wait until tomorrow. In the meantime, I will make another concerted effort to find Misty Morris and the real Melody.

I head for home. Our normally warm and welcoming house feels sterile and so very quiet. I put the television on for some background noise and open my laptop on the kitchen table. I spend hours searching online for a female model called Melody who would have been at the height of her career about fifteen years ago. It's futile; I find nothing conclusive. I think about that charming taxi driver in Manchester, but unsurprisingly, I never heard back from him. Nevertheless, I wrote the name of his contact in my phone: Bilal Ali from Wilmslow. I do a search for him. He's listed on the Companies House database as owning a property management business, and the address is an office in Hale. I go on 192.com and pay to see his full listing, but the telephone number is still blackened out. I ring directory enquiries, and they tell me that his number is withheld. I'm back to square one. I open a bottle of wine and drink nearly the whole bottle, and then I feel sick because I haven't eaten anything.

The next morning I send Alicia a message to tell her I won't be in the office today. I persuade my hairdresser to squeeze me in for a quick wash and blow dry; then I put on a slinky black dress that Stuart told me I looked sexy in and drive up to London. I find a parking space reasonably near the television studios, and I walk into the building to wait for my husband.

I know I look good. I get a few approving glances from various men, some much too young to be interested in me, and it bolsters my confidence. When Stuart walks out of the lifts and through the security gates towards the exit of the building, raising his hand to the guards, I stride up to him, my stilettos clip-clopping on the floor.

'Hello, darling,' I say, coming to a halt in front of him.

'What are you doing?' he asks, an unbecoming scowl on his face.

'Waiting for you. We need to talk.' I slip my arm into his.

'No.' He tries to break free of my grip.

'Not here, darling. You don't want to make a fuss here,' I whisper. He glances around to see if anyone is watching and then clearly decides I'm right. We walk out of the building together, but as soon as we're outside, he turns to me.

'What the hell are you doing?'

'Asking you to come home so we can talk things through.'

'No,' he says. 'I've made my decision, and I'm not coming back.'

'This isn't about you,' I say, standing directly in front of him, so close that he will be inhaling my scent. I hold his gaze and blink slowly, letting my tongue run slowly across my lips.

'No,' he says again.

'Alex isn't coping,' I say.

'What do you mean? He was fine yesterday.'

I choke back my words. How does Stuart know Alex was fine yesterday? And what has Alex told him? Does Stuart know the truth? I try to hold it together and smile at my husband.

'My car is parked around the corner. Why don't we go and have a chat and work out what to do about our son?'

'I'm not sure there's anything to discuss, Chantal.'

'Please, Stuart. I'm genuinely worried about him, and standing on the pavement outside the television studios isn't the right place to be having this conversation.'

He sighs and nods. We walk in silence along the street towards the car. If anyone is watching, they'll think we're a harmonious couple.

'Whose car is this?' he asks as I open the door to the white Fiesta.

'It's a courtesy car. Someone bashed into mine in the office car park.' I climb into the driver's seat, letting my tight dress ride up high. But to my disappointment, Stuart keeps his gaze straight ahead.

'What do you want?' he asks.

'Oh, come on, Stuart. It's me you're talking to. Your wife.'

'I know exactly who you are, Chantal. What's the matter with Alex?'

'I think he's on the verge of a breakdown. He's been saying all of this crazy stuff, and he's really distraught.'

'He was perfectly rational yesterday and told me he was staying with Debbie.'

'She's very worried about him. She wants us to take him home, you and me together.' I put my hand on his knee and run my fingers up his thigh.

'Stop it, Chantal!' he says, roughly removing my hand. 'I've told you that our relationship is over. I want a divorce. I know it's not what you want, and I'll give you plenty of time to get used to the idea. I don't want you to suffer, Chantal. You can keep the house, and we'll split everything else in half.'

'This isn't about me!' I know my voice sounds a bit screechy, but I can't help it. 'Don't you care about our son's life? I think he might be suicidal.'

'That is nonsense, Chantal. I had lunch with Alex yesterday, and yes, he's hurt, but he's far from suicidal. When was the last time you spoke to him?'

'If anything happens to him, then it'll be on your head,' I say. 'He's emotionally vulnerable, and you're breaking up our home.'

Stuart rolls his eyes at me, and I have to dig my fingers into the palm of my hand to stop myself from slapping him.

'You really don't know your own son, do you?' he says. 'Yes, he might be a bit concerned about the blood disorder, and yes, of course he's upset that I've left home, but he's mostly worried about you.'

'That's nonsense,' I retort.

'I had lunch with him yesterday, Chantal. He's fine.'

What the hell was Alex doing skiving off school yet again? This is making my blood boil.

'The person I'm worried about is you, Chantal.'

'You shouldn't have cheated on me, then.'

'I am sorry I hurt you, but you have been so on edge the past weeks, verging on paranoia. If there's anyone who needs psychological help, it's you. We have cover under our private health insurance.'

I gasp at his audacity.

'I think it's best that Alex comes to live with me and Jill. Her boys can double up, and Alex can have his own room until we move somewhere bigger. He can't impose on Debbie for too long, and he obviously doesn't want to be at home.'

'Over my dead body,' I spit. 'Get out of the car.'

And Stuart does. He opens the door, climbs out, throws me a condescending look of pity and gently closes the door. I watch as he strides away without a backwards glance. When he's disappeared, I burst into tears.

26

ALEX

It's been two days, and I still haven't heard from Luna, which is weird. We normally speak several times a day and message constantly, even when I'm in college or she's out at a demo, and I'm unsettled. I want to share everything that's been going on with me, but now I've got that sinking feeling that she might have found herself another boyfriend and I'm being ghosted. I didn't think she was the type, but then again, I didn't think that Mum would have lied to me about Dad.

After college, rather than going straight back to Aunt Debbie's, I drive to Luna's place. I'm just getting out of the car when I see Luna's mum walking towards the front door of the building.

'Hello, Ms Williams, I was wondering if Luna was at home.'

'You're such a polite boy, Alex. Just call me Mel.' She then frowns, and her canvas bag slips off her shoulder. 'I thought Luna was with you.'

'No. I haven't seen her since before she went to Coventry, and she hasn't answered any of my messages.'

Mel sways slightly, and I can see the panic that crosses her face. 'I think we'd better go inside,' she says, as she fumbles in her handbag for her keys. I follow her up the stairs to her flat, and I know she's hoping, like I am, that the door will be unlocked.

But it isn't.

'Luna!' Mel shouts. 'Are you home?'

There's silence. 'I don't understand,' Mel says, letting both her bags fall to the ground and shedding her coat onto a chair. 'I got a text message from her saying that she had gone straight down to the demo with you after getting back from Coventry, and that you'd be camping together, and she'll be home at the weekend.'

'But that's still three days away,' I say. 'I'm revising for my A Levels. There's no way I could go away at the moment.'

Mel rubs her eyes. 'I didn't think about that,' she says softly. 'I just took her at face value. Luna's never lied to me about where she is before; she hasn't had the need. I try to be as supportive as I can.'

'Do you think she's found someone else? I mean, I'm younger than her and everything. Maybe she's fallen for another guy?'

Mel snorts. 'I've never seen her as lovestruck as she is over you. I even told your mum that we jokingly call your parents the in-laws.'

'What? When did you talk to Mum?'

'I ran into her the other day. She thought I was someone else, and then I realised I recognised her.' Mel glances to the floor, slightly abashed. 'You'll understand one day when you have children of your own, Alex; you'll want to check out who they're dating. I'd seen a picture of your mother on her law firm's website. We had a nice chat, your mum and me.'

I find that hard to believe. Mum has made no bones about the fact that she doesn't approve of Luna, but then she's so worried about what other people think of her, I guess it makes sense for her to be polite to Mel.

'If Luna's not with you, then where is she?' Mel asks, sinking into a chair.

'I can put some messages out to the people in our group,' I suggest. 'Some of them will have been with her in Coventry.'

'Yes, love. Please do that, and I'll make us both a cuppa whilst you get on your phone.' Mel walks out of the small living room with sloping shoulders. If I'm feeling worried, I can't imagine what she's feeling.

I message the whole group.

Anyone seen Luna in the last couple of days? Neither her mum or me know where she is, and we're worried.

I get an immediate response from Vince.

She was in Coventry with us. We said goodbye at Victoria Station the day before yesterday, late afternoon. She went off towards the platform to catch the Horsham train, and I went to Brighton. It's not like Luna to be out of contact. Hope all's good. Keep us posted.

Shit. That means something's happened to her between London and home, and that was already two days ago. I pace around the living room, glancing at the pictures of Luna on the mantelpiece from when she was a little girl, wearing a pink tutu and looking absolutely nothing like the rebel she is today. Mel walks back into the room, holding two white mugs, which she places on the small Formica table. I show her Vince's message, and she looks like she's about to burst into tears.

She takes her phone from her handbag and dials Luna's

number. As before, it goes straight to voicemail. Mel's voice cracks when she speaks. 'I'm going to call the police.'

She's on the phone for a while, and I feel awkward sitting there listening, not doing anything. When she finishes the call, she looks so disconsolate, I feel like I should give her a hug, but it's not as if I really know Mel. This could be a big worry about nothing, or it could be that something terrible has happened to Luna. I say a silent prayer. I've never used the word *love*, but I think I might actually love Luna. I can't bear the thought of her being hurt.

Mel clears her throat. 'Here's what we're going to do, Alex. I'm going to talk to my colleagues in children's services, and I'm going to wait until the police arrive to find out what they're going to do. In the meantime, can you ring everyone you know and just ask around? Put messages out on social media or any other forums that you use. Leave me your telephone number. Then I want you to go home and stay safe. Don't do anything silly like roaming the streets looking for her, will you?'

It's like Mel can read my mind, because that's exactly what I intend to do. I can't believe how calm she is, so very unlike Mum, who would be screaming and shouting and all panicky.

'I'm not staying at home at the moment,' I admit.

She cocks her head to one side.

'I'm staying with my aunt.'

'Is everything alright?'

'Mum and Dad are splitting up, and I needed to get away.'

'Oh, I'm sorry to hear that. Your mum seemed so composed when I met her.'

I don't say anything, but that's Mum all over. A split personality. We smile at each other awkwardly, and I leave.

. . .

I SLEEP FITFULLY, checking my phone when I wake in the night, but there is still nothing from Luna, and no one seems to have a clue where she is. I hope the police have already started looking for her, because I'm freaked out now. I suppose I'll be one of the first people they interview, because they always think it's the boyfriend when something happens to someone, but in this instance, I'll be happy to talk to them.

When my alarm clock goes off, my limbs feel heavy, and I've got a nauseous feeling in my stomach. I reach for my clothes, but realise they're all dirty. This is the third day that I've been staying at Aunt Debbie's; I really need to go home to collect some more of my things, as well as getting a textbook that I've left on my desk in my bedroom. I doubt I'll be able to concentrate on any studying with everything that's going on, but it's only four weeks until my exams start, and I'm getting twinges of panic.

I message Luna's mum, who replies immediately, saying that the police have officially started a missing person's investigation. I don't know if that makes me feel better or worse. I just pray nothing bad has happened to her. I can't believe I'm thinking this, but I'm even hoping she's gone off with someone else, because at least that'll mean Luna's well and happy.

Somehow, I get through the morning in college. There's still nothing on the news about Luna going missing, but I'm sure if there was any information, Mel would let me know. I decide to go home during my lunch break so as to avoid seeing Mum. I just can't face her histrionics at the moment, or the fact that she has blatantly lied to me. At some point I'm going to have to confront her and demand to know who my real father is, but the way she acted after Dad left, frankly, I'm scared. I'll discuss it with Aunt Debbie, and perhaps we can talk to her together.

To my relief, the house is quiet, and the curtains are still pulled in the upstairs bedrooms. There's a strange white car parked in Mum's space, but it might be our cleaning lady's. I put my key in the front door, and it's open, so I walk inside and shout, 'Hello!'

I expect Gail, the cleaning lady, to poke her head around the door, but to my dismay, it's not Gail who appears but Mum.

'Hello, Alex. Have you come home?' She's talking to me in a perfectly normal voice as if nothing is wrong.

'Um, no. I've just come to collect a few things, and then I'm going back to Aunt Debbie's.'

'Before you do that, we need to talk.'

'I've got to get back.'

'No, this is more important. In the kitchen, please.'

Reluctantly, I follow her into the kitchen, and she pulls out a chair for me, then she walks to the fridge and takes out a carton of orange juice, which she pours into a glass. She places it in front of me and then sits down herself. Something's wrong, but it takes me a moment to work out what it is. Mum is wearing jeans and a sweater; she never wears such casual clothes during the working week.

'I know you've been blackmailing me, and I want you to explain why,' she says.

'What?' I haven't got a clue what she's talking about.

'There is no point in trying to deny it, Alex. If you do, you'll only make things worse for yourself.' Mum sounds weird. She's using her 'I'm a very important solicitor' voice, and she sounds cold and factual, and she's unusually calm.

'Mum, I don't know what you're talking about. What blackmail?'

She narrows her eyes at me and shifts her chair closer. She's really freaking me out.

'I've spent the last eighteen years trying to give you an amazing life, full of opportunities. You've been spoiled with all the latest gadgets, a car; we've taken you on holidays across the world, you've attended the best private schools, yet it's all been for nothing, hasn't it? I've slogged my guts out for you, juggling work and home life, always attending your school events, supporting you in every way I can, and this is how you repay me.'

'Mum, you've got to tell me what you think I've done.'

'Did you think you could scare me with blackmail? I suppose your girlfriend put you up to it, but it's finished now. You're to give me the money back, otherwise I'm taking you to the police, and believe me, your life really will be over.'

'Mum, I haven't got a clue what you're talking about. Is someone blackmailing you?'

'Yes, Alex. And I don't buy the wide-eyed innocent look.'

'It's not me! I promise. Why would I blackmail you?'

'Because you know something, don't you?'

I get up and pace around the kitchen. This isn't how I wanted to have the conversation. 'I don't know anything about blackmail, but I do know that I've got a blood disorder, and that you're type B blood, and Dad is AB, and I'm O. And do you know what that means?' I stab my forefinger in her direction. 'That Dad can't possibly be my real dad, which means you've lied to me and probably to him for all of these years. How could you do that, Mum?'

'I have never heard such ridiculous nonsense.'

'You might not know about genetics, but I do. I've told Dad to get his blood checked out, but there's no point, is there? Because he's not my real dad. But you need to be checked out, because I've probably got my faulty genes from you.'

Mum stands up now with such force that her chair topples over. She strides towards me with fury burning in her eyes, and for the first time in my life, I'm really scared of her. 'Your father has been a wonderful dad to you.'

'Yes, he has, but it doesn't mean he's my genetic father. Who did you sleep with, Mum? Why have you hidden this from us?' I flinch as she steps nearer.

'What have you told Stuart?' she asks in a strangely monotone voice.

'Nothing yet, but I'm going to. If you won't give me the answers I want, then perhaps Dad will.'

'And if you do that, I will tell him about your blackmailing, and I'll march you to the police station. Then your lovely little life will be all but over.'

She steps towards me with a terrifying look in her eyes, and then she glances at the knife rack; I swear to God I think she might be about to pull one out and attack me. She's totally unhinged. I know that I've got to get out of here now.

I step to the side of her, and then I bolt, running out of the kitchen, skidding into the hall and tugging the front door open.

'Alex, stop! Come back!'

But there's not a chance I'm going to do that. For one horrible moment, I think I might have left my car keys on the hall table where I used to dump them before Mum confiscated them. They're not in my jean's pockets, but then I remember, I put them in my back pocket. She's running out of the door now towards the garage. I tug open the driver's door, jam the locks on and start the car. I reverse out of the garage without looking where I'm going, and I have that horrible sensation that I had when I hit the deer, or whatever it was. I slam my foot on the brakes, but Mum isn't behind the car, she's level with my side window, gesticulating wildly. I carry on reversing, then shove the gear stick into first gear, and I'm away, pulling out of our drive. I glance into the rear mirror and see Mum crouching down on the driveway, her hands over her head like some tormented character out of a horror movie.

A van hoots at me as I pull out of our driveway without looking, but I just need to get away from here and back to the safety of Aunt Debbie's.

As I drive, I'm constantly glancing in my rear mirror, wondering if Mum's going to come after me, but it isn't until I pull up outside Debbie's little house that I realise tears are dripping down my cheeks. And then I realise that I'm meant to be back at school for a revision class at 2 pm, but somehow I've found myself here. It's probably safer for me at school, because Mum can't reach me there. I wipe the stupid tears from my face and restart the car, driving back towards my sixth-form college. It's only when I get out of the car that I realise I didn't collect any of my things.

I know Alex is lying. He has to be. He's worked out that Stuart isn't his father, and this is payback time. Both of them have let me down; it feels like they have ripped out my heart and trampled all over it. I have never, ever felt such fury. When I pull myself up from the ground after Alex leaves, I have an overwhelming urge to destroy things. I march into Stuart's study and swipe everything off his bookcase. I take the photos of the three of us and chuck them to the ground, enjoying the sound of splintering glass, and then with tears coursing down my cheeks, I stride back into the corridor, heading for the living room.

I hear a creak and then remember the broken window, the threatening note mentioning my top, and I catch sight of the blinking light in the alarm sensor in the corner of the hallway. Perhaps they're watching me. Perhaps Stuart got the monitoring service to put some extra software in the system so that they're watching me now, laughing as I trash this house. I telephone him and get no reply, so I call again and again, repeatedly. At some point, just as I'm screaming myself hoarse, he answers.

'Why do you keep calling me, Chantal?' His voice sounds weary.

'Has Alex called you?'

'No.'

'He hasn't told you some big secret?'

'I don't know what you're talking about. Is he alright?'

'Yes. Oh yes, our lovely son is just fine.'

'Chantal, you sound strange, upset. Is there anyone who can come and be with you?'

'That's what you're meant to do,' I sob, and then I end the call, because I don't want Stuart to hear me like this. I slam the phone down and grab a bottle of wine from the fridge, drinking directly from the bottle, drips running down my chin.

Everything is Alex's fault. If he hasn't discussed his suspicions about his paternity with Stuart, then at least I'm not too late. I can save this. I can save Stuart and me, but Alex will have to be the sacrificial lamb. How I used to love that boy, but now he's becoming a man, I see more of Jade in him. My life is disintegrating, and it's all his fault. Oh, how I wish I hadn't saved him. I had everything back then: on track for a good career, and I'm sure Stuart would have come back to me upon his return from Dubai, whether we'd had a baby or not. We'd have had a happy life, travelling, entertaining, and Stuart would have been my single focus. Our life would have been perfectly good without a child. But if Stuart finds out the truth, that he's not Alex's father and I'm not his mother, then I will have nothing. The ideal life will be gone for ever. There is only one choice.

Alex must die.

And it must be soon, before he opens his mouth. I can see us all grieving at his tragic funeral, Stuart and I clinging to each other, Debbie overcome with grief, and then I'll be able to resume our perfect life. The world's hearts will break for us. What a terrible tragedy for the Heatons, to lose their only child, who was just on the cusp of adulthood. As I think about it, I know that I have no alternative. A good mother may give up her life for her child, but that isn't me. Do I even love Alex anymore? He's caused me so many problems. I suppose I don't want him to suffer. He needs a death like his mother's, quick and painless – in his sleep, ideally. But how? I need to pull myself together and do some research, and do it quickly.

28

'Alex, what's happened?' Aunt Debbie says as I run up the stairs without saying hello to her.

'Nothing,' I say and rush into the tiny bedroom. I lie on the bed and thump my head back on the pillow. I wonder if Mum's having a nervous breakdown or something. It's totally freaking me out.

There's a gentle knock on the door, and Aunt Debbie puts her head around. 'You can tell me,' she says.

'Luna's missing, and Mum's gone crazy.'

Aunt Debbie sighs and walks in. The room seems much too small for both of us. She leans against the wall. 'What happened?'

I tell her about Luna, and I talk her through the weird conversation I had with Mum.

'It sounds like Luna's mum and the police are in control, and I'm sure she'll tip up very soon. You've got to try to stop worrying. Regarding your mum, she's obviously under terrible pressure because your dad has left. People can become quite delusional with heartbreak. I'll put the kettle on and give her a call.'

'I went home to collect my stuff, and I left without it.'

'Is there anything that's really important for you to have?'

'I guess not, but I'm running out of clothes.'

'That's no big deal. I'll do your washing for you. You've no need to worry. I'll find out what's up with your mum.'

After a few minutes on social media, trying to look for information on Luna, I give up and go downstairs. Aunt Debbie has made me a cup of tea and two pieces of toast with honey.

'I tried calling your mum, but she doesn't answer. I'll try again, and if she still doesn't pick up, I'll go around to see her tomorrow.'

'She won't do anything stupid, will she?' I ask.

'That's not in Chantal's nature. She's angry and hurt, and we always hit out at the people we love the most. Try not to worry too much.'

Twenty-four hours later and Luna is still missing. She's officially a missing person now; there's a news flash with a horrible photo of her in it. She'll be pissed that they're using an old picture before she got most of her tattoos. Mum hasn't called me either, and she isn't answering the phone to Aunt Debbie. I call Dad and ask if he's heard from her, but he says no, not since a conversation yesterday. He seems more concerned about how I am, which cheers me up, but I'm still not ready to ask him if he knows I'm not his real child. Besides, Aunt Debbie says I should get the truth from Mum first, and I think she's right.

I've got a revision class tomorrow for my politics A Level, and I realise I've left the main textbook at home. I really need to go back to collect my stuff. This time, I'm going to get as many of my belongings as I can, because either I'll stay living at Aunt Debbie's, or I'll go and stay with Dad.

When I tell Aunt Debbie that I'm going home to collect my stuff, she insists on coming with me.

'You really don't need to.'

'Perhaps, but I want to make sure that Chantal is alright, and that you are too. I'll drive you and wait in the car whilst you collect your belongings.'

My heart is thumping when we arrive back home, which is ridiculous because this is where I live, but everything I thought I knew has shifted. Although the house looks the same on the outside, I no longer have that sense of security that home always used to represent. Mum's car is still missing, although the white Ford Fiesta is there. I still haven't worked out who it belongs to. And then, I get a phone call from a withheld number.

'Is this Alex Heaton?' the man asks.

'Yes,' I say, gripping the phone tightly.

'My name is Detective Constable Seth Kennedy. I've been given your phone number by Melissa Williams, the mother of Luna Williams. I understand that you're Luna's boyfriend.'

'Yes,' I say. My hand is trembling, and Aunt Debbie peers at me with concern.

'We'd like to have a quick chat with you. Will you be at home in an hour?'

'I'm staying at my aunt Debbie's house at the moment, and we should be back by then.' I give him the address, and he says that he'll see me later.

'You don't think they suspect me, do you?' I ask Aunt Debbie as I shove the phone into my pocket.

'Absolutely not. The police are hardly going to give you notice that they want to talk to you if they think you've done anything wrong. I know you're under terrible stress at the moment, love, but try not to worry.'

I let out a puff of air and open the car door.

'Are you sure you don't want me to come in with you?' Aunt Debbie asks.

'Yes. Hopefully Mum isn't home, but if she is, I need to find out what's really going on.'

'Alright, love. I'll wait for you in the car.'

The air in the house is still as I walk through the front door; I can't put my finger on it, but it feels as if something is amiss. The hallway looks the same, with the vase of fake lavender on the side table and the umbrellas neatly stacked in the vintage brown stand, so I decide to go down into the basement first, to get a couple of suitcases. Our house has a weird kind of heating system that blows hot air out of grills in the floor, and in the summer it can be switched into air cooling. It's fairly common in America apparently, but unusual here. I told Dad he should change the system to renewable energy, an air source heat pump or a biomass boiler, but he said it was too expensive to change. The only good thing about it is that we have a big basement, large enough to house lots of boxes of junk that Mum and Dad have collected, and a big wine chiller for Dad. We also store all our suitcases down there.

I open the door to the basement from the utility room and press the light switch at the top of the stairs. Nothing happens. I wonder if the bulb has gone, so I open the torch on my phone and carefully walk down the steps. It's dark and damp, but what strikes me the most is the revolting stench of rotting food. It reminds me of when I was little and used to be terrified of this underground dungeon, as I called it, but there was never a stink like this. The light on my phone doesn't stretch far, but I catch a glimpse of something bright pink on the floor. I walk over to it and then bend down. It's a pink anorak, definitely not something Mum would wear. And then I remember where I've seen it before. The lady who was at our door when I ran out after Mum and Dad's argument was wearing a jacket just like this one. I take a step backwards, feeling confused, and step onto something squidgy. I swing around and angle the phone's torch onto the floor.

What the hell! There's a load of food spread across the floor. Stuff in ziplock bags and plastic containers, bags of peas and cartons of ice cream that have melted to create a congealed, sticky mess on the concrete floor. The smell is rancid, and I wonder how long it's been left out of the freezer. But more to the point, I wonder why Mum has taken it all out, because it must have been her. I can't see our cleaner Gail doing this. Gail would have put everything neatly into crates or freezer bags or taken the stuff upstairs to put in the fridge. I tiptoe in between the puddles of melted food, careful not to get my white trainers stained with raspberry sorbet, and reach over to lift the lid of the chest freezer.

It takes a long moment to compute what I'm seeing.

There is a woman lying in the freezer, her eyes milky and staring straight upwards, a grimace of terror frozen on her face, ice flakes on her eyelashes and in her hair. It's the woman I saw at the front door, the woman who was wearing the pink anorak. I let the lid of the freezer drop down with a thud. I step backwards and slip in a mush of something defrosted. I stagger back to my feet, my hands sticky.

I think I'm going to throw up. Gagging, I somehow hold onto my phone to light up the steps, but my hands are shaking so much the light bounces up and down. Who is this woman? Why is she lying dead in our freezer? I can't think coherent thoughts; I just know I need to get out of here. Now.

'What are you doing?'

It's Mum. She's standing at the top of the stairs, wearing her pyjamas, her hair all tousled as if she's only just woken up, yet it's nearly 6 pm.

'There's a woman in the freezer,' I say, my voice sounding weird, as if something is caught in my throat.

'What are you talking about?'

'A woman. There's a dead woman in the freezer.' I walk up to the top step, so we're standing just inches apart from each other in the utility room. Although I'm standing just a step below her, our eyes are almost level.

'Oh, Alex. I told your dad that you weren't coping with him walking out on us, that I thought you needed to see a psychologist. Are you hallucinating now, too?'

'I'm not bloody hallucinating! That woman, the black lady I saw on the doorstep, she's dead and in the freezer. What the hell is going on? Did you kill her, Mum?'

'Darling, I think you need to calm down.' She takes a step towards me, but I hold the palms of my hands out, and I think she realises that I'm taller and stronger than her, so she stops.

'When we're under severe stress, sometimes we imagine things, sweetheart. We genuinely think they're real, but they're not. Why don't we go into the kitchen? You can sit down, and I'll get you a drink and call the doctor.'

'Mum, you're mad! That lady, wearing a pink anorak, was standing on our doorstep, asking to speak to you the evening that Dad left. I saw her there. I spoke to her, and you can't deny it. What did you do to her? Was it an accident?'

My heart is thudding so quickly it feels like it's going to burst out of my chest. This woman, who has been my mum for my whole life, is terrifying me. I don't recognise her. And then all the smiles and the cajoling go away. Mum's eyes lock onto mine. She becomes icy calm, her breathing shallow and her face so pale.

'She had to die, Alex. Tammy is her name, and I killed her to protect us. To protect our family, and most of all to protect you. She was trying to destroy our lives. I simply had no choice.'

'You always have a choice in life, Chantal.' Mum swings around to face Aunt Debbie, who is standing behind her. I have never felt such relief; I'm not alone, and Aunt Debbie is here to support me. 'It's up to you and your own moral compass to decide whether to choose what's right or what's wrong.'

'What the hell?' Mum says. I see a flicker of concern in her eyes now as she glances from me, where I'm standing on the top step, to Debbie, who is standing in the utility room behind her. None of this is making sense, yet here we are, standing in the room that represents normality: the washing machine and dryer and the dark blue cupboards and the pile of laundry in the basket on the side and all of our coats hanging from wooden pegs on the wall.

'Where are Alex's adoption papers?' Aunt Debbie asks.

'What?' Mum narrows her eyes at her sister.

'Why are your and Stuart's names on Alex's birth certificate when he can't genetically be your child?'

'But it's only Dad,' I say. They both ignore me. 'She just lied about Dad.'

'You and Stuart could not have given birth to Alex. Your blood types cannot produce a type O child, which is what Alex is.'

'You don't know what you're talking about, Debbie,' Mum says.

'Oh yes I do, and Alex knows it too. He knows that Stuart isn't his father, but what he doesn't know is that you're not his mother, either. I worked it all out, Chantal. You're such a terrible mother, your son didn't even want to tell you that he'd had a car accident. It was me who took him to the hospital, and it was me who discovered that he has a blood disorder, and it was me who worked out that you've been lying for the past eighteen years. There is no point in denying it, Chantal, because I know the truth. I think the time has come for you to reveal to your son who his real parents are.'

Mum takes a step closer to Aunt Debbie, her eyes

narrowed and her right-hand index finger jabbing at her sister. 'You've always been so sanctimonious, Debbie, so judgemental and jealous of me. Everyone thinks it's you who has the big heart, but it's not, it's me. I saved Alex from a terrible life with a drug addict mother. I gave him everything I could, but this is how he repays me. By forcing my husband to leave me, by getting me fired from my job, by turning me into a social pariah, by hitching up with that dreadful girl and plotting to blackmail me.'

'Mum!' I shout, trying to make sense of what she's saying, but both Aunt Debbie and Mum ignore me.

'Who did you steal him from, Chantal?'

Mum laughs, but it's a nasty, hard-edged laugh. 'I didn't steal him. I saved him. I did it out of the kindness of my heart. I did it for Stuart, so we could have a family and be together for the rest of our lives. And yes, I did it for me, because I yearned so very deeply for a child of my own. But most of all, I did it for Alex, who at best would have ended up in care, and at worst would have had an early death at the hands of his negligent, drug-addled birth mother. I gave him a good life, but now I regret it all. If I hadn't saved Alex, my marriage would still be a happy union, and I would be working on the best case of my career. This boy is controlled by his genes. I honestly believed that nurture would trump nature, but I was wrong. He has bad blood in him, and there's nothing I can do about that.'

I take a step upwards, and Mum steps backwards into the room.

'Are you saying you're not my birth mother?' I ask, trying to absorb what she's telling me.

'That's exactly what I'm saying. I saved you.'

I glance at Aunt Debbie, but her expression is impossible to read. I don't think she's as shocked as I am.

'So where is my birth mother?'

There's a pause, and I can barely utter the words. 'Oh my god, is she the woman in the freezer?'

Mum rolls her eyes. 'No. Forget about your birth mother.'

'What woman in the freezer?' Aunt Debbie interrupts. 'What are you talking about, Alex?'

'There's a dead woman in the freezer,' I murmur, the memory of that poor woman's unseeing eyes making me feel nauseous again. I grip my stomach.

Mum ignores us both. 'Your birth mother drowned. She was a nobody, a drug addict, and you'd have died of starvation or neglect if I hadn't gotten rid of her.'

Aunt Debbie is leaning against the wall now. She's gone so white, I wonder if she's going to faint. 'What did you do, Chantal?' she whispers.

'I'm not a bad person, Debbie. I did it for the best, to save Alex and bring me and Stuart back together. You'd have done the same; you know what it's like to want a baby. Besides, she didn't suffer. She was as high as a kite at the time and wouldn't have felt a thing. The honest truth is I've thought about her a lot over the years, and I even have dreams where I try to save her, but I'd do it all over again. She didn't deserve a baby, and look what a great life I've given Alex.'

I can't stop staring at Mum. It's as if my brain can't or won't compute what she's saying. Then Aunt Debbie grasps my arm and tugs me hard.

'We have to get out of here!' she says. I see the fear in her eyes, and then I feel it too. Mum is a killer, and now she's told us what she's done, are we going to be next? And what about the woman in the freezer? If she's not my birth mother, who is she?

Mum pushes Aunt Debbie, who releases her grip on my arm. 'What are you going to do, Debbie?' Their two faces are centimetres away from each other.

'I'm going to call the police. You've killed two people and

stolen a baby. What kind of fantasy land are you living in to think that I won't do that? You say you're a good mother, but you're not. You're a bad wife, whose husband has been playing away because he can barely stand the sight of you. You're a bad mother and a bad sister.'

'What?' Mum looks taken aback. 'A bad sister?'

'You're loaded, yet you refused to give me money for my IVF. You told me that I was too old and that it wasn't worth it, but I got the money for the IVF anyway.'

And now it's Mum's turn to look shocked. Her jaw drops open, and bright red patches appear on her neck.

'What, you're the blackmailer? You're the person who threatened to tell the world about how I stole Alex if I didn't give you money? You're the person who sent those notes and who slashed the tyres and roof of my car?'

'What the hell are you talking about, Chantal?' Aunt Debbie shakes her head. 'I took out a second mortgage on my house.'

'No, it was you! You fleeced the twenty grand out of me.'

Now I'm totally confused. My mother isn't really my mother; she stole me. She's accusing Aunt Debbie of black-mailing her, and she killed some woman to protect me. None of it makes any sense.

'But what about the woman in the freezer?' I ask again.

'Who is she, Chantal? What have you done?' Aunt Debbie asks, her eyes narrowed. I've always seen the gentle side of my aunt, but now I can see how scary she might be to the little kids she teaches. I thank god that she's on my side.

'She didn't need to die,' Mum whispers. And then she turns on Aunt Debbie, stabbing her finger into Aunt Debbie's chest. 'This is all your fault! If you hadn't sent me those notes, none of this would have happened. I thought Tammy was blackmailing me, but it was you! Her blood is on your hands!'

'I didn't do anything, Chantal!' Debbie says.

Then Mum punches Aunt Debbie in the face, and Debbie swings around and slaps Mum. They're screeching at each other and pulling hair and kicking.

'Stop! You need to stop!' I shout, but they ignore me. Mum punches Aunt Debbie in the gut, and Aunt Debbie grabs onto Mum, and they both fall backwards. I watch in horror as they tumble head over heels down the concrete steps. There's a horrible bone-chilling thud, and then silence.

'Help!' I shout, but I don't know who's going to hear me. I listen. Silence. Are they both dead? Have I witnessed my mother and aunt die? The utility room spins around me, and I concertina to the floor. What now?

I know I should get up and look around for help, but it's like I'm frozen to the ground. And then I think again of that poor woman in the freezer whom my mother killed, and I whimper. Is Mum coming back for me? I haul myself up and on wobbly legs run through the utility room into the kitchen and grab a knife out of a drawer.

And then I hear a distant shout. I stand stock-still, barely breathing. It comes again. I can't be sure, but I think it's a female voice shouting *help*. I stagger to the back door, pulling it open.

'Help!' The voice is distinct now.

'I'm coming!' I yell, glancing all around the garden, holding the knife out in front of me, trying to work out where Luna's voice is coming from.

'Help! Here!'

The summerhouse. I race towards it and tug on the door. It's locked.

'Luna?'

'In here,' she replies. I peer through the windows, but they've been taped over with newspaper. I try to force the door open, bashing it with my shoulder, but nothing happens. It's only a flimsy glass-and-wood door, so next I try with my foot, kicking it as hard as I can. There's the sound of splintering wood, so I try again with my shoulder, and this time the door gives way.

'What the hell!' I exclaim, my hand rushing to my mouth. Luna is strapped to a chair, which has been tied to the wall with chains and ropes, her wrists and ankles bound to the chair's framework. Her eyes are red and sore, her hair matted to her head. One of Mum's prized Hermes scarves is lying on the ground. Luna looks at me and sobs.

'What has the bitch done?' I throw my arms around my girlfriend.

'She's mental.'

'I'm so sorry,' I say as I try to undo the plastic ties around Luna's wrists and ankles, grateful that I'm holding a kitchen knife. 'Keep totally still.' Her skin is raw and bleeding as I gently ease the ties away and slice through them. 'The police have been looking for you. Your mum and I have been going crazy with worry. How long have you been here?'

'I don't know. The last thing I remember was your mum stopped her car as I was walking out of Horsham station. She said that you were waiting for me at home, and she'd give me a lift. When we got back to your place, she gave me a cup of tea. And then I woke up in here. She interrogated me for hours – days, maybe. I've lost track of time. She thought I was blackmailing her, which is crazy.'

'I know,' I mutter, thinking of her accusing me and then Aunt Debbie.

'She gave me food and water, though, and let me pee in a bucket. When I told her just now that you broke into your home because you were trying to get money to pay back your aunt for the car repairs, she went berserk. She stormed out, saying she was going to come back with a knife and do me in. Is she coming back?' Luna's voice trembles.

'I don't know. She fell down the stairs.'

'Get me out of here, Alex! Away from her.'

'She's killed someone,' I whisper. Luna flinches away from me.

I put my arm around her shoulders. 'Come on. Don't be scared of me. We need to get out of here.'

'How do I know you're not going to take me straight back to her?' Luna asks. She's standing up now, but seems unsteady on her feet.

'Because that woman isn't even my mother, and she's evil. I need to call the police and an ambulance. I have to make sure that Aunt Debbie is safe and that Mum is restrained.'

Somehow we make it back to the house, with Luna leaning heavily on me. My heart is thumping, and my throat feels like I'm choking, terrified of what we might find.

And then the back door opens. Debbie stands there, her arms clutching her stomach. Blood is trickling down her forehead, and a massive swelling is growing on her cheekbone, getting larger as we stare at her.

'We need to get to the hospital,' she murmurs before sinking to the ground.

29

ALEX – A YEAR LATER

As the airplane breaks through the fluffy clouds, I see the green fields and clusters of trees and snaking grey roads that make up the Sussex countryside. It's so lush and gentle in comparison to the landscape that, just hours ago, I left behind. The plane lands gently, and the air stewardess's voice comes out over the loudspeaker system.

'Welcome to England, where, as you can see, the weather is surprisingly summery. On behalf of your captain and the crew, thank you for flying with us. We wish you a safe onwards journey.'

I am coming back, but to a very different home to the one I left eleven months ago. To be honest, I'm not sure what to expect. It takes a while to get through customs, but once I'm at the luggage carousel, I can see my bulging, knackered rucksack is already going around. I grab it, haul it onto my back and stride out through the nothing-to-declare gate.

'Alex!' Dad is standing right at the front. He throws his arms open wide and pulls me into a massive hug. I hadn't realised how much I'd missed his bear hugs until now. When he's released me, he stands back and gives me the once-over. 'You're looking good, son. The sun and altitude must have suited you,' Dad says.

And then Aunt Debbie steps forwards. She looks different, with a new haircut that suits her and a baby strapped to her chest.

'Hi, Alex,' she says, standing on tiptoes to give me a kiss on the cheek. 'We're so happy to have you home.'

'Hello, you,' I say, gently touching the soft downy head of her baby. 'It's great to meet you.'

'I've been telling baby Ava all about her cousin,' Aunt Debbie says.

I smile. At least there's one good thing that has come out of this mess. Against all odds, Aunt Debbie got pregnant.

'You will agree to be her godfather, won't you?' she asks.

'It would be an honour,' I say. I bought Ava a little silver bracelet and Aunt Debbie a pashmina, which I'll give them when we get home.

'Come on. Let's get you to the car. You must be exhausted,' Aunt Debbie says. She slips an arm into mine, and we walk alongside Dad, who is pushing the trolley.

I stayed on in Nepal for as long as I could, but freshers' week starts in a fortnight, and Dad thought it would be a good idea for me to have a couple of weeks in the UK to settle back into some sort of normality. I glance around the crowds of people waiting in the arrivals hall, worried that Dad, Aunt Debbie and I might be recognised, but no one is looking at us. Dad has always told me that people have short memories; I guess he's right. Even being four and a half thousand miles away hasn't protected me from the horrors of what Mum did. The media dubbed her as the 'murderess baby thief' the world over. There were even pictures of me in the press – fortunately, from when I was a kid. It would have been easier if Mum hadn't survived the fall down the basement steps, but she did.

Dad paid for me to go to Nepal. He wanted me out of the country so I wouldn't have to deal with the awful publicity. Although the headlines were all about Mum, on the whole, the media has been sympathetic to him. It's not like Dad did anything wrong. He resigned from his post as a presenter, though – the media interest was too much – and he's sold our old family home. I'm glad, because I never want to go back there.

We walk together to the car park, where Dad pays for the parking ticket and then helps put my rucksack into the boot of a car. It's a new car, an all-electric one, which pleases me. Aunt Debbie opens the back seat door.

'It's fine. I'll sit in the back,' I say.

'Absolutely not. You've been cramped up in an airplane for hours. Besides, I need to sit next to Ava. I've brought you a bottle of water and I've made you a sandwich in case you're hungry.'

I can't imagine Mum ever turning up with a sandwich. And that's the trouble; I can't stop thinking about Mum, yet I wonder if I ever really knew her.

The official diagnosis is that she suffers from psychosis. All that stuff about blackmail was in her head. I still can't fathom that, but apparently, she genuinely believed that someone was blackmailing her. She told the police that she had messages on her mobile phone, but they couldn't find anything to support that. She seemed to think that text messages can be deleted by the sender long after they've been sent, but that isn't the case. According to Dad, the police checked all her social media accounts and analysed her computer and her phone, but there was nothing to suggest she'd received threatening messages. It seems so weird that Mum – who by all accounts was a great solicitor right up until the end – was seeing, hearing and believing things that just weren't true.

As Dad reverses out of the parking space, a Mercedes Cabriolet is waiting to pull in. I haven't seen a car like Mum's in a year. It gives me a jolt.

There were some things that Mum didn't make up, though. The slashing of her car tyres and roof was a random act of violence. It happens when you leave a fancy car parked all alone in an unmanned car park, but Mum put two and two together and made five.

The other thing that wasn't in her head was the rubbish lorry. The prosecution managed to track down the refuse collectors, who remembered a demented woman asking about an envelope being removed from behind a bin at the crack of dawn one morning. I guess her twenty thousand pounds in cash is in a landfill somewhere. Or perhaps someone deserving found it. That would make me happy.

After Dad has pulled out onto the motorway, he glances at me. 'I guess it's hard for you, being back in the UK.'

'Yeah, but I couldn't stay away forever. I'm looking forward to starting uni.'

'And I'm happy to have you back.'

I wonder if Mum knows I'm home. I've been thinking about what to say when people ask me about my mum, and I've decided I'm going to say she's dead. She kind of is, or at least, her mind is.

Dad says that the guilt must have eaten away at her, nibbling her mind from the inside until it made her totally irrational. She genuinely thought that poor Tammy was threatening her, so the woman was killed for no reason what-soever. Tammy might have been an opportunist, but that's the only thing she was guilty of. At the trial, Mum was charged with manslaughter rather than murder for Tammy's death, because the jury found that she was suffering from such abnormality of the mind to substantially impair her mental responsibility for the killing. In other words, she genuinely believed that Tammy was threatening her. I feel desperately sorry for Tammy's family, especially her two young kids.

Mum also got sentenced for kidnapping me and then Luna, and of course for Jade's death. The court didn't believe the defence, who claimed that Jade's stolen car slipped into the lake and that Mum was just guilty of failing to save her. It was deemed that Mum was of sound mind back then, so she was charged with manslaughter, and the kidnap of me and all sorts of other things relating to the forging of my birth certificate. Some people thought she should have been charged with murder, that it was likely that she premeditated Jade's death. Dad and I disagree; we think she was an opportunist and that she probably got the correct sentence.

Dad researched Jade for me, but she'd been in foster care all of her childhood, so we couldn't find anything about her real family. We found my original birth certificate, but the father section was left blank. I don't mind too much, because I've got Dad and no one could ask for a better father; besides, there's nothing I can do about it. I've accepted I'll never know anything about my birth parents.

'Have you stayed in touch with Luna whilst you've been away?' Dad asks.

'Not much. I've got a new girlfriend now. She's from Newcastle, studying at Cardiff. I think you'll like her.'

Dad smiles.

Luna and I couldn't stay together, not after what Mum did to her. When she drugged Luna, she took Luna's mobile phone and removed the sim card, both of which the police found stuffed into a kitchen drawer. Thank goodness Mum didn't kill her, and thank goodness I arrived before she took a knife from the kitchen.

So it's not surprising that my relationship with Luna is

over. I'm sad, but I totally understand. Besides, we probably wouldn't have survived a long-distance relationship. I've heard on the grapevine that Luna and Vince are an item now. I'm happy for them.

I glance at Dad. He looks so content, and younger, too. 'What was it you wanted to tell me?' I ask, recalling the text message he sent me yesterday.

'Jill and I have done a lot of thinking and talking, and we're going to set up an ecological consultancy, looking at sustainable building methods. We're well on the way, actually. It helps that Jill was a geography teacher.'

'Was?' I interrupt. 'Has she quit teaching?'

'Yes. And we're hoping that when you graduate, you'll come and work with us, too. We want to set up a charitable and educational arm to the business.'

'Wow,' I say. 'It sounds great.'

We're quiet for a while, and then Aunt Debbie speaks from the back seat.

'Will you go and see your mum?'

I shake my head. Mum's in a secure psychiatric unit, and she'll be there or in prison, probably for the rest of her life, having been charged with so many heinous crimes. Sometimes I feel sorry for her because she's obviously sick, but the psychiatrists don't think she was ill when she pushed Jade's car into the reservoir. That was pure and simple opportunistic evil.

So no, I think I'll stay away. I'm just glad that we're not genetically related.

A LETTER FROM MIRANDA

Thank you very much for reading *The Only Child*.

The working title for this book was Guilt. I wanted to explore what happens to someone who is living with a terrible secret. Does it make them ill in body and mind? Can something so dark remain repressed for ever? And what is the balance between nature and nurture? I haven't answered any deep philosophical questions, but I certainly had fun writing this book, and hopefully you enjoyed reading it! As always, I try to draw upon locations that I know. For those of you who are familiar with the beautiful Peak District, you may recognise the reservoir when Jade met her untimely death. I've set the rest of the story in and around Horsham in West Sussex, and once again I apologise for filling the lovely town with horrible characters!

The plotting of *The Only Child* was truly a collaborative effort with my amazing editor, Jan Smith. If anyone tapped into our lengthy Zoom calls, they would be very disturbed listening to us plot all the horrible things that befall my characters! Every day I count my blessings that I'm published by Inkubator Books. Thanks to Brian Lynch and Garret Ryan, Jan, Jodi, Claire, Stephen and the rest of the team, my writing dreams have come true.

I would also like to thank the book blogging community who so generously review my books and share their thoughts with readers.

Lastly but most importantly, thank *you* for reading my books. I love to chat with readers via BookBub, Goodreads or Instagram so please reach out and say hello. Reviews on Amazon and Goodreads help other people discover my novels, so if you could spend a moment writing an honest review, no matter how short it is, I would be massively grateful.

My warmest wishes,

Miranda

www.mirandarijks.com

ALSO BY MIRANDA RIJKS

THE VISITORS

(A Psychological Thriller)

I WANT YOU GONE

(A Psychological Thriller)

DESERVE TO DIE

(A Psychological Thriller)

YOU ARE MINE

(A Psychological Thriller)

ROSES ARE RED

(A Psychological Thriller)

THE ARRANGEMENT

(A Psychological Thriller)

THE INFLUENCER

(A Psychological Thriller)

WHAT SHE KNEW

(A Psychological Thriller)

THE ONLY CHILD

(A Psychological Thriller)

FATAL FORTUNE

(Book 1 in the Dr Pippa Durrant Mystery Series)

FATAL FLOWERS

(Book 2 in the Dr Pippa Durrant Mystery Series)

FATAL FINALE

(Book 3 in the Dr Pippa Durrant Mystery Series)

Published by Inkubator Books
www.inkubatorbooks.com